Murder is Only a Number

Phillip Strang

ALSO BY PHILLIP STRANG

MURDER HOUSE

MURDER IS A TRICKY BUSINESS

MURDER WITHOUT REASON

THE HABERMAN VIRUS

MALIKA'S REVENGE

HOSTAGE OF ISLAM

PRELUDE TO WAR

Copyright Page

**MYS
Pbk**

Dedication

For Elli and Tais who both had the perseverance to make me sit
down and write.

Chapter 1

Part 1

Stephanie Chalmers realised that her life was not as it should be. On the one hand, she had a husband who loved her; on the other, he was a lecherous bastard who would chase anyone half decent in a skirt.

It was not as though she was beaten, or impoverished, or even neglected. Gregory Chalmers, she knew, had been a good catch when she had met him ten years previously. He had only been thirty-two then, two years older than her. Already, he had his own legal practice and was doing well. He had an easy way with words and an attractive physique with a full head of black hair. Sure, she had heard about his reputation, but she was confident she could tame him, the same way she had tamed a previous boyfriend, but that damn fool went and got himself killed in a motor accident. A tragedy as she saw it, considering all the effort she had put into the relationship.

She had loved the previous boyfriend with the all-consuming passion reserved for the young and susceptible; she had no intention of repeating that mistake by falling for Gregory, her future husband, only ultimately to be disappointed. It had taken six months before he proposed to her, wed her, and then bedded her, but not necessarily in that order. She knew that he would continue to love her intensely; she knew how to do that,

1

but she would only feel a strong affection. Still, she had reasoned, it was a good arrangement, and for nine of the ten years they had been fine.

Two children had resulted, both healthy, both obviously intelligent – a trait inherited from both parents. Stephanie had always assumed that her husband would not cheat on her, but in that she had been wrong.

Gregory Chalmers was a womaniser; he could not help himself. It had upset her the first couple of times, but then, she reasoned, he would calm down in time, and besides, the pretence of enjoying the act of procreation every other night was wearing thin; she was glad of the rest.

Regardless, Chalmers loved his wife, even if he had to sneak in late at night every few weeks, hoping that his wife was asleep – she never was.

***

It was Stephanie who first suggested they needed someone to help with the children. She was busy running her interior design business, her husband was occupied with more legal cases than he could handle.

Ingrid was the first woman to apply, a fresh-faced, clear-skinned young woman. 'I'm studying in London. My hours are flexible, so helping you out would be all right,' she had said.

Both the parents agreed that she would be good for the children, as she would pick them up from school and ensure they had their evening meal and completed their homework.

It was three months later that Stephanie first suspected something was amiss. She had come home earlier than usual one night. The children were next door with friends, although Ingrid was in the house, as was Gregory.

Upstairs, a little dismayed after the innocent looks from the two downstairs, she had seen that the marital bed was not as tidy as usual. She pulled back the cover, the evidence clearly visible. The sheets on her husband's side of the bed were creased, and they had been fresh on that morning.

2

Stephanie had sat down, shed a tear, drunk a glass of brandy, and then returned downstairs. By that time, Ingrid had left, and no more was said.

Two weeks passed before another occurrence with Ingrid and Gregory; two weeks where Stephanie had an opportunity to reflect on all that had transpired.

Still, she reasoned, he left her alone, and after that night the marital bed had not been used for the coupling of the man of the house and the children's helper. Stephanie Chalmers decided to let sleeping dogs lie. No point in creating unpleasantness when it was not needed. She remained civil to Ingrid; agreeable and available to Gregory, which was not too often.

***

'Ingrid, this has to stop. My wife is suspicious,' Gregory Chalmers said, four weeks into their affair. It was Thursday night, and as usual Stephanie would be home late. It was also the one night of the week when it could be guaranteed that the children were elsewhere, either next door or at a school friend's place somewhere in the area.

Chalmers had realised that the first flush of the affair with Ingrid, who was in her mid-twenties, had been incredible, but he was tired of her. She was becoming neurotic, wanting to touch him inappropriately in the house when Stephanie was there. It was fun the first couple of times but after that…

Gregory Chalmers, a philandering man who needed to chase other women, needed to feed his ego, was, he knew, at heart a one-woman man, and that woman was Stephanie.

He was aware that she knew about him and Ingrid. He had sensed it the last couple of times he and Stephanie had made love. Sure, she had been affectionate and yielding, pushing all the right buttons, but something was missing: a lack of tenderness, a tightening in her body that he had not seen or felt before.

She knew about his activities at the office with one of his clients, an attractive woman in her forties. He was almost certain that she knew about him and the wife of the local golf club captain. One of his so-called friends had called him twentieth hole Greg in front of Stephanie. Gregory knew that his wife's laugh was purely for the friend's benefit; to show him that she was naïve and silly, both of which she was not.

Only once in their years together had Stephanie referred to Gregory's wrongdoing. 'Don't bring it home,' she had said, and here he was, doing just that.

'I thought you cared,' Ingrid said in the kitchen of the house, a substantial three-storey terrace in Twickenham.

'You knew what it was,' Chalmers replied.

'Just a screw, is that it?' Ingrid said. The woman was becoming irrational, and he knew that Stephanie was due home within fifteen minutes. He now regretted that he had not resisted one last act of seduction in the elder child's bedroom.

'What did you expect? That I would leave my wife?'

'I love you, and now you are throwing me out.'

'No, I'm not. The job is still here.'

'I took the job because of you,' Ingrid said.

It had not been normal for Stephanie to phone when she left her business to drive home. It was a fifteen-minute drive when the traffic was flowing, thirty when it was not, and he knew after her phone call which of the two it would be.

Gregory Chalmers was frantic, attempting to reason with a hysterical woman and to ease her to the front door and out of the house. There was no way that either he or Ingrid could pretend to be idly conversing when Stephanie entered, and she would wonder what Ingrid was doing in the house anyway. After he had noticed that first time that Stephanie had checked the bed and seen the crumpled sheets, they had been extra careful. In fact, apart from their arranged meetings at the house, he had rarely seen Ingrid. She had wanted to meet at a local hotel, take a room, but he had declined. He had been with Stephanie a long time, and though he had seduced a few women, none had become clingy like this one.

Maybe she was too young, too immature, too unknowledgeable, he had thought, but he had discounted that very early on in their short relationship.

He knew now that Ingrid Bentham was a troubled woman, possibly delusional.

'Take your hands off of me,' Ingrid screamed as Gregory Chalmers took her firmly by the arm and marched her to the door.

'Stephanie will be back soon,' he shouted.

'Good. Then you can tell your wife that you love me, and we are to be together.'

'We cannot be together. I will stay with Stephanie, and you will leave.'

'You have never loved me,' Ingrid said. The woman had freed herself from Chalmers and was back in the kitchen, opening drawers, slamming them shut, picking up pans and hurling them to the floor. She even tipped the casserole that Gregory had prepared for Stephanie over on the floor.

She will be home in five minutes, Gregory thought. He knew there was no way he could clean up by then, and no way the woman causing mayhem would leave. He was unable to think straight, unable to even contemplate an explanation that would satisfy Stephanie when she walked in.

'Go, please go.' Gregory grabbed her again, manhandled her towards the back door. He knew that whatever happened, the evening would end badly.

Ingrid freed herself, using superhuman strength. She opened the drawer next to the sink. She took out a razor-sharp knife.

'You bastard. The same as all the other men,' she said as she drove the knife hard into Gregory Chalmers' rib cage. He fell back, stunned by what had just happened, but still alive.

'What have you done?' he gasped. He held his hand over the wound, the red blood staining his white shirt.

'I thought you were different; someone I could love, someone I could trust.'

With Chalmers leaning back against the pantry door, Ingrid came forward, her eyes ablaze, her mouth grimacing, as she thrust the knife forward, again and again. Chalmers collapsed to the ground, and died.

***

Stephanie Chalmers burst into the kitchen; she had arrived within fifteen minutes, as her now-dead husband had predicted. 'What have you done?' she screamed.

Ingrid stood at one end of the kitchen, the bloodied knife in her hand. 'He deserved to die,' she said.

Stephanie, unable to comprehend the scene, stood mute. Her husband lay on the tiled floor, covered in blood. The children's helper, a person she had trusted with the safety of her children, had murdered her husband.

Ingrid Bentham moved towards Stephanie, grabbed her by the hair and struck her across the body with the knife. Stephanie reacted, grabbed the knife, and threw it away. Ingrid, fiery mad and no longer in control, grabbed a thin knife that had been on the wooden table in the middle of the room and thrust it into Stephanie.

Stephanie Chalmers collapsed, apparently dead. Ingrid then walked over to Gregory's body and ripped open his shirt.

With the thin knife, she carefully carved the number 2 on his exposed chest. She then removed all her clothes, took a shower, helped herself to some clean clothes from Stephanie Chalmers' wardrobe, and walked out of the front door.

Chapter 2

The first notification of the events at the Chalmers' house was the blubbering voice of a child on the phone. 'Daddy and Mummy are dead.'

The operator at the emergency control centre responded at once, immediately instigating a trace on the mobile phone.

'Is there an adult there?' was her first question.

'Daddy and Mummy are dead.' This time the voice more unsettled than before.

'Can I have an address?'

'Glenloch Road.'

'Can you give me a number?'

'Daddy and Mummy are dead.'

'I need you to help me if I am to help them. What is the number in Glenloch Road?'

'64.'

Even before the name of the street had been given, the police and the ambulance services had been mobilised. Glenloch Park had been identified as Twickenham, and triangulation based on the mobile phone masts in the area had confirmed this.

It would only be seconds before the mobile number had been identified and a registered owner and address confirmed.

Local police officers were the first on the scene, only one minute before an ambulance arrived. 'It looks grim,' Police Constable O'Riordan said over the phone to his superior.

'Murder?'

'Judging by the blood, I would say so.'

'How many?'

'One, definitely; the other one looks to be in a bad way.'

'Ambulance?'

'It's here now.'

'There's a child here; he made the discovery. I would assume him to be the child of the house.'

'Okay, I'll send someone down to look after him. In the meantime, you know the procedure.'

The paramedic who had arrived with the ambulance had made a cursory check on the bloodied man lying on the floor in the kitchen.

'Careful with the evidence,' PC O'Riordan, a red-haired young man in his mid-twenties, said. Three years out of training and this was his first murder. He knew the procedure: secure the area, ensure that any evidence was left undisturbed before the crime scene examiner and his team had a chance to conduct their investigation, phone Homicide, although his superior, Sergeant Graves, back at the station, would almost certainly have dealt with that.

'The woman is still alive,' the paramedic, a middle-aged man, said.

'Serious?' O'Riordan asked, preferring not to look too closely. His first murder, his first time being confronted with so much blood. He had been trained to react calmly, although he had not yet attained the ability to detach himself from a scene of violence. He went outside and threw up, splattering some daffodils with his vomit. Taking a drink of water from a tap in the garden, he returned to the scene.

Detective Inspector Sara Stanforth was there. 'What is your preliminary report?' she asked the police constable.

'Male, clearly dead; the female is still alive, although in a bad way.'

'I can see that myself,' DI Stanforth said. O'Riordan knew her from the police station. He had only spoken to her on a couple of occasions, and both times she had been unpleasant. He assumed that their third meeting would be no different. Sean O'Riordan, ambitious and smart, but still, as yet, only a police constable, did not appreciate her style, but he knew that she was efficient.

'I arrived on the scene at 20.52 in response to a 999.'

'Yes, but what else?' Sara Stanforth said. A smartly-dressed woman, she was determined to succeed in an establishment clearly dominated by men. She knew of the glares from the men down at the station, men who should know better. Some had been friendly, especially Detective Chief Inspector Bob Marshall: so much so that they were now an item, having moved in together three months previously.

As for the others, some had been willing to treat her as an equal while the rest saw her as a bit of fluff, suitable only for making the coffee and whatever else. The whatever else she knew. Sara Stanforth knew she could be a bitch and overbearing, particularly in the station, but it came with the territory. She had to establish her credentials quickly before the typical male chauvinism took over.

'Family name, Chalmers. The dead male is probably Gregory Chalmers.'

'Probably?'

'The young boy, his name is Billy, said that it was his father, and this is the house of Gregory and Stephanie Chalmers.'

'Confirmed?' DI Stanforth asked.

'There are letters on a table in the hallway with their names on.'

Sara Stanforth had brought another woman from the station. She was with the boy, attempting to find out who he knew that could come and look after him. It was clear that he was a witness, but for now his well-being was more important.

'And the woman is Stephanie Chalmers?'

'According to Billy, it is.'

The crime scene was quickly being established, and the crime scene examiner was on his way. A neighbour, identified as a friend of Stephanie Chalmers, had come over and was tending to the young boy. His sister, known to be at a friend's house, would be staying the night there.

'Anymore you can tell us?' Sara Stanforth asked the paramedic as he removed Stephanie Chalmers from the murder

9

scene, knowing full well that the paramedic's responsibility was to the seriously injured woman, not to the police.

'Knife wound to the lower body, loss of blood. No more than that for now.'

'We will need to interview her.'

'At the hospital, but not today.'

'When?' Sara Stanforth asked.

'Not for me to say. You'll need to check with the doctor.'

It had only been a brief conversation, but DI Stanforth knew that the paramedic had been correct. However, this was her case, her first murder as the senior police officer, and she did not intend to let anyone else take it from her.

'Constable, Sean, what else can you tell me? At least, before the crime scene examiner and his people move us out.'

'It's not a suicide pact.'

'Why do you say that?'

'If you look again, you will see some clothes stuffed in a corner and some footprints made in the blood. There was a third person.'

'The murderer?'

'That would be the assumption.'

'What else?'

'Female, judging by the discarded clothes.'

'Anything else?'

'There is a number carved into the male's chest.'

'What does that mean?' Sara Stanforth asked.

'No idea, but there it was. Number 2.'

The crime scene examiner arrived, briefly spoke to the DI and the PC, donned his overalls, put gloves on his hands, protectors over his shoes, and commenced his work.

'A full report as soon as possible,' Sara Stanforth said.

'You'll have a preliminary within two hours. The full report sometime tomorrow,' Crime Scene Examiner Crosley replied.

Stanforth phoned DCI Bob Marshall. 'I want this case,' she said.

'It's yours. Don't stuff it up.'

'I won't.'

Sara could see that PC Sean O'Riordan was a good man, and his analysis of the murder scene had been spot on. If he wanted, she would see if he could transfer over to her team.

The DI donned a similar outfit to the crime scene examiner and re-entered the murder scene. PC O'Riordan intended to remain at the scene as well. A murder investigation excited him, even if the sight of the blood had not.

***

It had been forty-eight hours since Gregory Chalmers had been murdered.

CSE Crosley had filed a preliminary report: verbally at the crime scene, in writing later that night. The full report would be coming through within a couple of days, subject to forensics.

'Gregory Chalmers died as a result of multiple knife wounds to the chest; in his case, a Mundial carving knife, with death as a result of severe blood loss. The number 2 was carved on his chest after his death,' he had said.

'How long after?' Sara Stanforth had asked.

'Difficult to be certain, but less than five minutes. And a different knife to the one that killed him. Almost certainly the knife that was used on Stephanie Chalmers. Forensics can confirm.'

'And the third person?'

'Female, mid-twenties, blonde hair.'

'Any more you can tell me about her?'

'Not really. I am only confirming the blonde hair and that it was a female. The age is assumed due to the style of the clothing found at the scene. She used a downstairs shower and helped herself to some clothes from the wardrobe upstairs. She was probably in the house for another fifteen minutes after the crime was committed. We can ascertain that she acted calmly after the earlier violence.'

'How?'

'The shower was still wet. On getting out of the shower, she dried herself and hung the towel on a hook. She also wiped the bathroom floor. Not the actions of someone frantically attempting to leave a crime scene.'

'Anything else?'

'No sign of forced entry, so we are assuming it is the woman in the photo that we found in one of the children's bedrooms.'

'Is there a name?'

'Not on the photo, although the young boy who dialled 999 mentioned an Ingrid.'

'The photo shows a woman in her twenties,' Sara Stanforth said.

'The assumption is that the murderer and the woman in the picture are one and the same,' Crosley said.

'That's it at the present moment, an assumption?' Sara asked.

'You're the lead detective on this case. It's for you to find out.'

***

'It was her,' the heavily-bandaged woman said as she sat up in the hospital bed.

'Her?' DI Stanforth asked. She had been warned that Stephanie Chalmers was still under sedation and had nearly died on the operating table. According to the doctor, she had only just made it; a miracle, he had said, which, to Sara, were not the words that she expected to hear from a doctor. Besides, she had no time for miracles. To her, there was no such thing, only hard work and sheer dogged perseverance. She realised that she was a driven woman, and the only time that she would relax her guard was in the confines of the small apartment that she shared with her DCI, and then only when the door was closed.

'Ingrid. I trusted her with my children.' It was evident to Sara that the woman's slow speech was a result of the sedation. Apart from that, she appeared coherent.

'I need to ask some questions.'

'I want that bastard woman brought to justice. She killed Gregory.'

'Yes, I know. I need your help,' Sara said. She was not an overly sentimental woman, but she could feel a profound sadness for Stephanie Chalmers.

She had noticed the two children outside and had briefly spoken to the woman who was looking after them. Stephanie Chalmers' sister had told her that the children were as well as could be expected under the circumstances. Sara Stanforth could only agree; the first time she had seen a dead body, fished out of the River Thames, bloated and naked, its hands tied behind its back, she had been upset for weeks. And the young boy, a sensitive soul according to his aunt, had seen his father covered in blood, his mother dying.

It was remarkable that he had the clarity and the intelligence to phone the emergency services and to give an address, Sara thought.

The aunt had said that she would have expected no less, but now Billy Chalmers and his sister Emma were detached from reality. They had seen their mother, asked when she was coming home, and where was Daddy.

'Ingrid?' Sara asked the woman lying in bed.

'I took her on to help with the children.'

'Did she?'

'The children loved her. She would pick them up from school. Not every day, as sometimes I would make the time for them.'

'What else did she do?'

'She would make sure they had something to eat, as well as do their homework. I trusted her until…'

'Until?'

'Do I have to tell you this?' The doctor had come in to tell Sara that she had five minutes only, no more, as Mrs Chalmers was still critically ill and in need of rest.

'If you want us to find her, bring her to justice.'

13

'It was Gregory.'

'Yes.'

'He couldn't help himself.'

'Take it slowly,' Sara said.

'Gregory strayed.'

'Other women?'

'Not that I gave him any reason, but that was Gregory. Any bit of skirt, and he wanted some of the action.'

'Ingrid?'

'Not for the first three months that she's with us, and then he's using our bed.'

'With Ingrid?'

'With her.'

'Did you confront him?'

'I had become used to his behaviour, but not to him using our bed to seduce the hired help.'

'You said nothing?'

'No. I know it seems silly, but he was a good man, and I did like Ingrid. After that night, I assumed they had cooled the relationship, and I had not seen any reason to doubt for some time.'

The doctor returned. 'Two minutes, no more. I must be firm.'

'What happened at the house?' Sara asked. She still needed to know, two minutes or no two minutes.

'I entered the kitchen, and Ingrid was standing over Gregory. She was holding a knife. I shouted out to her. She came over to me, grabbing me, forcing me to the ground. She was wild and out of control. I pushed her away. After that, I do not remember.'

'Why do you think she killed your husband?'

'He probably told her that the relationship was off. They only last a few weeks with him, anyway.'

'A lover's tiff?'

'I assume it was, but Ingrid was always so placid. If I had not seen her there, I would not have believed her capable.'

Sara left soon after. A nurse came into the room and administered an additional sedative to the wife of the murdered man.

Chapter 3

'This is your case. How are you going to handle it?' Bob Marshall asked. He was sucking a mint, careful not to let Sara know that he still enjoyed the occasional cigarette. There'd be hell to pay if she knew, he knew that, and for two months he had gone cold turkey, but the occasional drag, he thought, would do no harm.

In the office, Bob was always demanding of Sara. Everyone knew they were living together, and it had led him to receive a warning from Detective Superintendent Rowsome about fraternising in the office.

Not that it was any of his business, Bob had even told him, but the superintendent was a pedantic man who worried obsessively about the Key Performance Indicators in his department.

'Look here, DCI, you can sleep with whoever you like, but stuff up and you know what happens,' Rowsome had said. 'Just make sure it doesn't impact on the efficiency of your department.'

Bob Marshall, keenly aware of his senior's concerns, and also conscious of the other members of his department, kept the pressure up on Sara. Not that he had any concerns, as she had proven herself to be competent; she had even acquired begrudging respect from DI Greenstreet, a curmudgeonly old-school police officer. He did not hold with the modern ideas on policing with their emphasis on graphs and charts and performance indicators. In his day, the police dealt with the criminals using a kick up the arse and a slap around the head.

Nowadays, they had to read them their rights, accord them respect, and then lock them up in prison, three meals a day, and the luxury of a three-star hotel. He knew what Sara Stanforth represented the moment she joined the department: political correctness, policing by the book, female equality.

Still, he had to concede that she had done well dealing with a serial rapist in the area; even arrested him on her own and brought him to the police station in handcuffs. *Not many men would have stood up to him*, he had thought at the time. Even Keith Greenstreet had to admit she was a good police officer, although, to him, her relationship with their DCI was something else. The sideways glances in the office, the passing too close to each other, the occasional whisper in each other's ear. Greenstreet knew what they were talking about, even if it was a long time since he had experienced any of it.

'Find Ingrid Bentham,' Sara replied to Bob's earlier question.

'Do you need any help?' Bob Marshall asked.

'DI Greenstreet, if he's willing. Also, the police constable at the Chalmers' house, Sean O'Riordan. I know he is keen to get into plain clothes. He was there at the scene; he's a smart man to have with the team.'

'Okay with you, Keith?' Bob looked over at Greenstreet.

'Fine by me.'

'Thank you, sir,' Sara said. 'Thank you, DI.'

'Don't go wasting my time,' Keith Greenstreet replied. He was approaching sixty, not in the best of health: high blood pressure, an irregular heartbeat, and carrying twenty pounds more weight than was healthy. His temperament in the office varied from morose to cheerful and back to morose; it spent more time at morose. He was not sure why Sara Stanforth had chosen him, and besides, he was the more senior of the two officers. He knew that he should be leading the investigation, but then he reasoned, DI Stanforth had something that he did not: a tight arse and the bedroom ear of Bob Marshall.

***

Police Constable O'Riordan arrived in the office at the police station later in the day. He had thanked Sara earlier when she had phoned to offer him a position in Homicide.

17

No longer expected to wear the regulation police uniform, he arrived in the office dressed in a dark blue suit.

Keith Greenstreet shook his hand limply. *Another young upstart,* he thought.

Sara had set up a crime board close to her desk; she was excited, and it looked like being a long night ahead. She had phoned the hospital. Stephanie Chalmers was recovering but suffering from delayed shock. Her house was still a crime scene, and on release from the hospital, she would go and stay with her sister.

'What's the plan, guv?' Sean O'Riordan asked Sara. He had found himself a desk in the far corner, as well as a police-issue laptop.

'Find Ingrid Bentham.'

'Easier said than done. She will have scarpered by now,' Greenstreet said.

Ignoring Keith Greenstreet's negativity, Sara focussed on the facts.

'We have an address for Ingrid Bentham, although she is not there.'

'What did you expect? That she would be at home waiting for you with a cup of tea.'

Sara knew why she had brought Keith Greenstreet on board. His experience would compensate for Sean O'Riordan's youthful enthusiasm, even hers. She knew that he did not respect her, other than begrudgingly, but when it was needed, it would be him who would find the woman.

'What do you want me to do?' Sean asked.

'What did you find out about Ingrid Bentham?'

'Twenty-four, blonde, spoke with a northern accent.'

'Northern is a bit vague,' Keith said.

'It's the best we've got.'

'If the woman has disappeared, she will probably head back home to the nest. You need to be more specific.'

'Do we have a recording of her voice?' Sara asked.

'Not sure,' Sean said.

'Well, then you'd better find one. Run it past someone who knows about regional accents,' Keith said.

'Keith's right. Can I trust you to deal with this?' Sara asked.

'Leave it to me,' the constable responded with his usual youthful enthusiasm.

Sara realised that this case was different. Usually, a murder would not give a definite murderer, only suspects, but in this instance there was a known killer: fingerprints and foot marks at the scene, and enough DNA to prove a case. However, the murderer had disappeared.

Stephanie Chalmers had provided an address for Ingrid Bentham. Two officers from the department had visited the address after Sara had phoned them, only to find that the woman was not there, although her flatmate was.

Sara and Sean O'Riordan visited later after their meeting at the police station had concluded.

Her flatmate confirmed that Ingrid was a quiet, pleasant young woman, friendly at the college she attended, liked by all that knew her, no boyfriends. The two women had met at college and had decided to pool their resources and to rent a small two-bedroom apartment. Apart from that, they had not socialised, other than the occasional Friday night at a local pub, where both had drunk too much on a couple of occasions.

'What else can you tell us?' Sara asked Gloria, the flatmate.

'Not much. Ingrid did not speak about her family or her childhood. I told her my life story: how I came here from Nigeria as a child, everything there was to tell. I talk too much sometimes, but with Ingrid, nothing.' Gloria spoke pure London, even though she had been born in Africa.

'Did she phone anyone?'

'Not to my knowledge. She had a mobile, but she did not use it much. She had a laptop.'

'Is it here?'

'Nothing is here; not even last week's contribution for the rent. She even took a bottle of wine that belonged to me.'

'Clothing, personal belongings?' Sara asked.

'She took all hers as well as some of mine.'

Sara had asked Crosley and his crime investigators to check the flat. The fingerprints and the DNA found at the apartment matched the crime scene at the Chalmers' house.

On leaving the flat, Sara phoned Keith Greenstreet. 'Can you follow up on Ingrid Bentham's movements after she left the flat: buses, railway stations, taxis, the normal?' Sara asked.

'Leave it with me,' he said. Even though it was late in the evening, he put on his coat as protection against the inclement weather and ambled out of the office.

'Thanks,' Sara said.

'Don't thank me now. Friday night, you owe me a pint.'

'If DI Greenstreet can work late at night, then so can I,' Sean said.

'Where are you going?'

'Back to the Chalmers' house. There may be some recordings of Ingrid Bentham's voice. It's a long shot, but it's worth a try.'

'Let me know how you go,' Sara said.

'What about you, guv?'

'Paperwork for now, and then I need to talk to Crosley.'

'The crime scene examiner?'

'Yes. See what else he can tell us,' Sara said.

***

Sara left the office late, way past midnight. Bob Marshall had waited for her.

'You're on your own on this one,' he said as they left the office. 'I'll need to ride you hard, and I can't protect you.'

'I know, Bob,' she said. It was strange: in the office, he was officious and demanding, but outside, and in the bedroom, he was caring and considerate. That was what she loved about him: his devotion to work and fair play, his ability to separate work from home. Sara knew that she had not attained that ease yet; not sure if she ever would. She would go to sleep and dream of the murder of Gregory Chalmers, the attempted murder of Stephanie. She knew that she would wake up during the night and start writing notes, surfing the internet looking for insights into the mindset of someone, in this case, female, who could murder with extreme violence, then detach herself mentally, take a shower, clean herself up, go home, pack and leave.

To her, Ingrid Bentham would need to be a callous, cruel-hearted woman, but according to Stephanie Chalmers, the children had loved her, and for a short while so had Gregory Chalmers. The children's love had been unconditional, the love of a child for an equal, whereas the husband's love had been carnal.

Sara had seen the photos of Ingrid. She was a beautiful woman, slim but not skinny. Her complexion was very pale; that may have been the photo's exposure, although more likely indicative of a woman from the north of England; her Viking heritage showing through. Sara imagined that if the woman stayed in the sun for too long, she would burn, not go brown.

Sara, objectively taking Gregory Chalmers' point of view, could see the attraction to a man in his forties, feeling for the first time the lessening of passion in his loins, the need to bed someone as fresh and sensual as Ingrid. According to her flatmate, Ingrid had been with no other man, yet she was the sort of woman that men would have lusted over.

In an age where sexual equality was taken for granted, it was strange that Ingrid Bentham remained the wallflower when all around were engaging in musical beds. That had been her life too, Sara reflected, until she had met Bob. Now, all she wanted him to do was to propose and put a ring on her finger.

Chapter 4

Sean O'Riordan arrived at the Chalmers' house at ten in the evening. A uniform stood outside. As he had driven up the road, he could see the uniform relaxing: the night was cold, and the policeman at the door was struggling to stay focussed. Crime scene tape had been placed across the front door to the house. Sean showed his badge, ensured to put on foot protectors and gloves.

The kitchen was clearly off limits, and besides, it was not the place to find a recording. The sitting room appeared to offer no possibility. There were several DVDs, but they were commercial, mainly children's cartoons and films. He was looking for something with a hand-written label. The house was still officially on lockdown as a crime scene, and Sean was aware that blundering around was not advisable. He made his way upstairs. The first bedroom was obviously the parent's room where the Chalmers had slept, and the husband had first seduced Ingrid. The next bedroom was not used, other than as a hobbies room.

The third bedroom, belonging to Billy, judging by the computer and the plane models, offered more of a prospect. It was clear that the young child was well-organised. His school books and DVDs were all lined up and in their place. Sean thought it offered the best chance of finding what he wanted.

He stood back and scanned the room, reluctant to move anything other than was necessary. He took a few photos before he touched anything. At the end of the row of DVDs, six in total, he saw one labelled 'birthday party'. The label had been printed, probably by the printer next to the computer.

He removed the DVD, placed it in a plastic bag, identified it, took a photo of where he had taken it from. The girl's room he checked on the way out of the house. He then returned to the office. He knew that his girlfriend would be fast asleep by the time he got back home in the early hours of the morning, and was aware that she would not object if he woke her up on his arrival.

Back in the office, Sean took a copy of the disk and placed it in his laptop, the screen lighting up after a few seconds with a group singing an out-of-tune rendition of 'Happy Birthday.'

There were two children and one adult; the one adult they wanted to hear.

'Billy, it's your birthday. You get to cut the cake,' Ingrid said.

Sean texted Sara, knowing that she would want to know immediately.

'Great. Six in the morning in the office. We'll need to find an expert on regional accents,' Sara replied.

She had been wide awake when the SMS had come through, going over her notes, evaluating the case, and what to do next. Bob was lying next to her; he was fast asleep. She had not heard from Keith. She called him.

'Still up,' he said.

'The same as you.'

'I've been staking out Ingrid Bentham's flat. Her flatmate has only just arrived home, drunk by the look of it. I was just about to knock on her door. Give me thirty minutes, and I'll message.'

'Thanks. Six in the morning. Okay by you?'

'I may as well not go home,' he said sarcastically, but Sara knew it was only his dry humour.

Keith gave the flatmate fifteen minutes before he knocked on the door. She had brought company home; a male voice bellowed for her not to answer the door, and to get back in the bed.

The door to the flat opened. 'Detective Inspector Greenstreet. I have a few questions.'

'It's late?' the drunk woman slurred back at him. She was naked.

'It's a murder enquiry. It's not a nine to five, sociable hours' investigation. You spoke to Detective Inspector Stanforth before.' Keith knew he was verging on harassment, but he was determined to get a result.

'I've told her all I know. Go away. I have a man here, and he's more attractive than you.'

Keith Greenstreet, not an attractive man, he knew, had been insulted enough times over the years, even shot at on a couple of occasions. The last time put him in the hospital for three weeks, while he recuperated after they had removed the bullet from his spleen.

'That may be, but he will have to wait.' Keith wedged his shoe in the door as she attempted to close it.

'If you're not going away?'

'I'm not. Tell your boyfriend to get some rest, build up his energy.'

Keith entered the apartment. It was evident that housekeeping was not Gloria's forte. The place was a mess, with clothes strewn everywhere. The kitchen sink was stacked high with dirty plates and cutlery.

'I'd better put on some clothes,' Gloria said.

'Suit yourself. I've seen enough naked women in my time.'

Gloria returned two minutes later, an oversized tee-shirt barely covering her modesty. She still wore no underwear.

'What do you want to know?'

'We need to find Ingrid Bentham.'

'Don't look at me. The bitch has left me with her share of the rent to pay, and now I need to find another flatmate.'

'How about him in the next room?'

'Him! Are you joking? He's just an idle screw. Apart from his dick, he's not much use.'

'Have you known him long?'

'Three hours. Long enough for you?'

'It's hardly the basis for a lasting relationship, is it?' Keith said.

'I don't need lasting relationships, just a man when I need one.'

24

'And Ingrid?'

'She never brought a man here. I asked her why not.'

'What did she say?'

'She said that she'd had enough of men, and did not need them.'

'Lesbian?'

'Not at all. I was lonely one night, made a play for her. She was angry, did not speak to me for several days.'

'Any medication?'

'Ingrid? Every day, although I don't know what it was.'

'Did you ask?'

'As long as she paid the rent, and she didn't screw the men I brought round here, what did I care?'

It was evident to Keith that Gloria, was at best an unreliable witness; at worst, a slut who screwed men as it suited her. Keith imagined that if he asked around the area, he would find out that Gloria was not as well respected as Ingrid, except in the opinions of the local studs.

The plaything for the night could be heard snoring loudly in the other room. 'It seems as if he will be no use tonight,' Keith said.

'Him? Give me five minutes, and he will be,' Gloria replied.

'What else can you tell me about Ingrid?'

'Nothing. We shared a flat, that was all.'

'Clothes, jewellery. Any that you borrowed?'

'Nothing.'

'If you lie to me, and it comes up in a court of law, you could be charged with obstructing the police.'

'Well…' There was a pause.

'Yes.'

'There was this ring.'

'And?'

'I sort of borrowed it.'

'Stole or borrowed is not my concern. Do you have it?'

'Yes.'

'Where is it?'

'In my bedroom.'

'I will need it as evidence. I'll fetch it.'

The sight in Gloria's bedroom was not pleasant. The man, a strapping tattooed individual, was lying naked on his back. The smell of stale beer was overpowering. Keith found the ring in the drawer, as Gloria had described. He placed it in a plastic bag and wrote on the outside: location, time.

He left soon after, stopping only to make a phone call on his mobile. 'I have a ring that belonged to Ingrid Bentham. It's engraved on the inside.'

'Six in the morning. Great work,' Sara replied.

***

Sara regretted that she had asked her primary team to meet at six in the morning. Not that the idea was not good, it was. It was that she was not an early morning person. Some, she knew, were at their best in the morning; others, in the afternoon and through to late at night.

It was evident the next morning as to which category her new DC belonged. There Sean O'Riordan was, bright and alert, as she staggered into the office at just after six. At least Sara had to admit that she looked better than Keith Greenstreet; the man looked as though he had slept on a bench in the park, but then, he was nearly thirty years older than her.

'Foul hour of the morning,' Keith said.

'Sleep well?' Sara asked.

'What little there was.' A singularly unexciting reply.

Sean O'Riordan, newly elevated from police constable to detective constable, was anxious and biting at the bit to get started. Sara had to concede that he suited plain clothes. His first day in the office, his suit had been brand new, off the rack, and here on the second day, there was another suit, this time a lighter shade.

Must be costing him plenty, she thought. She reflected on her early days as a detective inspector. She had served her dues, five years in uniform, initially administrative. In the past Keith Greenstreet would have said it was woman's work, but now political correctness forbade such words, and he had received a reprimand behind closed doors from his DCI on more than one occasion.

Sara was not a person to dwell on the past, and her time at her first police station north of the metropolis of London had not been the most exciting period of her life. There she was, a policewoman, a career that she had always wanted, and what did she have: a dingy bedsit; a man in the room next door who drank, and then snored, and then swore in his sleep. It had not been that many years before, and the memories were fresh. There had been a boyfriend back home in Liverpool, but she wanted a future; he wanted her at home and pregnant. Not that she did not want children, she did, but on her terms, and with Bob Marshall. It had not always been that way. Before Bob Marshall, she had been career-driven, probably a workaholic, but he had brought out maternal feelings in her.

Keith Greenstreet had been a policeman longer than Sara had drawn breath; his days with the police force were rapidly coming to an end. In the office, he would talk about how much he looked forward to the day he could hand in his badge and devote himself to personal pursuits. It was a defence mechanism on Keith's part: he had no personal pursuits, other than the occasional drink, no friends, no family other than his wife. Their marriage had been childless, not because he and his wife had not wanted children, they did, but that was how it had turned out. They had tried in the early years, but when it was clear that no children were to result, their lovemaking became infrequent; no more than the passionless coupling of two sad people, not happy with each other, unable to be apart.

Sean O'Riordan saw life differently. He was in his mid-twenties, a period in anyone's life when they are full of optimism and derring-do. To him, life offered endless opportunities, and he was a person who saw the world brightly, even at six in the morning. Apart from his police duties, he was studying for a

Master's degree. He already had a Bachelor's, but it would not suffice if he wanted to become a detective superintendent.

'So, what's the plan?' Keith asked.

'The ring that you recovered. What does it tell us?' Sara asked. Keith had placed it on the table; it was still in the plastic evidence bag.

'Only that it belonged to Ingrid Bentham. As I said yesterday, there is an engraving on the inside.'

'What does it say?'

'Not much, certainly not an address as to where to send it in the case of loss.'

'Apart from that.'

'"With love, M". That's all.'

'So, unless we can tie it in, it doesn't give us very much,' Sara said.

'You know it does. What did they teach you at police training college? Every little piece of information helps, even when it seems irrelevant,' Keith said. He immediately regretted the put-down of a fellow DI. He had to admit that Sara was handling their latest case with the required professionalism. He would apologise later.

Sara chose to ignore his comment. 'What have we done to find Ingrid Bentham?'

'The usual,' Keith replied. 'Description out to all police departments, watching the airports, railway and bus stations for the woman. She'll not be easy to spot.'

'Why do you say that, DI?' Sean asked.

'You've seen her picture?'

'Yes.'

'Tell me, what did you see?' Keith asked.

'An attractive blonde woman, twenty-four to twenty-six years of age, medium height, slim.'

'No distinguishing features, tattoos, scars?'

'None,' Sean replied.

'Keith's right,' Sara said. 'Statistically, Ingrid Bentham fits the norm for at least half the white females in this country; at least in that age group.'

'Apart from the hair colour,' Sean said.

'Bottle of hair colouring will sort that out soon enough,' Keith said.

'Sean, what can you tell us about the recording you recovered?' Sara asked.

'Northern accent, nothing more, but the recording is clear enough. I'll get someone to analyse it today.'

'Fine. Keith, can you concentrate on the ring. Long shot I know, but It may help. See if you can ascertain where the ring was purchased.'

'Police databases?' Keith asked.

'It's always a possibility. This woman's deranged. We need to find her soon,' Sara said.

'Why do you think that, guv?' Sean asked.

'She murders Gregory Chalmers, almost kills his wife. Then she showers, cleans herself up, dresses in some of Stephanie Chalmers' clothes and walks out of the door.'

'And then she returns to her apartment, packs her belongings and leaves,' Keith added.

'Not the act of a normal person,' Sean conceded.

'Correct. Most people, if they kill someone in anger, will panic, rush out of the door, leave clues as to where they are, but with this woman, nothing. It's as if she knew what she was doing; as if she had killed before,' Sara said.

'The number 2,' Keith said.

'It's a possibility.'

'That's more important than the ring,' Sean said.

'The ring is still important. More pieces of the puzzle,' Sara said.

Chapter 5

Behind the scenes, a full department was focussing on the death of Gregory Chalmers. People were collating information, preparing cases for the prosecution, filing the evidence, and looking for the prime suspect.

Bob Marshall had complete faith in Sara to handle the case, although his superiors were not so sure. As usual, the media were speculating, especially the more scurrilous. Apparently, they had found out about the mysterious blonde, the 'blonde in the bed' as she was referred to. Sara realised that information could have only come from the aggrieved wife, now a widow, but why?

Nobody appreciated their dirty laundry being hung out in public, and the most scurrilous rag was emblazoned with headlines alluding to the unusual arrangement in the Chalmers' household, speculating as to whether it was a lovers' tryst, whether all three enjoyed the bed together, and if the children were safe in the house of Stephanie Chalmers.

Unfortunately, Sara realised, if you want irresponsible reporting, then the newspapers in the United Kingdom were supreme.

Stephanie Chalmers was sitting up in bed when Sara entered her room at the hospital. 'Are you better?' Sara asked, realising that it was not the most appropriate question considering that her husband had just been murdered. Still, the woman had smiled when she arrived. Around the room, there was a collection of 'get well soon' cards, and someone had sent flowers.

'Fine, although I'm probably doped up on drugs,' Stephanie said.

'I was here the other day.'

'I remember. Detective Inspector Stanforth, isn't it?'

'Sara Stanforth, as you say. Are you able to answer any more questions?'

'I don't want to remember, but I suppose I must.'

'Tell me about your relationship with your husband.'

'Gregory was a good man, a good father, but…'

'Why the hesitancy?'

'He couldn't help himself.'

'Women?'

'Not often, but every month or so there would be the signs. The late nights, the smell of perfume, the dash for a quick shower to wash off the evidence – a woman knows.'

Stephanie Chalmers held a handkerchief to her eyes and wiped away the tears. Sara could see that she had been fond of the man, even if his behaviour on occasions had been unforgivable.

'And you accepted it?'

'Reluctantly. More for the children than for me, but yes, I accepted it.'

'Ingrid Bentham?'

'That was different. I knew he had been sleeping with her, at least that one time. I had assumed that the affair was over. I thought to get rid of her, but the children adored her, and she was reliable.

'You regret that you did not get rid of her?' Sara asked.

'What do you think?'

'There have been reports in the newspaper concerning your husband's death.'

'And on the television.'

'The newspapers are speculating that you knew of your husband and Ingrid Bentham. That you encouraged the relationship.'

'Why would they say that?'

'Is any of it true?'

'No. I had learnt to accept Gregory's behaviour outside of the house, but inside the house, never. What if the children

31

had seen the two of them? I may have my faults, but I'm still a good mother.'

Sara sat close to the window, allowing the weak sun outside to warm her back. She had not liked hospitals ever since she had spent three days in one as a child.

'We can't find Ingrid,' Sara admitted.

'I'm not surprised.'

'What did you know about her?'

'Nothing really. Only that she came from up north, and that she was studying in London.'

'Family, friends?'

'I asked once, but she said that her parents were dead. I'm not sure if it was true.'

'You had no reason to doubt her?'

'Not until she started sleeping with Gregory.'

'Do you know why she would do that?'

'Gregory was a charming man, but he was older than her. Have you seen pictures of Ingrid?' Stephanie Chalmers asked.

'Yes.'

'She was a beautiful young woman. What would she want with an older man? We may be financially secure, but we are hardly rich, and besides, I was not going to let him go.'

'We found a ring, a gold ring. Did you ever see her wearing a ring?'

'I remember it. I asked her once about it.'

'What was her reply?'

'She said it was from her mother. It was the only time she spoke about her.'

'Her father?'

'Nothing. She would always walk away if her parents were mentioned. I don't know what the secret was, but on reflection there was always something dark about her.'

'What do you mean?'

'Hindsight. Most people are easy to read. You can tell from how they move, how they talk, whether they are educated or not, gregarious or introvert, willing to chat or more silent. With

Ingrid, I was never sure. Almost as if she had an impenetrable veil in front of her.'

It became clear that Stephanie Chalmers was starting to fall asleep, and her children were waiting patiently outside with their aunt. Sara left them alone and went to see the hospital administration. In her sedated condition, the widowed woman could have mumbled something; something that one of the hospital staff could have sold to the newspapers.

***

Keith had remained in the office. His skills with a computer were limited, but he persevered. One of the things he intended to conquer once he retired. He knew that retirement meant another milestone in his life, and there was only one more after that: a quiet spot in the cemetery with a headstone, the only remembrance that he had ever existed. It was not as if anyone would be coming to place flowers on his resting place. As miserable as he appeared in the office, he knew that it was the one place where he felt at peace; the one place where he could feel content.

An engraved ring presented problems. It was not the easiest item to trace, and apart from the engraving on the inside, there was nothing more, certainly no indication as to who had manufactured it, and where it had been engraved.

The police database was comprehensive. If someone had spent time in prison, for instance, he should be able to check their personal possessions on the date of imprisonment, although there was no indication that Ingrid Bentham had spent time inside.

On the contrary, the woman gave every impression of being an average woman, friendly and attractive, except for one undeniable fact: she was a vicious murderer. But why?

Keith Greenstreet had encountered a few murderers over the years, arrested a few. With them, it had been easy. Virtually all had shown aggressive tendencies, or else they were in an abusive relationship, or they had a long history of criminal activity, but with Ingrid Bentham, nothing.

The woman did not fit the mould, yet her slaying of Gregory Chalmers and the attempted murder of Stephanie Chalmers indicated a savagery he had not seen before. And then, the woman calmly walks out of the door. It was as if she was two people. Keith could see severe psychological tendencies in Ingrid Bentham.

Keith realised that a criminal psychologist would be a good person for the team to contact. He would let Sara know on her return.

As much as he wanted to dislike his senior, at least in this case, he could not. Sure, she could be overbearing, pushy sometimes, but she was a good police officer, determined in her pursuit of justice. He would put aside his prejudices, outdated he knew, and give her all the assistance she required. He would also apologise for his earlier outburst when he inferred that she was not trained well enough to conduct the investigation.

***

Sean, eager and keen, had found a speech analyst; in fact, a person who trained actors in how to speak regional and foreign accents. The man was on the books, approved by the police for their use.

Sean made an appointment for one o'clock in the afternoon. He decided on an early lunch, and then he would take the train up to the centre of London; no point in taking a car, as the traffic was horrendous and parking was a nightmare, even with a police pass.

Anton Schmidt – an unusual name for an expert in the English language – opened the door to his office in Mayfair.

'My father was German, but I was born in England, not far from here. A true Cockney. My mother said that I was born within earshot of the bells of St Mary-le-Bow, but I'm not sure if it's true,' Schmidt said.

'I have a video recording of a birthday party. A woman is speaking. I need to know where she is from,' Sean said.

'Fine, let me see it.'

Sean put his laptop on Anton Schmidt's desk and pressed the play button once the recording was ready. Ingrid Bentham's face was clearly visible.

'That is the woman in question?' Anton Schmidt asked. 'She is very attractive.'

'And deadly.'

'The woman in the newspapers?'

'Yes.'

'Nasty business. Let me watch it for a few minutes, and then I can give you my considered opinion.'

Sean moved out of the office and left Schmidt with the recording. He took the opportunity to purchase coffee from a café below the office. He returned after ten minutes.

'Northern,' Schmidt said.

'Anything more specific?'

'Originally from the Newcastle area.'

'Age when she left?'

'Newcastle, up to her late teens.'

'And then?'

'Hard to say. There are indications of London idioms, but they are formed relatively quickly. She has probably been in London for some time, but the original accent remains noticeable. Most people's accents are formed in their youth. It's unlikely to stay hidden, no matter how hard they try to conceal it; at least, not to me.'

***

After the first couple of days, progress slowed. Sara and her team now had a clear idea as to where the woman had come from, although no firm information as to who she was. Ingrid Bentham was the name she had been using, but there were no bank accounts in that name, at least none that had any money in them, and the only address they had was the flat she had shared with Gloria. The Chalmers always paid Ingrid in cash, and there was no record with HM Revenue & Customs that any tax had ever been paid.

When questioned, Stephanie Chalmers had said that was what Ingrid wanted. It was a minor point, and the murder investigation team were interested in solving the murder of Gregory Chalmers, not indulging in a tax investigation. The ring, so far, had drawn a blank, other than the assumption that it could have been from the mother, but an uppercase 'M' did not seem conclusive.

Bob Marshall, as the DCI in charge of the team, was feeling the heat. It was on record that he and his lead detective in the murder investigation were involved in a personal relationship. Detective Superintendent Rowsome was being questioned by his superiors as to whether this would impact on the effectiveness of the investigation. He had allayed their concerns with a ringing endorsement of his DCI. He knew he had lied. As far as he was concerned, Bob Marshall was after his job, and he did not intend to let him have it. Rowsome knew that he had climbed the promotion ladder as far as he could. There were still another ten years before retirement, and he was hanging on for dear life.

'I've gone out on a limb for you,' Rowsome said in his phone call to Bob Marshall, two minutes after receiving a grilling from his seniors.

'The investigation is going well,' Bob Marshall said. It was not entirely correct, and he half-expected Rowsome to fire back at him.

'Not from where I'm sitting,' Rowsome said before hanging up his phone.

Bob Marshall knew that his decision to appoint Sara as the lead instead of Keith Greenstreet was sound, but defending that decision was not so easy. Unless there was a result within the week, he would need to consider replacing Sara. He knew what her reaction would be. He hoped it would not affect their relationship, but if he had to do it, he would.

Sara, increasingly frustrated, wondered what they could do. Each day they met and discussed what to do next. Each day they went over the evidence so far, but there was precious little.

There was no shortage of fingerprints, no question as to the murderer and no stone had been left unturned, but Ingrid Bentham had disappeared. They had traced the name back, only to find that it had come into existence four years earlier. That aligned with Anton Schmidt's analysis of the woman's accent. A check of births in the UK had revealed no Ingrid Bentham, other than a woman in her seventies.

It was clear that Ingrid Bentham was not the woman's birth name, but what was it? Keith had considered travelling up to Newcastle, utilising some of the contacts he had made over the years in other parts of the country.

Sara believed it to be a good idea, only to have it rejected due to budgetary constraints.

'Sorry, but that's how it is,' Bob Marshall had said in the office that day. Sara knew that he had refused not out of any concern over the budget, but because he thought it would be a wasted trip. He received a cold shoulder that night in the bed they shared.

Sara knew that he was under pressure to rein in costs, and under pressure to remove her from her position, but he had no right to place restrictions on her. She was angry and rightly so.

'Don't worry about it,' Keith said when told of Bob not approving his trip.

'We need a breakthrough,' Sara said, not mentioning the cold shoulder and the cold bed to Keith.

Sean had visited Gloria on Keith's suggestion. Keith had felt that a young man would have more success in finding out information than he had. Sean had knocked on the door, introduced himself, asked a few questions, and then made a quick retreat as the overly-amorous Gloria had come on to him.

Next time, the two men agreed, Sara could accompany them.

'I still reckon the number carved on Chalmers' chest is significant,' Keith said.

'We have checked,' Sara said. 'There is no record of another body with the number 1.'

'Maybe she only intended to kill one person, so there was no need for a number. With the second one, it reminded her of the first, and she decided to keep a count.'

'Keeping score?' Sean asked.

'Why not?' Keith said. 'What is the state of this woman's mind? She's clearly unhinged.'

'She's still smart enough to disappear.'

'Maybe she's done it before.'

'What do you mean?'

Keith leant back in his chair; not a pretty sight, Sara thought, but did not intend to mention it. She valued her DI's experience, even his dry humour, and the man had been big enough to apologise to her for his earlier behaviour.

'She wouldn't be the first murderer who acted and looked normal,' Keith said.

'We know that, but what are you suggesting?' Sara asked.

'She's clearly psychotic. We need an expert to analyse her behaviour.'

Sara consulted Bob; he approved the cost.

Chapter 6

Grace Nelson seemed too young to be a criminal psychologist. At least she did to Keith, although Sara had checked and found her to be in her early forties. The police database showed that she was highly qualified and able to give evidence at a trial.

Keith had to admit she had enough initials after her name. He had none, apart from two General Certificates of Education, one for geography, the other for religious studies, but as he had not travelled far, other than to France and Spain, and he professed to no strong religious views, they both seemed irrelevant. They had, however, allowed him to join the police force as a junior constable. From there on, it had been hard work that had allowed him to rise to the rank of detective inspector.

'I've studied the case,' Grace Nelson said. Sean thought her accent was from the west of the country. He had been reading a book on the subject, but he knew he could be wrong. Regardless, she was remarkably well educated.

Sara, an ambitious woman, envied Grace her education, but the idea of sitting down to study was anathema to her. She had managed to secure a BSc in Policing and Criminal Investigation, but it had been hard-won.

So much so that she had crammed the last six months, and had completed the degree in under three years. Bob Marshall was working on a Master's, and often when she was fast asleep, or in need of attention, he would be slavishly sweating over his studies. She knew that DCI would be the limit of her career. It was not because she did not want more, but she had come to realise that a Master's degree was beyond her, and besides, she had decided that she wanted a child, Bob's child, in the next couple of years. Her biological clock was ticking, and it was winding down.

'What are your thoughts?' Sara asked Grace Nelson.

'Carving a number with a knife indicates a logical mind.'

'Sane?' Keith asked.

'Unlikely,' the psychologist replied.

'It may be best if we let Dr Nelson present first,' Sara said.

'My apologies,' Keith said.

'Paranoid schizophrenia would be my preliminary diagnosis. Ingrid Bentham displays some of the behavioural traits. Of course, my analysis is incomplete. Without seeing the woman, it is hard to be precise. Was she on medication? Have you managed to ascertain that?'

'She was on medication, but we don't know what it was.'

'It's important.'

'There's only one person who would know.' Keith looked over at Sean.

'Okay, I'll go with Sean and hold his hand,' Sara said. Her mood had improved with the psychologist in the office.

'You mentioned medication,' Sean said.

'There are some antipsychotic drugs: Chlorpromazine, Thorazine, Loxapine, Fluphenazine are just a few. There may be more than one drug, and they would need to be taken on a regular basis. The patient would need to be checked every few months, in case of issues.'

'And if the medicine is not taken on a regular basis?' Keith asked.

'Hallucinations, delusions, anxiety, anger, suicidal thoughts, obsession with death and violence, plus a few more.'

'Are you saying that Ingrid Bentham fits the profile?' Sara asked.

'I am raising the possibility. Without a close and detailed examination of the person, I can't be sure.'

'What causes paranoid schizophrenia?' Sean asked. He knew he would be reading up on the subject that night.

'Yet again,' Grace Nelson said, 'there are a number of possibilities: family history, stress, problems during the mother's pregnancy, sexual or physical abuse. There are more, but until you have the woman, my analysis remains speculative.'

***

'Come on in,' Gloria said in a friendly voice upon seeing Sean in her doorway. She was dressed provocatively, almost as if she had been expecting him. 'It's great to see you,' she said. The tone of her voice changed when Sara poked her head round the door.

'Detective Inspector Sara Stanforth. We have a few questions for you.'

Reluctantly, the door was opened, and the two police officers entered. It was clear that Gloria had been entertaining, a few empty wine bottles testament to the fact.

'What do you want? It's my weekend. Don't you ever take a rest?'

'Not when someone has been murdered,' Sara said as she looked around the room. She could not claim to be the world's greatest housekeeper, but compared to Gloria, she was fastidious.

It was evident to Sara that Gloria was high on something, and it was more than alcohol. Sara could see that the woman was a vulture when men were around. She understood why Sean had been reluctant to approach the woman again without a chaperone.

'Maybe, but what do you want from me?' Gloria said. 'I haven't seen Ingrid since she walked out. I told him that.' She looked over at Sean. He was not sure whether it was the look of anger or of disappointment. Although he knew what he felt: relief.

'Ingrid was on medication. Is that correct?' Sara asked.

'I told the old man that.'

'Detective Inspector Greenstreet,' Sara corrected her.

'Yes, him.'

'Do you have any of that medication here?'

'She took it all when she left.'

'Are you sure? You lied about the ring.'

'The ring would have covered her rent money.'

'Gloria, we need the name of the medicine.'

'Something "zine"; that's all I know.'

'And the name of the patient?'

'Ingrid Bentham, who else?'

'Did you see the name? It's important.'

'Not really. As I told the old man, sorry, Detective Inspector Greenstreet, I was not interested. Ingrid paid her rent, and we got on well enough. Apart from that, she left me alone, I left her alone. Satisfied?'

'Not yet,' Sara said. 'Do you have a man in the other room?'

'What if I do? None of your business.'

'As you say, none of my business, but if you want to get back in there with him, you'd better answer our questions, or we'll take you down to the police station.'

'You can't do that. I've committed no crime,' Gloria shrieked. A man's head appeared at the bedroom door.

Sean flashed his badge. 'Police.' The head retreated back inside the bedroom.

'Okay. The name was scratched off. I don't know where she got it from, or what it was. I never asked, and she never told me.'

'Did she take it every day?'

'How would I know? She was a good flatmate, nothing more. Some of the others have wanted to take my men, but with Ingrid I was safe. Not that she couldn't have if she wanted; she was beautiful, I'm not. Just an easy lay, that's me.'

'And the medicine's name?'

'Only what I told you.'

***

'Not so easy to obtain high-potency prescription drugs,' Keith said back in the office. He had stayed back, pleased that he had not been asked to accompany Sara to meet Ingrid Bentham's flatmate.

Not that interviewing the promiscuous Gloria was a problem, but she had reminded him of certain unassailable facts:

he was getting old and he was not an attractive man. It had not worried him when he had been younger; unattractiveness had a particular lure for certain women, especially his wife. Back then, he had been young and fit, even played rugby for the local police station every weekend; just friendlies with the other stations in the area. Always good fun, always a few too many beers afterwards.

But he was no longer young or fit, and now his age had committed him to a life of celibacy; not that he minded, but… the mind was still young, even if the body was not.

The sight of the naked Gloria had caused a twitching in his loins, although he didn't fancy her. He had to admit that it was probably drunken men who found her attractive; sober, they would have looked the other way. Still, even she had tempted, and then the great put-down: old and ugly.

Sara, as always eager to push on, held court in the office. A team player, she had brought a pizza back with her. Keith was pleased at the gesture. He had worked with some miserable sods during his career, and he had to admit that working with Sara was alright.

'Where can you obtain these drugs?' Sara asked.

'Black market,' Keith's reply. 'And then some of those who obtain them legitimately sell them to make extra money.'

'Assuming that the drugs in the bathroom were antipsychotics, she may have had a prescription,' Sean said.

'If she did, then under what name, and what were the drugs?' Keith said.

'We've checked for an Ingrid Bentham. There are no prescriptions against that name,' Sara said.

'Her flatmate said that the name on the labels had been scratched off, anyway,' Keith added.

'She's hardly a reliable witness,' Sean said, ever eager to add his input. Keith Greenstreet intimidated him: the experienced DI and the wet-behind-the-ears detective constable.

'As you say, hardly reliable,' Sara conceded.

'Did she make a play for you?' Keith asked dryly. 'Was she prancing around with no underwear again?' He knew he was winding up the young constable, aware that Sara appreciated the humour.

'Apparently that is reserved for you, DI,' Sean responded. He knew he was being baited, and he had no intention of biting.

'Okay, boys. We've got a case to solve, and the DCI wants a result,' Sara said.

The drugs, assumed to be Chlorpromazine or possibly Clozapine, although not confirmed, were, according to Grace Nelson, dopamine blockers, with known side effects. Long-term use, which seemed possible with Ingrid Bentham, could cause nausea, vomiting, blurred vision and some other complaints, and Clozapine required regular blood checks.

'According to Grace Nelson,' Sara said, 'the drugs prescribed and their dosage are regularly evaluated. If Ingrid Bentham has slipped off the radar, no longer taking the right dosage, then she could be volatile, subject to change in her mental stability.'

'Likely to kill again,' Sean said.

'She's hardly likely to be taking them now,' Keith said.

'There's no way that we would know.'

'She's killed once, another murder may not concern her.'

'Twice, if the carving on Chalmers was correct.'

'As you say, Keith, her second murder. Any ideas on how to find out?' Sara asked.

'Newcastle. I have a contact there. I've already phoned him on a couple of occasions, but a personal visit always works best.'

'I'll work on the DCI,' Sara said.

Keith smiled back at her but said nothing. What he wanted to say would have broken every rule in the book of political correctness. He was certain she would get permission.

***

'If it's vital,' Bob Marshall said. As usual everyone, including Sean and Keith, was in the office late. It was past nine, and Sara needed two more hours before she had completed all the paperwork. The one unfortunate aspect of policing was the need for reporting. It wasn't that she was not good at it, as she was, but there was a murder enquiry, and sitting in the office filling in reports for senior management to survey briefly, and then file in the box of disinterest, did not excite her.

However, a deranged woman interested them more than usual. It was not the first time that a psychotic individual had been on the loose, and each time it raised interest in the media. Their interest ebbed and flowed depending on local and international events – a terrorist attack in the Middle East, an election somewhere else – but the death of Gregory Chalmers continued to appear on the internet and the television news programmes.

Bob had been asked to bring in additional help, but he was still holding firm against a recommendation from Detective Superintendent Rowsome to do it now.

'On your head,' he had said. 'I've made my recommendation. If this goes pear-shaped, then it will protect me. If you don't follow through, don't blame me if you find yourself back on the street in uniform.'

Bob Marshall recognised the threat. He had had little respect for Rowsome before; now, he had none. As far as he was concerned, Sara was doing fine, even Keith Greenstreet had admitted that to him, and he was not a man known for his benevolence to a fellow police officer.

The detective chief inspector had argued the case with his detective superintendent, put him off for the present, but he could only afford to give Sara another week at most. Then, girlfriend or not, he was going to have to pull her off the case, or at least, out of the senior officer's chair. He considered Keith Greenstreet, but he was slowing down. It would have to be someone from another station. If Sara wanted Keith up north, then she would have his permission.

'You've got your permission,' Sara said. Keith was wrapping up for the evening; more likely falling asleep in his chair.

'Don't expect me in the office tomorrow,' he said.

'Surprised he gave in so quickly.'

'DCI Marshall is under pressure for us to give him a result,' Sara said.

'Is that it?' A grin spread across Keith Greenstreet's face.

'Keith, wash your mouth out.'

'Late night bit of fun, that's all.'

'I'll forgive you if you come back with a result. What's the plan?'

'Check with a DI there, my age.'

'Retirement age, is that it?' Sara touched on a sensitive subject. He had had some humour at her expense; she was only returning it.

He did not like being reminded of the subject but accepted her comment gracefully. 'Put out to pasture, more like.'

Sean walked out with Keith. He still had another two hours' study at home, part of the requirements for his Master's degree. He was not being put out to pasture; he was only on the first rung of the promotion ladder. He had charted his course: DI in four years, DCI in six. After that, armed with a Master's degree and the experience in Homicide, he knew he could make detective chief superintendent within ten.

Ambitious he realised, but he was determined, and failure was not part of his vocabulary.

Apart from the studying at home, his girlfriend was always supportive, but becoming tired of the lack of attention she was threatening to move out. Sean thought she wouldn't, hoped she wouldn't, but sacrifices had to be made. She wanted marriage, children, and a house in the suburbs, and that needed money, especially the house, as house prices in London were going through the roof. He could barely manage the payments on a two-bedroom apartment, and it was nothing special. Even a DI could not afford the house she wanted, and he only knew one way to circumvent the slow progress to senior management, and that was hard work, lots of it.

He knew that he was up to the challenge. He only hoped his girlfriend was as well.

Sara stayed for another hour, as did Bob. With no one else in the office, their approach to each other was less formal. Once, when everyone else had gone home, they had made love in his office.

Sara was feeling the tension of the case, as was Bob, and both realised there was every possibility of a zero result.

History of previous cases had shown that paranoid schizophrenics were unpredictable, especially if they were killers. Sometimes, for no explicable reason, they would snap, commit murder, calm down, and then regain their position in society. Nor did they fit the characteristic criminal mould. They could be council workers, lawyers, professionals, even police officers, although that seemed unlikely given the rigorous scrutiny that the police went through on joining and during their career.

Chapter 7

Keith met Detective Inspector Rory Hewitt in Newcastle as planned. They had worked together on a few cases in the past, and each regarded the other as a friend.

'Good to see you, Keith. Nasty business,' Hewitt said. He was a few years younger, but closing in on retirement, the same as Keith, although he relished the prospect. An ardent golfer, he intended to try out the best courses around the world, courtesy of a substantial bequest from a favourite aunt on her passing.

'Not the first time, is it?' Keith said. It had been a hard drive, rain for most of the time, and he could feel the weariness in his bones. He knew deep down that retirement for him would not last for very long, whereas Rory Hewitt was still fit, even sported colour in his hair, although it was thinning. Keith assumed the colour came courtesy of a bottle. For Keith, what you are given is all that you get. He had no intention of dying his hair black or any other colour; there was not much left, and it was grey. And as for dieting and exercising, that was for others. Rory had tried to entice Keith to a game of golf once. Keith's comment at the end of the day was the same as Winston Churchill's, or was it Mark Twain, he was not sure which: 'A waste of a good walk.' Keith didn't have much time for walking either, but Rory had taken his comment with the humour intended.

'What do you need?' Rory asked.

'Ingrid Bentham, not her real name, carved the number 2 onto Chalmers' chest.'

'And you want the number 1? Long shot coming up here.'

'Maybe,' Keith said, 'but we've been around a long time. Our collective minds might find something not in the files.'

'No murders up here that fit the bill.'

'The best we have is that Ingrid Bentham had traces of a Newcastle accent. Apart from that, we have no idea who she is.'

'Then we need to review old cases,' Rory said. 'I'm free for a few days.'

***

Sara considered the case so far. They had a woman who had killed once, possibly twice, and there was the very real risk of a third time. Yet they had no idea who the woman was. Keith was trying to fill in some of the blanks, but Sara still had her concerns. Ingrid Bentham had arrived in London several years previously, and there were photos available to confirm that. The college she had attended had not provided much information, other than to say that she was an adequate student, hardworking, although she struggled at times.

Sara had seen reports like it before; to her, it was a euphemism for not being too bright. Sean had seen it differently, in that his research had shown that with the drugs she was almost certainly taking, she would have had difficulties in focussing.

Regardless of her educational record, she had certainly been astute enough to have gained the confidence of the Chalmers, as well as employers in a few previous jobs, mainly shop work.

As far as Grace Nelson, the criminal psychologist was concerned, Ingrid was extreme, and she needed to be found at the earliest opportunity. Sean had taken up the search for the person who had purchased the ring that Ingrid Bentham had worn, hoping to find out where it had been engraved, but it seemed a pointless exercise. As keen as he was, he had to concede that the chances of success were slim.

It was almost certainly a wedding ring. The condition of the ring, according to a local jeweller, placed its date of manufacture as thirty years ago. Sean assumed that it had belonged to Ingrid's mother, which would indicate that the mother had given it to her. The engraving showed that to be possible.

Sara advised Sean to put the ring to one side and to focus on something else, but what? They were out of ideas on how to proceed. An all-points warning had been put out for the woman, but they had little faith in it producing a result. Ingrid Bentham had no distinguishing features, her face was symmetrical, her height and figure average for a woman of her age, or what they thought was her age. Her college records indicated twenty-four, although that was not certain.

Bob Marshall could see that Sara was floundering. The chief superintendent had already voiced his concerns over Sara's competency.

It wasn't out of any discrimination against women, Detective Superintendent Rowsome had insisted, but Bob Marshall could see the man shifting responsibility, leaving him to carry the can. As far as Rowsome was concerned, a person's ability was suspect until it was proven. This was Sara's first murder trial and it was not going well. She knew how it worked, as did Bob. Ten successes and everyone respects you enormously; one failure, even after the ten, and your reputation is shattered.

***

Keith and Rory reminisced over old cases they had worked on in the past. Keith had spent his working career in London, Rory predominantly in the north of the country, but villains are villains, and they are mobile.

They had first met twenty-six years earlier when a gang of drug pushers attempted to expand their operation throughout the country. Both of them had been detective sergeants then. Rory had dealt with the case in his part of the world, Keith in London. After that, they exchanged information about suspected criminals, or about crimes that appeared to have similarities. They had met up on a few policing courses since then, sharing a few pints of beer of a night time.

'What do you have?' Rory asked, after they had found an empty room near the back of the police station.

'What I've already told you. Female, mid-twenties, almost certainly a paranoid schizophrenic, and a murderer.'

'The photo doesn't tell us much, does it?'

'She could dye the hair, cut it, and she'd not be recognisable.'

'If she has, then it indicates that she is in control of her faculties.'

'And aware that she had committed a murder,' Keith said.

'Guilty conscience, or is she paranoid enough to believe it was the voice in her head, or Gregory Chalmers deserved to die?'

'Does it matter, at least to us? If she is as nutty as a fruit cake or as sane as you and me is not the issue.'

'Agreed. We have dealt with enough in either category over the years. Whatever she is, she's dangerous, but I don't see how I can help.'

'Rory, you keep records of people deemed dangerous. Assuming she has not committed a murder, would there be a record?'

'Mental Health Register, although I'm not sure if it would record a minor, assuming that she was in Newcastle. Any idea as to age?'

'Focus on female child offenders.'

Rory and Keith spent the day poring over old cases. Apart from the death of a youth in a school playground, there were no other incidences that looked possible, and besides, the school playground murderer had been a ten-year-old boy high on drugs.

'What about suspicious deaths?' Keith asked over a pint of beer that night.

'In the case of a minor, we may not have kept the records; always sensitive, dealing with children.'

'We're not dealing with a child now.'

'You're aware of the need to protect the rights of children.'

'Even when they grow up to be murderers?'

'Even then.'

***

The day had started with a whimper more than a bang at the police station in Twickenham. Sean, always wanting to be active, had found time on his hands. Sara was in her office drafting reports, attempting to portray the investigation into the death of Gregory Chalmers in a better light than was actually the case.

Bob Marshall had told her officially in the confines of his office the previous day that her time was running out, and unless she came up with something concrete, then he would need to take her off the case, find someone more experienced.

'You can't do that,' she had said.

'Unfortunately I must,' was Bob's reply. He had not wanted to say it, especially to Sara, but in the office, he was a policeman. At home, and out of hours, then he could be someone else. He regretted his actions after she had stormed out of the office, slamming the door hard.

Bob had slept on the sofa that night. He did not even receive the benefit of a goodnight kiss.

They had managed to eat breakfast together and to maintain a civil conversation before driving separately to the police station the next morning. Once in her office she finally forgave him, sorry that she had treated him so harshly when he had only been doing his job.

Keith was up in Newcastle, probably drinking more than he should, attempting to find out who the missing woman was. Sean, from what she could see, was at a loose end. Otherwise, the office was buzzing as usual.

***

Sara made two cups of coffee: one for her, the other for Bob, by way of a peace offering.

'Sorry,' she said when she placed it on his desk. She returned to her desk, planning to phone Keith. Apart from a brief call the day before, she had not heard from him. The key to the case seemed to lie in Newcastle, and Sara was anxious for news, any news, that would take them out of the current quandary. Until Ingrid Bentham made the next move, which could mean another murder, there was no way to move forward.

Sean busied himself looking into cases of known psychotic killers. Their ability to kill at random or in an orchestrated pattern could change due to unexpected factors. He had wandered over to Sara's office to discuss his findings when the phone call came through. Sara picked up the phone.

'Egerton Road,' she said to Sean. 'There's been a death.'

Sean grabbed his jacket; Sara picked up her handbag and phone. Within ten minutes, Sean driving, they had arrived at the address. They had not needed the number; they knew exactly where they were heading.

The road was blocked off, two uniforms on duty. Sara flashed her police badge. Sara and Sean parked twenty yards away from the apartment and walked the remaining distance.

'I found him,' Gloria said as soon as she saw them.

'Does he have a name?' Sara asked. For once, she felt pity for the woman. Gloria sat on the stairs leading up to the flat she had shared with Ingrid Bentham. It was a cold day, and she was not wearing a jacket. Sara removed hers and placed it around the shoulders of the distraught woman. Sara could see that she needed medical care, but first she and Sean had to check the murder scene.

'Hold on,' said a voice from behind. It was Stan Crosley. 'Overalls, gloves, shoe protectors,' he said.

'I have some in the car,' Sara said.

'Your car is down the road, and you were just about to check out the crime scene, so don't give me that nonsense.'

'Apologies.'

'Accepted, but I'm in charge now. What do we have here?'

Sara sat down next to the distraught woman. 'Gloria, what's his name?'

'Brad.'

'Does he have a surname?'

'Howard.'

'Have you known him long?'

'For a couple of years. We used to meet up occasionally. He fancied Ingrid, I know that, and look what she's done.'

A uniformed policewoman came and took care of Gloria, escorting her away from the building. Sara reminded her not to take her far, as she needed to question Gloria at the crime scene.

Stan Crosley led the way into the flat. 'It's a pigsty,' he said.

Sara could only agree. She could see that no attempt at housekeeping had been made since her last visit, the only difference being the increased height of the pile of unwashed dishes in the kitchen sink. 'How can anyone live like this?' she said.

Sean ignored the condition of the room.

'Get behind me,' Crosley said. 'I don't want your hobnail boots destroying the evidence.'

Sean could have said that they were not hobnailed, and his shoes had cost him plenty, but did not respond to Crosley.

In the small corridor separating the main room from the two bedrooms at the rear there were footprints. 'Probably the woman outside. I'll check later. She must have stepped in some blood,' Crosley said.

'She had blood on her dress,' Sara said.

'Find her something else to wear. I'll need forensics to check it out. Are you sure she's not responsible?'

'We are confident that she's not,' Sean said.

CSE Crosley entered the far bedroom. 'Whoever she is, she's a bloody savage,' he said. So far, Sara and Sean had not seen the body. 'Watch your step. You can see the blood on the floor. Keep to one side of it.'

Sara followed Crosley, almost felt as if she wanted to throw up, an acidic taste in her mouth. She looked away and regained her composure.

Sean came in and saw Brad Howard lying on his back in Ingrid's room. He was naked. In his chest there was a thin knife, its handle protruding.

'Straight in the heart,' Stan Crosley said. 'Mid-coitus.'

'What do you mean?' Sean asked.

'What I just said. A few more checks to confirm, but it seems conclusive. He was engaged in sexual intercourse when the knife was inserted.'

'Ingrid Bentham?' Sara asked.

'It looks as though it is. Fingerprints and DNA will confirm. She's a nasty one if it's her,' Crosley said.

'Nasty and malevolent. Evil.'

Sean shuddered at the thought of what had happened in that room; Sara remained impassive, surveying the scene.

'If you two are finished gawking, I've got a job to do,' Crosley said.

'We're finished.' Sean was feeling unwell. He had seen Gregory Chalmers, as well as his wife. On that occasion, he had vomited on some flowers in the back garden; this time, he would not vomit, but he needed a hot drink. The policewoman outside with Gloria had organised a flask of coffee from a café not far away. Sean took a plastic cup and helped himself to a drink. Gloria was sitting in the back of an ambulance; a mild sedative had been administered to her.

'He's dead, isn't he?'

'Unfortunately, he is,' Sara replied. 'Were you close?'

'Sort of, but he fancied Ingrid.'

'Had she slept with him before?'

'Saint Ingrid of the perpetual virginity?'

'Yes.'

'Never. She never had a man over, and then she kills the first one that she invites in.'

'But why?'

'It was because of me. That's why Brad is dead.'

'What are you not telling us?'

'She phoned me last night.'

'Why didn't you tell us?' Sara asked.

'She wanted the ring; the one you took. She said it was important to her, and if I had stolen it, or given it to the police, then...'

'She threatened you?'

'Yes, I was scared.'

'But you stayed here in the apartment knowing what she is capable of?'

'I've nowhere to go, and besides, this is my home, or it was.'

'Then why Brad?'

'Revenge, I suppose. I told her that the police had found the ring, and they were keeping it as evidence. I wasn't lying.'

'She didn't believe you?'

'Not at all, but then I do lie occasionally. She knew me well enough.'

'You were not here last night,' Sean asked.

'I stayed with a friend.'

'Male?'

'Female. I only came back today to pick up some clothes. That's when I found him.'

'Did you know that Brad was coming over?'

'No, but if Ingrid had phoned him, he would have come.'

Stan Crosley came out from the apartment for a break. He was carrying a change of clothes for Gloria. He saw Sean and Sara by the ambulance. 'A word, if you don't mind,' he said.

'Sure, what is it?' Sara asked.

'Did you take a look at the wall behind the door?'

'No.'

'I've got a photo here on my phone.'

Sean and Sara looked at the display as Crosley held it up to them. There was a large sheet of paper secured with tape. On it, written in blood, *Murder is only a number*. Below it was the number 3.

'She's playing with us,' Sara said. 'What kind of woman can behave like this?'

'One that is crazy; one that will kill again,' Sean said.

Chapter 8

A door-to-door investigation, conducted in the vicinity of Gloria and Ingrid's apartment, had proved negative. The night before the discovery of the body it had been raining and miserable, and very few people had been out on the street. One woman believed she had seen a man heading up to the apartment, but she had been vague in her recollection of events and certainly had not seen a woman.

Brad Howard's body, once Crosley and his team had completed their investigation at the murder scene, had been removed and taken to Pathology. An autopsy would be conducted, although the cause of death was not in any doubt. Whether he had been stabbed mid-coitus, as the crime scene examiner had said, would need to be determined.

For a woman who had been dedicated to chastity, Ingrid Bentham had indeed come a long way. The assumption with Gregory Chalmers had been that it was misguided love, coupled with paranoia, and a lack of the drugs needed to moderate her condition. But now, with Gloria and her sometime boyfriend, there seemed to be another element, even more disturbing.

Ingrid Bentham had apparently discovered the joy of killing, although it may have always been there, and now it was number 3. Sara wondered how long before number 4, and where and whom?

And what was the significance of the ring?

Sara and Sean wondered how the woman was able to appear and disappear at will. London was awash with street cameras, yet none had picked her up.

Stephanie Chalmers had left the hospital and moved in with her sister. The house where her husband had died was firmly locked up. His widow had no intention of ever entering the house again, which seemed illogical to Sara, as it was a beautiful home, but she supposed painful memories are always hard to deal with.

It had been the same with Sara when her parents had died five years before. They had been returning from a holiday when their car slid off an icy road, plunging them into a freezing river. According to the doctor, they would not have known what happened, but it gave Sara sleepless nights for months afterwards.

***

'We had better find this woman before anyone else is killed,' Rory said to Keith. Both men were nursing sore heads from the previous night.

So far, they had only drawn blanks. There were no murders attributed to minors, certainly not females, but the team back in London felt, as did Keith, that the number 1 was significant. If Ingrid Bentham had committed a murder as an adult, she would still be in prison, or at least a secure hospital for the criminally insane.

And her fingerprints would have been easily traceable, which concerned everyone. It was assumed that even if there was only a suspicion of wrongdoing as a child, her fingerprints would be on record, but in fact that was subject to the discretion of the department handling the case and the local legal jurisdiction.

Rory thought that there should always be a fingerprint record, but he was aware that there had been a period when the rights of the child, innocent or otherwise, had been paramount. Pure foolishness, he thought, but the rules were the rules.

'What do you reckon? Think carefully,' Keith said. He was getting edgy, wanting to get back to London. There was another murder. Keith assumed it was the man he had seen in Gloria's bedroom that night. He wanted to be involved, and Newcastle was even colder than London.

At least in London, he reasoned, there was always a warm fire in his favourite pub, although he wasn't much of a drinker nowadays, apart from special occasions such as the night before. He had been in his younger days, but now the bladder could not take the punishment, and the hangovers, mild and quickly dealt with in his youth, played havoc with the migraines that he had become prone to. He knew that his body had seen better days, but apart from the occasional moan, he did not complain.

'There was a case some years ago. A young boy, nine years old if my memory is correct. He died under suspicious circumstances,' Rory said.

'Suspicious, what do you mean?' Keith asked.

'There was an old quarry out near where he lived. He was found at the bottom of it. His death was recorded as death by misadventure, but…'

'What does that mean?'

'The marks at the top showed scuff marks, as if there had been a tussle of some sort.'

'Who was involved with the investigation?'

'I was, but it was some years ago.' It concerned Rory that it had slipped his mind. His mother had suffered from dementia; he hoped he was not starting to suffer the same condition.

'How many?' Keith asked.

'Thirteen, maybe fourteen.'

'It's around the right time. Do you still have your notebook?'

Rory fumbled around in a filing cabinet that was close to his desk. 'Here it is,' he said.

'12 December, 2004. Duncan Hamilton, aged nine, discovered at the bottom of Titmarsh quarry, no suspicious circumstances.'

'You said it was suspicious,' Keith reminded him.

'I've just read you the first entry. Later on, we found the scuff marks at the top of the quarry. It was a hell of a drop; the poor kid would have been dead on impact with the ground below.

'14 December, 2004. Interviewed Charles and Fiona Hamilton, parents of the deceased. One other child, Charlotte, not present.'

'Not the most enjoyable part of policing,' Keith said.

'Not at all, but it comes with the job description.'

'Do you remember what they said?'

'In my notes. "Parents distraught. Fiona Hamilton heavily sedated on doctor's advice. Broached the subject of a possible fight or altercation at the quarry. Charles Hamilton was furious and stormed out of the interview."'

'What did you expect?'

'His reaction was understandable. There they were, coming to terms with their son's death, and I'm there, casting doubt as to whether it was an accident. Even so, his storming out seemed to be an overreaction.'

'You persevered?'

'Had to. If he had been pushed, then it was murder.'

'15 December, 2004.' Rory Hewitt referred back to his notes again.

'"Charles Hamilton stated that his son, as well as the other children in the neighbourhood, often went up to the quarry, although they, or at least his son, had been warned not to."'

'Tell a child, especially a boy, and they will want to go,' Keith said. He remembered his youth. There was a fast-flowing river near his parents' house. They had warned him about the dangers, but the chance to catch a few fish always drew him there. He remembered that he had almost drowned once as he was attempting to manhandle a fish onto the bank. He didn't tell his parents, but he never went fishing there again.

'Exactly, and we were willing to accept the fact that maybe they were playing there, and he had slipped. Ready to accept that the scuff marks were as a result of Duncan attempting to hold on, or someone trying to prevent him falling.'

'It didn't end there, did it?' Keith said.

'I thought it had. Pursuing other children, possibly raising a case against them for the accidental death of a minor, would have tainted them for life. Young boys do stupid things, believing in their infallibility; most survive, although Duncan Hamilton did not. Maybe they were daring each other to look over the edge. Who knows?'

'What happened to change your mind about the case?'

'It's in my notes. "17 December, 2004. Travelled to the Hamiltons' house to interview. Charlotte Hamilton, the elder child, was in the front garden."'

'And?'

'She was singing a song.'

'And the song is significant?'

'I wrote it in my notes. "*Stupid Duncan up at the quarry, along came a sister and gave him a push.*" It was eerie.'

'Did you question her?'

'She would not speak. Psychological problems according to her parents.'

'Did you tell the parents about their daughter's singing?'

'Yes. This time Charles Hamilton sat mute; his wife spoke for both of them.'

'What did she say?'

'Fiona Hamilton stated that her daughter had an imaginative mind and to take no notice.'

'And did you?'

'What could I do? There was no proof, no witnesses, and no assistance from the Hamilton family.'

'How old was Charlotte?'

'Ten.'

'But you always suspected?'

'The song gave me the creeps. It sounded like a theme song out of a horror movie, yet it came from the mouth of a child.'

'What happened to Charlotte Hamilton after that?'

'I've no idea. The inquest was a formality. I made a statement, purely the facts, and the death was recorded as accidental. Both of the parents were present, although they did not speak, at least to me.'

'The daughter?'

'She was not there.'

***

'We need to interview the Hamiltons,' Keith said. It was a murder enquiry, and if Ingrid Bentham and Charlotte Hamilton were one and the same person, the inconvenience to the Hamiltons was of minor concern.

'Understood.'

Keith made the phone call. 'Detective Inspector Keith Greenstreet. I need to question you about your daughter, Charlotte.'

The voice at the end of the phone, female and initially friendly, went quiet. A masculine voice took over. 'She is not here.'

'Then where is she?' Keith asked.

'We have not seen our daughter for some years. We have no idea where she is.'

'Are you Charles Hamilton?'

'Yes.'

'I am requesting a formal interview. It can either be at your house or at the police station.'

'Come to the house, one hour.'

As the phone call ended, Keith could hear the faint sobbing of a woman in the background. He assumed it was Fiona Hamilton.

Rory, reluctant to venture near the Hamiltons' house again but mindful of his duty, accompanied Keith.

'It was over there,' Rory said as they entered the front garden through a small gate. 'That's where she was singing.'

The Hamiltons, on opening the door, were polite, although obviously not pleased to see DI Rory Hewitt. However, they acquiesced and invited them both in. Keith saw that the house was beautifully presented, everything in its place. Trained to be observant, he noticed the photos of a young boy lined up on the bookshelves and on the mantel over the fireplace; it could only be Duncan Hamilton. He saw no pictures of a daughter, other than of a very young child, a babe in arms almost.

Keith, realising the importance of the interview, followed procedure and notified them of their rights.

'Mr Hamilton, we are anxious to contact your daughter,' Keith said.

'We have not seen her for some years.'

'I need to ask you why not.'

'It's a family matter.'

'I'm sorry,' Rory said. 'That statement needs to be clarified.'

'DI Hewitt is correct,' Keith said. 'We believe that your daughter is a possible witness to a number of serious crimes in London. We need to find her.'

Rory handed the Hamiltons a photo taken from the Chalmer's house. Charles Hamilton took one look. His wife averted her eyes.

'After the death of our son, we decided that it was best if Charlotte received counselling,' Charles Hamilton said. He showed no emotion.

'Because of Duncan?' Rory asked. Keith realised the advantage of having someone with him who knew the family history.

'She was traumatised by his death,' Hamilton said. Keith could see Fiona Hamilton was barely able to contain her emotions. It was clear that Charles Hamilton was stoic, but his wife was of a nervous disposition.

'According to the records, Charlotte had some problems,' Keith said.

'She was always a sensitive child,' Fiona Hamilton said. Keith could only assume it was a mother's love for a child that failed to accept the reality. He wondered if they had the same suspicions about Duncan's death as did Rory.

'It was more than sensitivity, Mrs Hamilton,' Rory said.

'As you say. She had emotional problems,' Charles Hamilton conceded.

'I need to know where you sent her and the medical treatment she received,' Keith said.

'Is this necessary? Our son is dead; our daughter is missing. What more do you want from us?'

'I am truly sorry,' Keith said. 'But this is a murder investigation. It is my responsibility to bring the perpetrators to justice, to make them pay for their crimes, to prevent more deaths.'

'And you believe that Charlotte is a murderer?' Fiona Hamilton stood up, screaming. Her husband took hold of her and held her close to him. She buried her head in his shoulder.

'It may be best if you phone for the family doctor to come here, or I could arrange one for you. Mrs Hamilton could do with a sedative,' Rory said.

'That's fine. I'll make a phone call,' Charles Hamilton said. He took out his mobile and dialled. 'Five minutes, Doug. It's important.'

'Family friend, he'll come straight away,' he said to Keith and Rory on concluding the call.

It was no more than two minutes before there was a knock at the door, only ten before Fiona Hamilton was mildly sedated, allowing the interview to continue. There were questions to be answered, and the answers were needed now.

'Mr Hamilton, as you know I always had a suspicion regarding the death of your son,' Rory said. This time, Fiona Hamilton stayed calm.

'Do you have a recent photo?' Keith asked.

'It is five years old.'

'Can I see it, please?'

Charles Hamilton went over to an old writing bureau. He opened the top drawer and withdrew a photo that he handed over. Keith knew what he was looking at. Apart from the short hair and the younger face, it was Ingrid Bentham.

Keith's instinct was to phone Sara immediately, but he knew that first he had to conclude the interview.

'I need to know the name of her doctor and whether she remained in this house after the death of her brother,' Keith said.

'I will give you the contact details. After Duncan's death, her condition worsened. In the end, it became impossible for her to stay here. We found a good place for her, a well-respected mental institution, where she received the best care.

'At the age of nineteen, no longer a minor, and not subject to any restraining order, she left. After that, we have not heard from her.'

'Thank you,' Keith said.

'You believe that Charlotte killed those men in London, don't you?' Fiona Hamilton asked, her voice very quiet.

'That is not for me to comment on,' Keith said.

Charles Hamilton sat quietly for a while. He eventually spoke. 'Unfortunately, Detective Inspector Hewitt, you may have been right about Duncan's death.'

Keith could see a broken man, a broken family: one dead child, almost certainly murdered by his sister; the sister now a serial killer. He felt great sorrow on leaving the house. He knew he needed to be in London, although not before he had interviewed those in charge at the mental hospital where Charlotte Hamilton had stayed for eight of her twenty-four years.

He knew that, whatever happened, the lives of good people were forever altered due to the paranoia of one child, now an adult. He was glad that he was retiring: too much misery and despair during his time as a police officer. Informing the Hamiltons about their daughter was the last piece of bad news he intended to impart to anyone again.

Chapter 9

The mood in the office changed dramatically after Keith had phoned through from Newcastle. Finally, they had a name, even if the woman was not using the name in London.

Keith had sent a scanned photo through on his smartphone. Sara could see that it was Ingrid Bentham, as had Keith. Bob Marshall, pleased with the development, phoned through to Detective Superintendent Rowsome. The man unexpectedly showed up at the office thirty minutes later.

'Great policing,' he said. 'An arrest soon?'

'We hope so, sir,' Sara replied. Bob Marshall stood close by, absorbing the accolades, justified in his decision to keep Sara on the case, although it had been Keith Greenstreet who had provided the first significant breakthrough.

'Good woman you've got there,' Rowsome said to Bob Marshall as he left the office.

'She's a good officer.'

'That's not what I meant.'

'You're right, sir.'

'You'll not find anyone better than her.'

'I know, sir.'

The detective superintendent's comments had the tone of a command, not that Bob needed one; he knew exactly what he was going to do about Sara.

With the detective superintendent out of the office, Bob, back in DCI mode, turned to Sara. She was still glowing at the unexpected praise.

'It doesn't help much, though,' Bob said. He had found a seat close to where she was standing.

'You're right. We may have a name, even an understanding of the woman's state of mind, but no idea of her current location.'

'She's not finished her killing spree, you realise that?' Bob said. 'So far, she's killed a lover and her flatmate's boyfriend, but not the flatmate. What about her parents? Are they safe?'

'We assumed they were, but who knows?' Sara admitted.

'Then you'd better make sure they have protection.'

'Yes, DCI.'

'And tell the flatmate to make herself scarce. The woman has only killed men so far; we don't want a woman as well.'

'I will deal with that.'

'Sara, now that you're the shining star, at least in Detective Superintendent Rowsome's book, what's your plan?'

'Find Charlotte Hamilton.'

'But how? What do you have apart from a name? So far, this woman has killed two people, almost three. And one of them in her old apartment. She may be as mad as a hatter, but she is smarter than us. Why is that?'

'Luck on her part.'

'It's more than that. Ask Keith to check as to her intellectual capability. Even in her deluded state, she may be able to think rationally. She could kill again at any time.'

Sara realised that Bob, yet again, had brought her back to ground with a thud. He was right that Charlotte Hamilton could kill again, and there was nothing they could do to pre-empt her. Their only hope was to apprehend her, but if she could change her appearance as well as her identity, then the chances of picking her up on surveillance cameras or finding her at the haunts she had frequented seemed slim.

Regardless, Sara organised some uniforms to stake out the college she had attended, as well as her former flat and even the Chalmers' house.

Sara made a phone call to Charles and Fiona Hamilton. 'Charlotte had a ring; it was engraved on the inside.'

'I gave it to her the day she turned seventeen,' Fiona Hamilton said. 'It was a family heirloom. It had belonged to her grandmother.'

'How are you?' Sara asked.

'What do you think?'

'Not good, I suppose.'

The phone call ended. Sara assumed that the Hamiltons were beyond conversation.

***

The Mental Health Register showed that Charlotte Hamilton had been placed in a mental facility not far from the family home. There was no mention of Rory Hewitt's suspicion over the death of her brother, or that she was considered possibly violent.

St Nicholas Hospital, a forbidding remnant of Victoriana, the home of Charlotte Hamilton for eight years, was not a welcoming sight to Keith. The place gave him the creeps.

Rory Hewitt had accompanied him.

They negotiated reception; it was either sign in or they were not going any further, police badge or no police badge. They were ushered into a small waiting room on the first floor.

'Dr Gladys Lake, pleased to meet you.' A rotund woman came into the room and introduced herself. The top of her head did not reach Keith's shoulder. He bent his head forward and extended his hand. She shook it vigorously and with strength. He could see that she was an energetic woman; she reminded him of a teacher at the school he had attended as a child.

'We need to talk to you about a former patient,' Keith said.

'Charlotte Hamilton.'

'How did you know?'

'I've had Charles Hamilton on the phone. He's in quite a state. It seems that you have been making aspersions about Charlotte, something to do with her brother as well as the deaths of two men in London.'

'Unfortunately, they are more than aspersions. We have a warrant out for her arrest.'

'And you think that Charlotte could be responsible?'

'Is there somewhere we can talk?' Rory asked.

'My office, you'll need to excuse the mess.'

Keith could see why the woman had mentioned the mess. There were patients' files strewn across her desk, a laptop in the middle of it with a monitor to the side. Over on the far side of the office was a bookcase full of medical books.

'It's my bolthole away from all the cleanliness outside. It's the only place I can get some peace to study.'

'That's fine,' Keith said. 'What can you tell us about Charlotte Hamilton?'

'A beautiful child, no doubt a beautiful woman now.'

'She is.'

'Are you sure about this? When she left here, she had not had a relapse for a couple of years.'

'We have sufficient proof for a conviction.'

'Murder?'

'Yes, two murders now. We are worried there may be more.'

'Her brother?'

'We are not pursuing that. At least at this present time. The recent events in London concern us more.'

'Subject to patient confidentiality, I will tell you what I can. Charlotte entered here after the death of her brother; she was deeply disturbed. We evaluated her, placed her on medication, and with time and counselling, she calmed down. So much so that she attended a local school, visited her parents at the weekends.'

'Why did she not return to live with them?' Rory asked.

'It was difficult.'

'We need to know.'

'You are aware of Charlotte's medical condition?' the doctor asked.

'Not exactly. Our criminal psychologist believes that she displays the classic symptoms of paranoid schizophrenia.'

'Smart woman. With medication, Charlotte was able to lead a relatively normal life. However, ...' Dr Lake paused.

'There were some issues with the Hamiltons?' Keith asked.

'Once back at the family home, even with suitable medication, she would revert to type.'

'What do you mean?'

'She would become angry, frustrated, start lashing out at the parents, harming herself.'

'Razors, that sort of thing?' Keith asked.

'Yes.'

'And back here?'

'Five minutes and she was fine, although she hated it here.'

'Are you saying she switches on and off, medication or no medication.'

'Not at all. She needs the drugs, but the dosages were too high for her to be with the Hamiltons for too long.'

'But they came every weekend?'

'Here, she was all right, and if they took her out, she gave no trouble, but near that house she had problems.'

'Do you believe it was the memory of her brother?'

'That was my assumption.'

'What do you know of the death of her brother?' Rory asked. So far, he had let Keith do the majority of the talking, but Duncan Hamilton's death was a subject that he knew more about.

'A tragic accident.'

'Nothing more?'

'Are you saying his death was suspicious?'

'Charlotte has now killed two people. It is possible that Duncan's death was not as recorded.'

'And do Charles and Fiona Hamilton know of your suspicion?'

'Yes.'

'How did they deal with it?'

'Badly from what we can see. You realise that we're only doing our duty. Charlotte Hamilton could kill again. We need to find her.'

'I have to deal with trauma every day. I understand that you must do what is right.'

'We need your help,' Keith said.

'What do you want to know?'

'Charlotte has killed one lover, as well as the lover of her flatmate. Both crimes appear to be motivated by personal anger. Is there anyone else who could be a potential victim?'

'In her state of mind? Anyone she came in contact with over the years, even me.'

'So far we have ruled out anyone female.'

'I don't see why.'

'Would she regard her parents with ambivalence?'

'Possibly.'

'We have a police guard at their house.'

'That will not stop her,' Gladys Lake said. 'Charlotte may have mental issues, but she is still a smart woman. If, as you suspect, she has reverted back to a paranoid state, then she could find a way.'

'Medication?' Keith asked. 'We are aware that she was taking some medication.'

'Chlorpromazine most likely.'

'You're not sure?'

'I've not seen her since she left here. If she is on prescription, there should be a record.'

'According to our criminal psychologist, Grace Nelson, the dosage and the medicines change over time.'

'She is right, which would mean that Charlotte is under the care of a doctor. Or should be,' Gladys Lake said.

'Black-market prescription drugs are not that easy to come by.'

'Maybe, and what I prescribed five years ago may not be relevant today, especially the dosage. And besides, a lot of patients stop taking them at times due to the side effects.'

'If she failed to take her drugs or took incorrect dosages?'

'Probably what you see now: a belief that people are out to get you, aggression, violence.'

***

With the woman clearly identified as Charlotte Hamilton, an all-points warning was issued. This time it was more accurate than the previous one for Ingrid Bentham, not that Sara Stanforth held out much hope for it. A bottle of hair dye available in any supermarket, a different hairstyle, even plain clothes, and Charlotte Hamilton could go from attractive to dull and back to attractive at will.

Sean, pleased that the case was moving forward, disappointed that his studies for a Master's degree were slipping, focussed on detailing the murderous woman's movements in the intervening five years, from when she had walked out of St Nicholas Mental Hospital until the murder of Gregory Chalmers.

Legally prescribed drugs, especially the more potent ones, would be registered and on the record. Also, they needed to know if the drugs had changed over the years, and whether she was subjecting herself to regular medical checks.

If the records were meticulous, Dr Gladys Lake should have been able to access them. After all, she had been her primary doctor for many years, and someone with a known psychotic ailment would be monitored at all times.

His father, Keith Greenstreet recollected, was susceptible to blowing his top one minute, only to be calm the next, but with Charlotte Hamilton it was more than banging a fist on the desk in frustration. With her, it came with a knife, although no one, not even her doctor in Newcastle, had seen that possibility.

Sara, for once riding high in everyone's estimation, knew that it would not last for long.

'Five days maximum before they start questioning your ability and my judgement,' Bob Marshall had said the previous night. Detective Superintendent Rowsome was looking for an arrest; his Key Performance Indicators were slipping in a couple of key areas. With Charlotte Hamilton behind bars, he knew that his KPIs would be excellent for the next three months. The arrest of a murderer always counted for a lot, and Rowsome was looking for promotion.

Bob had an unusual way of initiating sexual congress, Sara thought. Discussing a murder was hardly the ideal conversation for a lead up to a romantic interlude, although it was not going to distract either of them. Sara knew that DCI Bob Marshall was the man for her, although he had been cagey on the subject of marriage. She knew that he had been married before, and even though there were no children, no complications, it had left him cautious.

Bob did not talk about his previous wife, which suited Sara, but sometimes the subject came up in conversation. According to Bob, she had a fiery temper coupled with a loving disposition. One wrong word on his part and she would not talk for a month, other than with monosyllabic replies.

Sara could see no problems for Bob on that account with her: she had no temper, said her mind and then forgot it. And as for not talking? She was a woman with a need. A woman in need of affection, Bob Marshall's affection, and she was not going to allow any temper tantrum to get in the way.

Next day in the office, after a successful romantic interlude the previous night, Bob Marshall was back into detective chief inspector mode.

'Sara, what are you doing about this woman, and is her flatmate safe? How about her parents?'

'We have uniforms watching out for them.'

'Not really good enough, is it?'

'What else can we do? We can hardly protect them day and night. Besides, Ingrid's, or should I say Charlotte's, flatmate is out of sight, visiting relatives in Nigeria. The woman was scared and rightly so.'

'You have an address, contact details?'

'Yes, DCI.'

'And the parents?'

'It must be tough for them,' Sara said. She remembered the brief conversation with Fiona Hamilton, the sadness in the woman's voice.

'Tough for any parent. Remember, five days and those in the office upstairs will be baying for my blood and yours. I've trusted you with this case, and so far, what do you have? Just a name. Where is this woman, what is her next move? Who is her next victim? Have you considered this?'

'Impossible to ascertain who the next victim will be.'

'Why?'

'One lover and then the lover of her flatmate.' Sara realised that her DCI was placing her under pressure for her benefit. After the praise of the detective superintendent, she had to admit that she had lost some focus. Bob was sharpening her up; she would deal with him later.

'So far, it's been people that she knows, and male.'

'Apart from Stephanie Chalmers, although we believe that was not intended. The woman walked in and found Ingrid with blood on her hands, as well as a knife. And Gregory Chalmers' death appears to be unpremeditated.'

'Brad Howard?'

'Premeditated. She calculated his death.'

'Why not kill Gloria?'

'We believe that she targets males.'

'At present. I suggest you tighten your operation. You have a full department here, and Keith will be back later in the day. I advise you to find this woman before there are any more deaths.' Bob walked away, only looking back to mouth 'Sorry.' He knew he had been a bastard, but it had only been to make her focus.

Fired up, she called in Sean. 'What do you have?'

'Not a lot. I can find clear evidence that she continued with her medication for a couple of years, but nothing after that.'

'Change of name?'

'Unlikely. No doctor would issue antipsychotic medication without a full medical history, and then he would probably check back with the primary physician.'

'Gladys Lake?'

'She told Keith that she had not seen her since the day she left the hospital.'

'It's possible.'

'Where did she get the additional medication?'

'London.'

'That gives us five years. Discounting the three years at college in London, we have two years unaccounted for. Where was she?' Sara asked.

'We'd better find out. There is an address for Charlotte Hamilton in London that Gladys Lake supplied. Supposedly, she had prescribed her medication the day she left. We should go there,' Sean said.

Chapter 10

Muswell Hill, five miles north of the centre of London, had recently been voted one of the five most desirable places to live in London. It was clear that the judging committee had not seen the address where Sara and Sean pulled up in Sean's car, a blue Ford Fiesta.

It was Charlotte Hamilton's first known address in London and not a welcoming sight. The terrace house looked to be run-down, which was incongruous given that every other house in the street was neat and tidy with fresh paint.

Sara got out of the car and knocked on the front door of the terrace house. 'What do you want?' called out a deep-voiced woman, her speech interspersed by coughing.

'Detective Inspector Sara Stanforth and Detective Constable O'Riordan. We have a few questions.'

'Very well.'

The woman, still coughing, opened the door, the security chain in place. 'We can talk here,' she said.

'Inside would be better,' Sara said.

'I don't like strangers.'

'We're here on official business. It is either in your house or down at the police station.' Sara knew what was behind the door. Sean, still naïve in many ways, did not.

'I'll get my coat.'

The door closed again. Two minutes later it reopened and the woman came out, a cigarette hanging from her mouth. 'I need to be back within the hour.'

'I can't promise you that,' Sara said.

'What's inside the house?' Sean whispered to Sara.

'This is where Charlotte Hamilton came to after leaving Newcastle. Somewhere she could earn some easy money; a place that paid in cash and did not ask too many questions.'

Sean understood.

Sara phoned a fellow police officer at the nearest police station. He agreed to them using an office there.

'Your name?' Sara asked in the quietness of the room, although it would have been better described as a broom cupboard, having just enough space for a table and chairs. All three had taken a coffee from the machine outside; the drink tasted of cardboard, the same as the cup. Sara and Sean took theirs black; the woman added milk and sugar.

'I run a clean house,' the woman said. Sara judged her to be in her fifties. Her face was blotchy from too little sun, not hard to achieve given the weather of the last few months, but this woman appeared to have had no sun for several years.

Sara went through the formalities before asking her name again.

'Mavis Williams.'

'Your age?'

'Fifty-eight. What's this all about?' The woman shifted uncomfortably in her seat, gasping for breath. Even on the trip in the back of Sean's car she had been desperate to light up, and now in the confines of the small office she was desperate to put another cigarette in her mouth. She fiddled with the packet, took out a cigarette, put it to her lips, returned it to the packet.

'We are looking for someone,' Sara said.

'Not one of my girls. They're all legal.'

'That is not our concern. If you're running a brothel, that is for the local police. We are from Homicide.'

'No one's been killed in my house.'

'Five years ago, a woman used your address. We believe she maintained that address for a further two years.'

'So?'

'We know her as Charlotte Hamilton. Does the name mean anything to you?'

'Most of my girls use fictitious names.'

'This woman was blonde. She would have been nineteen when she first used your address.'

'I don't employ anyone under twenty-one. Saves hassles with the police.'

'And your neighbours?'

'What do I care about them.'

'The woman, as I said, was blonde,' Sara continued. 'She was average height, slim and attractive. She would have spoken with a northern accent, from Newcastle.'

'Oh, her.'

'What do you remember about this woman?'

'She called herself Charlie. Unusual name, but not the silliest that I've heard. I've had my fair share of Blossom, Cherry, Honey, even had one who wanted to be called Buxom.'

'Miss Williams,' Sean said, 'what can you tell us about Charlie?'

'She was beautiful, I'll grant you that. She looked virginal the first day I saw her.'

'Was she?'

'How the hell would I know, although I charged extra on account of her supposed virginity. Men, they're all the same. Want to be the first, even in a whorehouse. At least thirty men took her virginity.'

'Did she have any inhibitions when she entered your place?' Sara asked.

'None that I could see. She took to it like a fish to water.'

'Do you know where she is now?'

'No idea, and I don't want to know.' Mavis Williams fidgeted again. 'I need a cigarette.'

'Not in here,' Sean replied.

'I'm gasping.'

'We still have further questions.'

'Not until I've had a cigarette.'

It was evident to Sara that the woman had information that could be vital. She had to give in to the woman's demand. Sean and Sara took the opportunity to have another cup of cardboard coffee.

Returning to the interview room, Mavis Williams exhaled the remains of her cigarette smoke over the two police officers.

78

Sean stood up and moved to the window. He opened it to let out the offensive smell.

'Can't give them up,' she said. 'They'll kill me, I know that. Anyway, we've all got to die eventually.'

Sara had to agree with the 'eventually' but not due to inhaling nicotine. Bob Marshall had appreciated the occasional cigarette; she had soon put a stop to that luxury.

'How long did Charlie stay with you?' Sara asked. She had shown a picture to Mavis Williams to confirm that Charlotte Hamilton and Charlie were one and the same; they were.

'Two years, on and off.'

'On and off?' Sean asked.

'Mainly on. She rented a room from me in the back of the house. If she wasn't servicing the men at the front of the house, she was there.'

'Did she like the work?'

'Screwing drunks and foul-smelling men with hygiene issues for money? What do you think?'

'I suppose not.'

'A lot of the women are spaced out on heroin or whatever, but she wasn't.'

'So why?'

'She said she needed the money. I never asked why. It's always best to maintain a distant relationship with the women I employ.'

'Over the two years, any unusual behaviour on her part?'

'At first, she was agreeable, but with time she became irritable, sometimes irrational. The reason she left eventually.'

'We need to know the details.'

'One of her clients, a particularly unpleasant character, I think he was Polish, or maybe Hungarian. I never asked, never cared, as long as his money was good.'

'And?'

'He wanted Charlie, although I had seen her earlier on and she was in a strange mood. I knew this man was a bit kinky. He liked a bit of violence, nothing serious, just a bit of slapping.'

'You allow that?' Sara asked.

'That's between the client and the woman.'

'Charlie went with this man?'

'She was always ready for another man. Most of the women spend their money on hard drugs, but not Charlie. She saved all her money, and after two years she must have had plenty. I pay well, and the men give generous tips.'

'What happened to the client?'

'From what I can gather, he starts getting a bit violent, and then Charlie snaps. She becomes aggressive, beating the man with whatever she can find. She had a small mirror in her handbag; she breaks the glass and comes at him with the sharp fragments. The man dashes out of the room stark naked. Charlie is in hot pursuit, screaming at him. It took three of us to calm her down.'

'And afterwards?'

'We cleaned up the man and then gave him one of the other women for free. He was not that badly hurt, although he could have been.'

'Charlie?'

'I gave her one hour to pack her belongings and leave.'

'What can you tell us about her after that?'

'Nothing. I never saw her again, and that's the honest truth.'

***

'Next time, I'll take the train,' Keith said on his return to the police station in London. It was apparent to Sara that he had not been home for a shower first.

She felt that she should tell him to go home first and clean himself up, but she desisted. He was a grown man, old enough to be her father, and she had grown uncommonly fond of him: almost like a warm blanket or a child's favourite toy.

Sure, his appearance could be disarming, and his humour was questionable, acerbic at times, but within that shell of a man she recognised a decent and honest person; a person aiming to make a difference. She had little time for the lazy and inept, and with Keith Greenstreet, she recognised a kindred soul.

Life had taken its toll on him, and he looked older in the office that day than any other in the past.

'Apart from a six- to nine-month period, we have accounted for Charlotte Hamilton's movements,' Sara said.

'It's not over,' Keith said. 'This woman is lethal.'

'And we've no idea where she is.'

'And we never will. Her movements are unpredictable, and every time she moves, she changes her identity. She could be one block from here, and we would never know. We could even walk past her in the street.'

'Your thoughts, Keith. Where to from here?'

'Keep looking.'

'It's not much of a strategy,' Sara admitted.

'I agree, but what else is there. We know of all known addresses that she has used. We are aware of her ability to conceal herself and her willingness to sell herself without guilt, and then we have a woman who is intellectually bright.'

'Brighter than us, and no longer on medication.'

'That's a fair assumption,' Keith said.

'She's going to kill again,' Sara said. 'And soon.'

Chapter 11

Liam Fogarty could not believe his luck. Not only had he been rewarded with a promotion at work, but here he was with a beautiful woman.

He knew that with a bulbous forehead and a receding chin that he hid with a goatee beard he was not the most attractive of men. He realised that it was the reason he had never been successful with women. In his early teens, there had been the occasional female, equally as drunk as he had been, and each had seen beauty in the other. The inevitable result: a casual attempt at lovemaking in the back of a car, or more likely lying on the cold grass in the local park, had been the limit of his sexual experience.

It had been two years since his last woman, discounting the one he paid for every month or so.

'What are you doing here?' he asked the woman who was obviously interested in him, judging by the way she looked at him and the suggestive moves she was making.

'Looking for you.' The woman realised it was a stupid line, but then the man looked silly to her. She had not known that he was smarter than he looked, smart enough to have obtained a degree in Economics, but then that was not why she needed him.

The woman looked at the man. She was not excited at what she saw, although he looked pliable and fit for purpose.

'Do you want to dance?' Liam asked. He was well plastered, on his fifth pint, and his mates were egging him on. He was in need of a visit to the Gents, but that would have to wait. He knew his mates would have been over in an instant to grab the woman. He took another drink, Dutch courage to him. Sober, he recognised his inadequacies; drunk, his persona changed, as the balance between gregarious and fast asleep in a drunken stupor was only separated by a short time span. Even now, he wanted to sit down and sleep it off, but not with this woman closing in on him. He believed he was Adonis reincarnated; even Paris stealing Helen away from Menelaus and taking her back to Troy.

'Give her one for us,' Liam's drunken friends shouted above the noise of the club. He looked at them with a smirk. He was the lucky bastard, and they could go to Hell.

The woman grabbed him firmly and pulled him towards the dance floor. He almost tripped as she dragged him to the centre, away from his jeering mates.

'What's your name?' Liam slurred, attempting to focus. He was desperate to stagger out and to relieve his bladder, but he held on. He regretted that he had drunk so much; concerned that he would not be able to perform. The woman was giving him the right signals. He knew he was on to a sure thing.

'Does it matter?' the woman replied when he pressed yet again for her name.

'I suppose not,' Liam said. He had been deprived of a woman who had shown interest in him for too long, other than the women who feigned interest as long as he paid, but this one, she was gorgeous.

He swayed as he spoke; he wanted desperately to sober up, but the woman continued to prime him with alcohol, even taking a drink from another drunk on the dance floor who was close to collapse. The drunk had attempted to complain but the woman had just leant over towards him and given him a kiss on the cheek.

'Thanks,' she said. The drunk could see the beauty in the woman, although the woman he had been fondling on the dance floor was not too happy and stormed off. The drunk tried momentarily to cut in on Liam. The woman pushed him away, as had Liam. *No bastard is taking this woman from me,* he thought.

The woman moved in closer at his sign of bravado. She was holding him tight, her breasts pressing hard against his chest, her legs close to being entwined around his. They danced, they kissed, and all the time Liam Fogarty could feel the need of the woman. He could see the beauty in the woman, but not the venom in her eyes, the searing hatred that coursed through her veins. He could not realise that the woman was working on him, bringing him to a crescendo.

***

The club where Liam and his woman were dancing was not far from London. It was heaving that night. The music was loud and getting louder, the drinks were flowing, and the noise was overpowering. A residential estate close by had tried to have the noise moderated a few months earlier. They had formed a residents' committee to make a submission to the local council. They wanted a noise abatement order as the first step, a closure of the club to follow.

A heated meeting in the council offices had come to nothing. A formal notice had been sent to the club. Its owner, Sam Goldsmith, a shrewd businessman who had made his money to the east of London with clubs and discos, legal or otherwise, knew more about local councils than the local residents, led by a busybody by the name of Betty Arkwright, did. She had the law on her side, and a write-up in the local newspaper had garnered widespread support for her and her residents' committee.

Sam Goldsmith, impervious to the man in the street as long as he could afford his extravagant lifestyle and his two mistresses, cared little for the Arkwright woman and her sanctimonious group of narrow-minded residents. The more they complained, the more he would bribe, by way of cash and trips overseas. The local residents' committee had no chance just by waving a copy of the Environmental Protection Act 1990 at the council.

Goldsmith knew that more music, the longer trading hours, the increased patronage could only mean one thing: more money for him and the greedy councillors, their snouts in the trough.

***

It was Liam Fogarty's first time in the club: a celebration with his friends, and he was paying. Not that he minded, as they were good friends he had known since his schooldays. They were still struggling to make their mark, but there he was, regional manager for a multinational bank. It had been hard-won, a lot of sweat and tears, a lot of study and sleepless nights, a lot of time without a woman. However, tonight was his night.

In his drunken mind, the woman he was dancing with was with him because of his self-assuredness. He had noticed her pale complexion; he had certainly seen her breasts, as had his friends. 'Give them a squeeze for us,' they had hollered when they had first seen Liam and the woman together.

Liam was drunk, almost close to comatose, but his friends were worse. The club did not tolerate excessive drunkenness officially, but Liam had the money. There were over five hundred in the club that night, and four hundred would probably fail a breathalyser if they attempted to drive home.

'Do you come here often?' Liam had asked when he first saw the woman making eyes at him, swaying from side to side to show her assets. He had thought that she would disappear as he made his way towards her, but she did not. He could see a good night ahead. He realised it was a clichéd chat-up line. He had moved in close to the woman, as the noise made it impossible to hold a normal conversation.

'First time. And you?'

'Celebrating with my mates. Are you on your own?' Liam hoped that she was. A promotion and this woman in the one day was more than he could hope for. He imagined her with him, somewhere more comfortable, somewhere more intimate. He had been put down too often in the past, and usually he would have given her a wide berth. His last girlfriend, a pleasant enough woman, had not been as attractive as the one standing in front of him, but he knew that he was not an attractive man.

The last girlfriend, they used to meet on a Friday, and he would sleep over at her place on that night, but apart from that he had not felt any great emotion for her. Not that she was not affectionate, she was, but she came with a history of too many men, too much promiscuity. He had known her at school when she had been slim and cute with firm breasts and a tight arse. Then, she had not wanted to know him, but with time and a preponderance to put on weight, she had changed. When he had met her seven years after leaving school, she had gained twenty pounds and an extra chin, and her body had sagged after the birth of a child that she loved but he could only see as an encumbrance. She had professed love, but he knew the truth. She wanted a provider and a father figure for the child, the result of her promiscuity and a former student at the school they had attended.

Liam knew that when he wanted a child, he would find a good woman, maybe the woman who now had her arms around him.

'We can dance if you want,' she said as she kissed him firmly on the mouth. His mates, pretending not to notice but unable to resist, cheered.

The woman looked over at them and smiled. *You bastards*, she thought.

***

At first the music on the dance floor had been fast and frantic, with arms flying this way and that, but within ten minutes of Liam and the gorgeous black-haired woman hitting the floor, it had slowed, so much so that they had no option but to embrace and to sway with the music.

'I want you,' the woman said, her body pressing close to his.

'We need to go somewhere,' Liam said.

'Anywhere is fine by me,' she said as she pressed in close. She knew the effect she was having on the hapless individual.

'My place is nearby,' he said.

'Too far.'

The conversation continued for several minutes. Garry, one of his drunken friends, attempted to cut in. Liam pushed him away.

'Go away, find your own woman,' Liam's female said. She was almost glued to him now, and her constant gyrations up and down his body had the desired effect.

'Can I see you again after tonight?' he asked. He realised the dancing and the movement of his body were starting to reduce the effects of the alcohol. He could not believe his luck. He had looked around the club earlier before he had drunk too much. He had seen some attractive women, but sober he would not have approached them. Too many rejections by the sort of women he fancied had made him reluctant to repeat the process. Too many times had he been told that he was unattractive or fat or he smelt. It was true that his facial features were not good, nor was his body. It was not fat, more like baby fat that had not gone away. He discounted his need for greasy fish and chips and pizzas washed down with beer as the cause. The smell that they complained of he could not understand, but he thought it may be to do with the garlic which he liberally dosed on his food every day.

And now, here he was, with the most attractive woman in the club. He had not seen her on entering; assumed she had come later.

'Why worry about tomorrow?' the woman said when Liam persisted with asking her out the following day. She wore a tight blouse and a short skirt, unfashionably short. She knew she looked to be an easy lay, the effect she was trying to create. Five nights she had hidden away to the north of London in flea-bitten accommodation where only money was required and no prying questions were asked. Not that it concerned her, as she was adept at changing her appearance and her behaviour. She knew the medical diagnosis of her mental condition, but they were wrong, part of a plot to belittle her.

It was those bastards who were at fault, not her. She was the sane one, and those who conflicted with her had a limited life span. She intended to rid the world of those who caused her anguish, and as for her parents, they were the worst of them all. She tried to remember them fondly, but she could not. They could wait for another day.

Men were the problem; men who had paid for her body, men who had professed love but only wanted to screw her. Once she had dealt with this one, she would disappear for some time, but she would return.

Gregory Chalmers had treated her badly, as had his bitch wife. Brad Howard, that bitch Gloria's boyfriend, had come over quickly that night. So much for his faithfulness to her. She had seen him undressing her with his eyes before; his death had been pleasurable. She imagined that the man she was with would not be as good as Brad, but she did not intend to waiver.

As she danced close to Liam, the gormless and charmless man, she reminisced. She thought of a happy childhood, until that stupid brother of hers had teased her and then broken her collection of dolls, even pulled the leg off one. She had been ten, too old for dolls, but she had loved her collection, especially the one with the missing leg. He had deserved to die, and she was glad that she had killed him.

And then there was that bitch doctor at St Nicholas who had been pleasant to her, but she had allowed them to attach electrodes to her scalp. She remembered the trembling in her hands and feet; the restraints that held her down. She was meant to be sedated, but sometimes they made a mistake, and the pain of the electricity passing through her body had been unpleasant.

Her parents had visited her, but they never took her back home, other than for short periods. They did not want her, she could see that clearly now, and as for the medication, to hell with it. She knew what it did, how it quietened her down, but she no longer needed it. She had a purpose in life, a purpose to rid the world of all those who had caused her pain and anguish, and this foolish man who thought he could dance. He believed that he was God's gift to women, but he would not be the first or the last. He would be another marker that she was here and she was determined.

'There's a toilet out the back,' she said. 'Take me there.'

The idea excited him, although a toilet did not. He imagined a bed with silken sheets, rose petals on the pillow, a bottle of champagne with two glasses.

The club was modern and clean, but the toilet out past the kitchen belonged to another era when the club premises had been part of an industrial complex; it had not been cleaned for some time and smelt. Liam imagined rats and cockroaches, and he did not like them, but the woman was hot and whispering in his ear, then sticking her tongue in his mouth. He wanted to be somewhere else with her, and his place was only five minutes away. The woman came closer, put his hand on one of her breasts. The desire to make love to the woman was overpowering.

She pushed him down on the toilet seat, pulling his trousers down to his ankles. He was erect and ready. She straddled him with no foreplay.

'Just stay there for me,' she said.

He sat still while he maintained his erection.

'Are you ready?' she asked.

'Yes, yes,' he said gasping for breath. The woman was beautiful, even if the surroundings were not. He was aflame and unable to hold out for much longer.

'Are you ready for your surprise?'

'Yes,' he said.

The woman put one hand inside the small bag she carried. She waited for him to be at his peak, and then she thrust the thin stiletto knife into his chest. Liam, at the moment of death, clutched the knife with one hand in an attempt to remove it.

The woman removed herself from the man and put one of her fingers on the blood oozing from his body.

The toilet was concealed from general view. On leaving it she found a tap outside. She removed the clothes she was wearing, washed herself down, put on fresh clothes that had been in the small bag, and walked out of the building by way of a back gate.

She smiled as she walked away, only to break into song after a couple of minutes. *Liam thought he was a stud until I stuck a knife in his heart.*

Chapter 12

'George Street, Richmond!' Sara Stanforth said over the phone to Sean O'Riordan. She had already phoned Keith Greenstreet and given him the same directive. Crime Scene Examiner Stan Crosley had also been notified.

'What is it?' Sean asked. It was one in the morning, and he was still studying. There was an important exam the next week, and he knew he was not ready.

'Joey's.'

'I know it,' Sean said. He had been there with his friends some years before.

'There's been another murder.'

'Charlotte Hamilton?'

'It looks that way. We'll have a clearer idea out at the scene. The local police are securing the crime scene and rounding up the patrons. They are none too happy from what I've been told, but if it's her, she's been out in public and very visible.'

'Someone must have seen her,' Sean said. He was dressing as he spoke. His girlfriend woke to ask what was going on. 'The usual,' his reply. She had become used to the hours that he worked, and rolled over and went back to sleep. He thought she looked delightful lying curled up in his bed, but now was not the time for romance.

It was only three days since Keith had returned from Newcastle. Three days when the team had mostly stayed in the office analysing, debating, and trying to come up with a plan on how to find this woman.

There were extra police out on the street, and random door knocks had been conducted, but nothing. The woman baffled them with her ability to appear and disappear at will.

Keith was first at the murder scene as he only lived two miles away. Sara arrived shortly after. Sean was two minutes later. Bob Marshall came as well in Sara's car.

'What do we have?' Bob asked.

It was Keith who replied. 'Male in his thirties.'

'Fatal?'

'That's why we're here,' Keith replied.

'Then we'd better take a look,' Sara said. She went round to the back of her car and took out gloves and foot protectors. The local police had waylaid the patrons, or at least those that had not sneaked around the cordon and down a side alley.

'It will take some time to interview all of them,' Sean said.

'We have to whether they like it or not,' Sara reminded him.

Two uniforms were outside the main door, another at the back of the building.

'Who found the body?' Sara asked.

'One of the cooks. It appears he went out back for a cigarette. That's when he found it.'

The four police officers moved through the club and out to the back. The cook, a big man who looked tough but had proven himself not to be, was sitting quietly. The dead body had upset him.

Careful not to disturb the evidence, the four police officers approached by a circuitous route. Standing on the other side of the yard, with the toilet door slightly ajar, they could see the body sitting on the toilet, the head drooped forward. There appeared to be a lot of blood.

'I need to check,' Sara said. She was aware of the CSE's reaction if he saw her, but she needed to know. Close up, she could see the knife in the man's body. She looked around, a small torch in her hand, as there was no light inside, and it was still night.

'It's here,' she said.

'What's the number?' Sean asked.

'4.'

'Rowsome is going to have my guts for garters after this,' Bob said, knowing full well the man's venomous tongue, a man short on praise, long on criticism.

This was his department, and his SIO, someone he had protected from criticism, and yet again the woman had come into his patch and committed murder, and from all accounts, in sight of five hundred patrons at the busiest club in the area.

Bob Marshall knew what was coming: an immediate directive to remove Sara from the senior role.

Sara, equally aware of what was to happen, but not willing to relinquish control without a fight, focussed on the job in hand.

Stan Crosley had arrived, and he was ushering them out of the area. 'I've got work to do. The same woman?' he asked.

'It looks to be that way,' Sara replied.

'Can't you find her?' his sarcastic response.

Out front, the patrons were getting restless. Most had been drunk or close to it, and the alcohol was slowly wearing off. The local police had identified the friends of the dead man. They were off to one side.

As for the other patrons, the local police could interview them, check proof of identity and ask the mandatory questions: did you see anything suspicious, did you visit the back of the club at any time, did you see a woman with the dead man? One of the dead man's friends had supplied a picture from his smartphone.

'Liam,' one of the friends said. 'I can't believe it.'

'What can you tell me about the woman?' Sara asked. Sean was interviewing another of the friends. Keith was dealing with two others.

'We saw her, of course. Liam never had much success with women, and there he is with a looker.'

'Can you describe her?'

'It's hard. We were all drunk, celebrating Liam's promotion at work. He had just been made regional manager, and the drinks were on him. Anyway, this woman starts wrapping herself around him.'

'Can you describe her?'

'Slim, extremely attractive, especially to us drunks.'

'She's attractive, even without alcohol.'

'You know her?' the friend asked.

'Not personally, but we know what she is capable of.'

'And she killed Liam?'

'Subject to confirmation.'

Liam's friend Ken was slowly recovering from his drunkenness. Sara organised a coffee for him, one for her. One of the uniforms obliged and went and found a café still open, or it had opened once it had seen the milling throng out on the street.

'Ironic, I suppose,' Ken said.

'What do you mean?' Sara asked.

'The first time he finds an attractive woman, and she kills him. Is it the one on the news?'

'It seems possible,' Sara replied, not wanting to comment too much, knowing full well that the media would certainly grab Ken for an interview.

'Mind you, she wasn't attracted to him for his charm, was she?' Ken said.

'No.'

'I tried to move him away from her on the dance floor. The woman told me to find my own woman. If I had succeeded, it would be me dead now.'

'Probably.' A one-word reply from Sara.

'Why does she do this?'

'That's the subject of our enquiries. Anyway, what else can you tell me about the woman?'

'Dark hair, almost black, or I assume it was.'

'Why do you say that?'

'There's not much light inside the club.'

'She was previously blonde. Are you sure she had dark hair?'

'Positive.'

Sara realised that if the woman was teasing them, she could be out the front: part of her ghoulish behaviour, revelling in what she had committed.

***

'Pierced the large artery coming from the heart,' Stan Crosley said later in the morning.

'Death came quickly?' Bob Marshall asked. He had heard from Detective Superintendent Rowsome already. The death at the club had become headline news, and he would have to make a press statement.

The DCI was not sure what to say: we are following all lines of enquiry; an arrest is imminent. He knew such words would not allay the demands of an eager media desperate for any titbit of information, but what else could he offer. He could hardly say that they knew the identity of the murderer but hadn't a clue where she was.

Stan Crosley answered Bob Marshall's earlier question. 'This woman does not understand the physiology of the human body. If she had, she would have known that a knife wound to the heart does not guarantee immediate death. She did, however, luck on piercing the large artery. Anywhere else, the man could possibly have regained consciousness long enough to raise the alarm.'

'Would he have lived?'

'Unlikely, but he would have lived longer. With Gregory Chalmers, she used a large knife, but a stiletto is much smaller. With Brad Howard she was lucky as well. Is she likely to strike again?' Crosley asked.

'We can't be certain, but all indications are that she has found a taste for murder.'

'And you can't find her?'

'Unfortunately, that is the truth at the present moment.'

Sara did not speak. She had been informed by Bob that someone more experienced was to take over the case. He had not wanted to do it, but she had lost the confidence of senior management, and whereas she had done an excellent job, he had no option but to remove her. However, she would stay with the team. Keith Greenstreet had made an impassioned plea for her to remain in charge, only to be told by Bob that it was beyond his control. He knew where he would be sleeping that night.

Chapter 13

Part 2

Three years later

Detective Chief Inspector Isaac Cook knew immediately on entering the crime scene the one person who could help him. He had read the case files of Charlotte Hamilton, and it was clear who had the most knowledge about her.

The murderous woman had become notorious some years previously, even revered by deluded fools around the world. In the USA, there were plenty of women who felt that their lives had been destroyed by men. There had even been a couple of copycat killers, who after murdering their spouse or ex-boyfriend with a knife if they had one, a gun if they did not, would paint a number on the man or else on the wall.

Somehow, these people, in their anger, would justify their actions by citing Charlotte Hamilton. They were wrong, of course. The gutter press and social media had elevated Charlotte Hamilton's star way above where it should have been.

There was nothing admirable about this woman, no attempt on her part to right the wrongs wrought against women by men, no ideological stance, and no act of retribution. Charlotte Hamilton had clearly been defined by the authorities as a psychotic killer suffering from paranoid schizophrenia. However, being psychotic and paranoid had not affected her ability to evade capture.

Liam Fogarty had died a tragic and violent death due to his drunkenness and the belief that a beautiful woman desired him, not because she needed to make a sacrifice.

Sara Marshall had been right. Charlotte Hamilton had been outside the front of the club in Richmond that night while the patrons were going through the interview procedure. She had even posed with a few other people who were waiting for the police to deal with them so they could go home to sleep it off, or in the murderer's case to post pictures on Facebook. She made sure that in one of the photos she had a police officer in the background, namely Sara Stanforth, as she had been known then.

There had been a few rough months after Detective Chief Inspector Bob Marshall had removed her from the lead role in the search for Charlotte Hamilton. Forced by his superior, Detective Superintendent Martin Rowsome, he had assigned the lead role to a more experienced officer with twenty years in Homicide and a good track record.

Not that it made any difference, as he had no more success. Two months after the hapless future regional bank manager had died, and with no more deaths, no more numbers carved into men's bodies, no more numbers painted onto walls with blood, the team were reduced in number.

Keith Greenstreet had finally retired; reluctantly, he had said, but Sara Stanforth could see that he was tired, and his health was not good. He had been a good officer, someone she had grown fond of in the short time they had worked together, so much so that when she married Bob Marshall, she asked Keith to walk her down the aisle. He had even spruced himself up for the occasion, taken to exercise and a healthy diet. However, it was of little benefit, as shortly after the wedding he had succumbed and passed away. The most he had was eight months of retirement.

Sara had continued to work in Homicide, but there had been no lead roles, other than in a case of straightforward marital strife, where the husband had shot the wife, and that was only because Bob felt some guilt over her treatment regarding the Hamilton woman.

Charlotte Hamilton's parents, suffering immense guilt and sadness, had become reclusive, shunning contact with friends and neighbours. The last Sara had heard of them, they had sold up and moved to a cottage in a remote area.

Dr Gladys Lake at St Nicholas Hospital, Charlotte's home for eight years, had been assigned a police guard for a few months, after receiving a phone call one night: 'I remember,' the only words spoken.

It was Sara who had found the cheap hotel where Charlotte had been staying after she moved out of the flat she shared with Gloria, and where she had murdered Brad Howard.

Charlotte Hamilton's death count was now at four. Rory Hewitt had reopened the case into the death of Duncan Hamilton. The verdict had been changed from death by misadventure to cause of death unknown, although no one, certainly not Rory Hewitt or Duncan's parents, believed in the 'unknown'. It was clear to all three who had given that fatal push.

***

'Sara Marshall, my name is Isaac Cook,' the voice said on Sara's mobile. 'Detective Chief Inspector Isaac Cook.'

'Yes, sir. What can I do for you?'

'I need you here. Are you free?'

'I will need to pass it by my DCI.'

'I'll deal with him. It's imperative that you're here.'

'Where do you want me?' Sara Marshall asked. She knew who Detective Chief Inspector Isaac Cook was. She had seen him on a couple of occasions, even been introduced to him, although his phone call gave the impression that he had not remembered.

'35 Easton Grove, Holland Park.'

'Thirty minutes.'

'I will be there,' DCI Cook replied. 'I need you to see this.'

For once the traffic was in Sara's favour. Within twenty minutes she arrived at the house. The uniforms were visible, as was the tape surrounding the crime scene. An ambulance was parked across the street.

'Not unless you cover up,' a voice bellowed at her.

'I have gloves and foot protectors,' Sara said.

'Apologies. I'm Gordon Windsor, the CSE here. It would be best if you put overalls on as well.'

'DCI Cook?'

'He's inside.'

Sara changed quickly and proceeded inside the house. It was clear that whoever lived there lived well.

'DI, I'm Isaac Cook. I believe we've met. I wasn't sure if you would have remembered.'

To Sara, it seemed naïve to believe that any woman would not remember Isaac Cook. He was over six feet, slim, and jet black. Even she had heard of his many romances, his straightforward manner with the average person as well as the top politicians in the country. She had seen him on television on more than one occasion.

'Not sure I could forget you, sir,' Sara replied.

'I need your opinion,' Isaac Cook said.

He led the way as they moved to the first floor of the house, and into the main bedroom. It was a scene that Sara had seen before. In the centre of a queen-sized bed lay the body of a man, naked and flat on its back.

'The cleaning lady found the body,' Isaac said.

'Similar pattern.' Sara looked up at the wall. She knew why she had been asked to visit the house.

'Copycat or is it the same woman?'

'It's been three years. After so long, most people have assumed that she committed suicide.'

'Had you?'

'Never. She may have been mad, but she was always in control. You saw the photo on Facebook with me in the background. And Charlotte Hamilton in the foreground taking a selfie.'

'Who hasn't,' Isaac said. In fact, from what he could remember, over five million had seen that photo.

'I knew she was still alive somewhere.'

'What do you reckon? Is this Charlotte Hamilton?'

Sara moved around the room. The man appeared to be in his fifties, a little overweight, but apart from that in good physical

100

shape. She observed the slight erection, assumed it to indicate mid-coitus, although that was for others to confirm.

The knife, with only the handle visible, was embedded in the man's throat. There was also blood congealing on his chest in the area of the heart.

'She's improved her technique,' Sara said.

'What do you mean?'

'When she killed Liam Fogarty, she only stabbed him once with a stiletto knife. Unlikely that he would have lived, but he would have lived longer had she not severed the large artery.'

'Are you certain?' Isaac asked.

'The crime scene investigators will confirm, but, yes, it's her. Did she take a shower?'

'Dried the floor, hung up the towel afterwards.'

'So much blood. Gave her plenty of writing material,' Sara said.

'The number on the wall?'

'It's the same style of writing.'

Both of them looked at the wall, an off-white colour before the blood of the victim had been used to paint the number 5.

'It's her,' Sara said. 'She's back, and she will kill again.'

'We need to work together on this.'

'The case was assigned to another officer.'

'I'll square it with your DCI.'

'Thanks. I would like to get even with this woman.'

'She's dangerous, and she knows you,' Isaac said.

'And I know her,' Sara said.

'Welcome on board.'

***

Procedurally, the responsibility for the murder investigation would lie with the Homicide team in the area where the crime had occurred.

Graham Dyer, a local businessman, had died in Holland Park, close to Challis Street Police Station, and would come under DCI Cook and his team. The other murders had occurred in the Twickenham area, Sara Marshall's area of responsibility.

Bob Marshall had no issues with his wife again taking the lead role in Twickenham, although his detective superintendent had, or at least had until Detective Chief Superintendent Goddard, Isaac's boss, had phoned Martin Rowsome and insisted.

The plan was that Sara Marshall and her team, currently only Detective Sergeant Sean O'Riordan, would stay at their office, while Isaac Cook and his team would remain in Challis Street. The stations were close enough, only thirty minutes to drive, although sometimes it could take as long as forty-five minutes.

Sara had no illusions as to what was going to happen. Isaac had been hopeful that the death of Graham Dyer was a one-off, although he had been involved in enough murder cases to know that once a murderer has acquired the taste for killing they need to feed that hunger, and Dyer had been number 5.

Isaac had read up on the previous four deaths. He had been visibly disturbed by the death of Duncan Hamilton. He had read the psychological reports from both Grace Nelson, the criminal pathologist, and Dr Gladys Lake. The behavioural patterns of Charlotte Hamilton were clearly identified; the analysis was the same from both women: highly dangerous, likely to kill again, no cognitive sense of right or wrong.

Isaac knew this time they had a problem. In the past, his murders had been centred around blackmail, revenge, anger, a need to conceal the truth, but with Charlotte Hamilton, it went deeper.

The woman was smart. IQ tests in Newcastle had shown that she was in the top ten per cent in the country, yet coupled with that was no moral restraint, no comprehension of the evil she was committing, no concern about the emotions of those who had loved her, still loved her.

The media, as ever aggressive for a good story, had soon latched on to the death of Graham Dyer. So far they did not

102

know about the number on the wall. They had been bad enough the first time, even attempting to portray her as some kind of folk hero, at least on one internet site dedicated to the bizarre and deluded. Isaac had checked it out; it had over twenty thousand followers, although most of them were just curious and could be considered harmless. However, taking the numbers down from twenty thousand to those who read the website, maybe ten per cent, and then to those who fantasised over Charlotte Hamilton, the lone ranger, wreaking revenge on those men who had subjugated women. Even if ten per cent of ten per cent of ten per cent of twenty thousand, there was bound to be one or two crazy enough to commit murder.

Isaac hoped that the deluded would do it elsewhere; Charlotte Hamilton was enough to deal with. His team were primed and ready: DI Hill was already interfacing with his counterpart, DI Sara Marshall. Detective Sergeant Wendy Gladstone was in communication with Sean O'Riordan, and Bridget Halloran was collating the paperwork.

A joint operations room had been set up in Challis Street. Detective Chief Superintendent Goddard had attended the first meeting, given them the obligatory pep talk.

'What do we know about this woman?' Isaac asked after Richard Goddard had left.

'You've read the report?' Sara asked.

'We've all read it, but what we need is to hear it from you.'

Sara, pleased to be a rising star again, not a has-been confined to the office more often than she would have liked, stood up to speak.

'After Liam Fogarty's death, we kept the investigation open for another four months. In all that time, we found no trace of Charlotte Hamilton, other than a hotel where she had stayed after killing Brad Howard.'

'Are all the murders attributable to Charlotte Hamilton? Could any be copycats?' Larry Hill asked.

'There's no doubt. Fingerprints and DNA at all murders, apart from Duncan Hamilton.'

'She killed her own brother?' Wendy Gladstone asked.

'Psychotic. No concept of right or wrong,' Sara said.

'Medical reports aside,' Isaac said, 'what do you believe she intends to do? What are her thought patterns?'

'She killed three people in London and disappeared.'

'Any thoughts as to why?' Larry asked.

'As to why she killed three people or why she disappeared?' Sara asked.

'The latter.'

'Either she went back on medication, although we could find no prescriptions in the names that she has used and no black-market sales, or she just stopped of her own free will.'

'Is that possible?' Isaac asked.

'According to the experts it is, although the psychotic thoughts would remain.'

'The triggers being men?' Wendy asked.

'That's what we believe. So far, there have been no attacks against women, apart from Stephanie Chalmers at the first murder. We believe that only happened as a result of her walking in just after Charlotte Hamilton had killed Gregory Chalmers. Gloria, her flatmate, was not killed, although her boyfriend was.'

'Gloria, where is she?'

'I've no idea. Probably back in London, but we've had no reason to contact her for over two years.'

'We need to find Charlotte Hamilton,' Isaac said. 'Any ideas where we should look?'

'Where she's stayed hidden for three years may be a good place to look,' Sean O'Riordan said.

'But you've no idea where to look,' Larry reminded him.

'As you say, no idea, and that is the problem.'

'Job for you, Wendy,' Isaac said.

Gordon Windsor, the crime scene examiner at the murder in Holland Park, joined the meeting. 'I can confirm that samples we found at Graham Dyer's house belong to Charlotte Hamilton. As expected, he died mid-coitus, seminal fluid found on the tip of his penis. At the moment of ejaculation, she thrust the knife into his heart. This time, she missed the large artery, and he would have still been alive. He had been stabbed an additional three times in the heart and once in the throat.'

'Any clues about the woman?' Isaac asked.

'Brunette, although the roots were blonde. Also, she showered, cleaned the bathroom and left. Nothing more.'

'We conducted door-to-doors,' Larry said. 'Nobody saw anything. Graham Dyer was a local businessman, successful by all accounts. He had been married but was living on his own. One neighbour stated that he occasionally brought a woman home with him.'

'Where did he meet Charlotte Hamilton?' Bridget asked.

'Good question,' Isaac said. 'Sara, any ideas?'

'Not really. Gregory Chalmers, she met when he and his wife had advertised for someone to help with the children. Brad Howard, she knew through Gloria. Liam Fogarty, she picked up at a club in Richmond. If she wants a man, she'll find one.'

'Wendy and Larry, you'd better get down to Holland Park and see if you can trace the murdered man's movements.'

Chapter 14

Charlotte Hamilton had seen the black police officer. She imagined seducing him, and then at the right moment sticking a knife into his black heart.

She knew she had been right to stay hidden for three years; three glorious years where no questions had been asked, and everyone had been courteous and friendly, even invited her into their houses. She had not been fooled. They were no better than her parents who had deserted her, allowed her to be drugged and then electric-shocked, with the confusion and memory loss after. Sometimes she wondered about her parents: where they were, what they were doing, even wishing her stupid brother was still alive. But what if he was?

He had only been an irritant to her, teasing her, breaking her dolls, getting between the love of her parents for her. She was glad she had killed him, even though she could have saved him. She remembered him squealing as he hung on to a branch protruding at the top of the quarry. How she had enjoyed pulling the branch away from him; how she had enjoyed watching him fall and fall and fall, and then hitting the ground with a thud. The sound had been music to her ears, and if she closed her eyes, the scene was still so clear.

She had seen the sorrow in her parents' eyes, especially her mother's, that he was dead and she was still alive. They should have embraced her with the love they had shown to him, but what did they do? They threw her into that place full of crazies. Sure, she had to admit that it had not all been bad, but it was a home for the insane, and she was sane. The man who had tested her before admission had said she was exceptionally bright, yet she was locked up behind bars with people who drooled and talked nonsense and threw their food on the floor.

She remembered the woman doctor, that Lake woman. She had told them to attach the electrodes to her scalp, and then told them to crank up the electricity. They had told her that it was good for her; something to do with dopamines and incorrect electrical paths in the brain. But she knew what it was; it was to punish her for being smarter than they were, for finding out how to beat the security and to climb over the fence. They had caught her once or twice, but she had done it many times.

She wanted to leave there at eighteen, but she had stayed a year longer. She had used their hospital because she had nowhere to go, but once she figured it out, she had left. They had tried to stop her, to reason with her, but she had a woman in London who was going to look after her. All she had to do was to offer her body to any man that was willing to pay, and where was the problem in that? Hadn't she given herself enough times to the local men in Newcastle, and what did they give her? Nothing, apart from a nasty rash. At least the hospital's medicine chest had dealt with that.

And then the men in that house in London with their breath smelling of beer, their bodies of sweat and lack of hygiene. They wanted to love her, to make love to her, but what did they really want? Just a quick screw, the opportunity to prod and poke her body, and once they were satisfied, they would leave her to clean up the mess. They were the same as all the other men. Gregory Chalmers had treated her well; she had loved him, but in the end he was only a bastard as well. And then there was Gloria's boyfriend, tattooed and well-built. He thought he was something special until she had stuck the knife in him. The feel of his body beneath her as she rammed the knife in. The spurting blood covering her body. The look on his face as he realised that he was not there for love, only for death, his death. He had died for all men, although he was only one. Many men were deserving of death; she would ensure them that right.

The club had been fun, although the man had not been. He had told her his name was Liam, and he had been ugly and small and unable to satisfy her; not that it mattered, as she had been pleased with the knife in his heart. She had read in the newspaper afterwards that he could have lived if she had not happened to put her knife in the right place. One day she would thank whoever had advised her on that. Graham Dyer had been her first after three years, and his death had been assured as she knifed him repeatedly; no point in a shoddy job. He had tried to paw her in the pub, and back in his house he had tried to love her. She had no need for love; no need for a man, other than to be the receiver of a violent death.

She could see another murder, maybe the black police officer, but he would be smarter than her previous victims. And then there was that female detective inspector. She realised that women were not to blame for the troubles in the world, but for that woman, Sara Stanforth, she would make an exception. And what did a man have that a woman did not? She knew the answer to that question: the power to subjugate women, the power to put her into a lunatic asylum, the right to hit her, just because they had paid for her. And with Gregory Chalmers, the authority to profess love and then cast her off, no more than an old shoe, not even worthy of contempt.

She had not wanted to harm Stephanie Chalmers. She had been a good woman with a bad husband: a husband that cheated on her, who did not love her, only himself. Charlotte wished it could have been different, that he could have loved her and she could have been with his children, but he had been no different. She had enjoyed carving a number onto his chest, although she had not carved another since.

She knew that her mind played havoc with her thoughts, and that medication would make her see everything the same way as other people, but who was sane? Her or them?

They were the mad people, not her. She knew that given the right environment, she could act as they did. It had been easy outside that club to masquerade as an innocent bystander. The photo she had taken had been shown around the world; she was famous, and she enjoyed the feeling. She would take another to show that woman police officer and that black man that she, Charlotte Hamilton, moved the streets of London with impunity.

They would never find her, and she would remove more men from society. She needed to pass the message on for other women to join her cause.

***

Isaac Cook's parents maintained an album of their son. They had photos of him as a child, as a youth, his graduation from university, and especially his time as a police officer.

They had recorded every press conference where he had spoken. They even had one of him with the prime minister, although Isaac was not sure that they would want a copy of the short video that had just appeared on Facebook. So far, Isaac could see that it had had over three thousand views, and that number was certain to rise.

Charlotte Hamilton had a Facebook account, and although it had been blocked a couple of times, it resurfaced soon enough with a different name. Those interested in her career always seemed to find it.

The video of Isaac leaving Graham Dyer's house with Sara Marshall had been clear enough, even if the camera, a smartphone, had been located on the other side of the road. It had been a cold day, and most people on the street had a hat on or a hooded jacket, which would have been the ideal disguise for Charlotte Hamilton.

Isaac checked the woman's Facebook account. Now she had fifteen thousand two hundred followers. Isaac knew that the world was full of idiots, but liking the Facebook page of a serial killer seemed macabre. He assumed that all mass murderers enjoyed their infamy, and it no doubt encouraged them to cause more misery. Next time a video of a slaying would be hard to stop. Facebook may put a block on a video portraying graphic violence, but there were other websites, and they would not be so scrupulous.

'How are you going to handle this case, Isaac?' DCS Goddard had asked on his arrival at the Homicide office.

'We need to find the woman.'

'Why do you think you will succeed? The other police station had three years, and they couldn't find her.'

'We're better, sir.'

'You may well be, but this woman is smart; smart enough to video you.'

'Unfortunate, sir.'

'Downright embarrassing. My best police officer videoed by a serial killer, and you never spotted her.'

'I was with DI Sara Marshall, and she never spotted her either.'

'That's the second time on film for her. Any more and she'll need to join the actors' union, Equity.'

'I don't think she would appreciate that, sir.'

'You must have a plan.'

'Not a lot to go with. We are checking on Graham Dyer's movements, attempting to find out when and where he met Charlotte Hamilton. Apart from that, we are at a loose end. The woman disappears, reappears and disappears again.'

'Then find out where.'

'Not so easy. She blends in seamlessly into the city. Apart from her predilection to murder, she's just an average citizen.'

'That may be, but I don't want any more deaths. Understood!'

'Understood, sir.'

DCS Goddard left, and Bridget came into the office. 'Bit hard on you, sir,' she said.

'He's right.'

Isaac was the best police officer in the department, but even he could not see the way forward. A murderer invariably gives themselves away eventually, but Charlotte Hamilton did not see herself as a murderer.

Back in Twickenham Sara was going over old notes. She had phoned Charlotte's father's mobile, told them to watch out for their daughter, although they had seen the news and assumed it was her. She also called Dr Gladys Lake to let her know that Charlotte had resurfaced.

Rory Hewitt, still working, although looking forward to his retirement, stationed some uniforms to watch the hospital. Bob Marshall, Sara's husband and DCI, was concerned for his wife. She was now the mother of a one-year-old, and she should be spending time with him. Murder always burned the hours, and a child needs more than a couple of hours of exhausted attention from its mother each day.

Sara, eager to prove her mettle after her unceremonious dumping by her husband on the orders of Detective Superintendent Rowsome, intended to make amends, to show both of them that she was as good as any man, and certainly better than the man who had replaced her.

He had had less success than her, and he had left soon enough: tail between his legs, but his reputation not tinged by failure.

Hers had been, she knew that, and while she still held the rank of detective inspector, the two words had not been split by 'chief'. She knew that may not be possible without a Master's degree, and in the past the department would have paid for her studies, but for two years they had been refusing. Budgetary constraints, the official explanation; unofficially, a black mark against the candidate.

***

DS Wendy Gladstone and DI Larry Hill visited Holland Park, positioning themselves where the video of their DCI and DI Sara Marshall had been taken. They knocked on a few doors close by; nobody remembered anyone specifically, although more than one person had been videoing the scene.

Graham Dyer owned an antique shop not far away. It was closed when they arrived, not unexpected considering that the owner was now in Pathology, and would be undergoing a detailed autopsy. He had been in his fifties, well liked locally, and led an active social life. Wendy and Larry visited some local establishments – clubs, pubs, cafés.

It appeared that he had visited most of them at one time or another, had been married and would take the occasional woman home with him. So far, nobody remembered the woman from the night of the murder, although he had been in one of the pubs earlier in the day.

An attractive female would not be noticeable, both Wendy and Larry agreed, in an area that boasted more than its fair share of beautiful women.

'The perfect disguise,' Wendy said, although, as she freely admitted, she would not have gone unnoticed. It had been some months since her husband had passed away, but she still missed him. She had joined a gym, taken up yoga, even quit smoking for a couple of weeks, but she was back on them again, although not as heavily as before.

Isaac Cook, their DCI, continued to have female trouble. Sue Smith, the latest in a long line of suitable women, had gone overseas, and he was alone again; not that he liked it, but there was not much he could do about it.

Wendy knew he could always find someone for a casual fling, but he had admitted to her on a couple of occasions that he wanted to settle down.

***

Isaac was pleased to be busy again, although troubled that a known murderer was walking the streets. The woman could be anywhere, he realised. With his other murder cases, it had been a case of sifting through the clues, interviewing people, aiming to solve the crime and to pinpoint the murderer, but with Charlotte Hamilton, none of this was needed.

The woman had been identified, the prosecution case was ready, and there was no question of her guilt. To Isaac, what he could see was a missing person's investigation, and the person in question was calculating and able to strike at will. She was a phantom whose appearances signalled another death, but where would she next appear?

Not only had she videoed him leaving Graham Dyer's house with Sara Marshall, but she was also videoing locations around London, including a distant view of the apartment block where Isaac lived. Her notoriety continued to gain momentum as she placed them on social media.

It was a world obsessed with celebrity, whether it was vacuous and worthless, talented or talentless, and it cared little that the person they sought out, even worshipped, was a psychotic murderer.

Some websites had been set up around the world by admirers, their hosting servers located in countries that did not enforce censorship, other than on their own people.

The copycat killings continued to occur: an unfaithful husband in North Carolina, a drunk homeless man in Alaska, even a male immigrant from Africa in Birmingham. And always a number had been painted on the man or on a wall, either in his own blood or with a felt pen.

None of the women involved in the copycats was as smart as Charlotte Hamilton, as they had all been caught and charged.

Isaac Cook, tall, black and intelligent, pondered the way forward. He had met Sara Marshall on a couple of occasions to discuss tactics, and to see if they could pre-empt the next murder, but both knew that Charlotte Hamilton did not commit murder by the book.

So far, she had killed five: the first, her brother, then a lover, followed by a flatmate's boyfriend. Her last murder, three years previously, had been chosen for no other reason than he had been male, and he had been willing to accompany her out to a toilet at the back of a club.

Then three years of nothing, only to return and kill Graham Dyer.

Sara Marshall thought that she could disappear again, but Isaac's instincts were more attuned. He knew she would strike again and soon.

Even he could see that the woman had a fixation on him, but why? He had seen her picture, even the video of the children's party at the Chalmers' house, and he had to admit she was beautiful. She had been twenty-four then; she would be twenty-seven now, and if she did not kill men, would be the sort of woman that he liked, her pale skin offsetting his shiny black.

'Larry, what's the plan?' Isaac asked. Both men were sitting in Isaac's office. There seemed little point in being out on the street looking for the woman.

'We can just follow up on leads.'

'Do we have any?'

'According to Sara Marshall, the woman stays within certain areas. The three murders, three years ago, were centred around Richmond and Twickenham. Now, she is close to us, here in Challis Street. There is every reason to believe that her next murder will be within four to five miles of this location.'

'Do you realise how many clubs, pubs, places of entertainment there are?'

'More than we can hope to cover.'

'Precisely,' Isaac said. 'We're being forced to wait for her to make the next move. Her increasing baiting of us indicates a change in her modus operandi. In the past, she has been a silent killer, driven by her neuroses, her belief that she was providing a service, but now she appears to want the adulation as well.'

'Plenty of sick people out there,' Larry said.

Wendy Gladstone had come into the office, bringing a cup of coffee with her. 'What do you reckon?' she asked Isaac.

'The best we can do is to issue a warning to the general public.'

'The male public according to profiling,' Wendy corrected Isaac.

'As you say, the male public.'

'Vague,' Larry said.

'Any better ideas?' Isaac asked.

'Not really, but what are they looking out for? A woman of twenty-seven, hair colour unknown, clothing unknown.'

'Miss Average,' Wendy said.

Chapter 15

A woman walked along Oxford Street, one of the busiest shopping locations in Europe. She drew no glances from the other people on the street. It was a warmer day than the previous four, but it was still cool. She wore a dark coat and jeans.

The day was drawing to a close, and it was becoming dark. She realised that she had been walking for hours, and had been deep in thought. She knew that life had given her a purpose, and she felt a degree of contentment.

For some years, she had been lost, unsure how to proceed. Integrating into a small country town had been easy. She had arrived there three years before. All that she owned or needed she carried in one suitcase and a backpack.

The old lady who opened the door at her accommodation had been pleasant and had welcomed her in with a cup of tea. Charlotte Hamilton knew that it was old-fashioned hospitality and that the woman meant well.

Dr Gladys Lake had meant well, but then she allowed them to torture her; Mavis Williams had meant well, but she expected her to let men use her body; Stephanie Chalmers had meant well, but her husband had used her.

She hoped that Beatrice Castle meant well, or...

'Call me Beaty, everyone else does,' the old lady said.

'Call me Cathy.'

A cat had climbed up on to Charlotte Hamilton's lap. It purred. Charlotte felt calm. She had had a cat as a child, but her brother had teased it, and then one day it had been run over by a car. She remembered her mother picking it up and placing it in a hole in the ground, next to the roses. 'It's the best place for him,' she had said.

Charlotte remembered that day well enough. She had made a cross out of two small branches that had fallen from a tree in the garden. Each day for a week, she visited the grave and placed a few flowers on it. Her brother had said she was crazy, and it was only a dumb animal and it had deserved to die. She knew from that day that she hated him.

It had been easy to hate him, to hate a lot of people, but she could not hate Beaty or her cat. She did not know why, but it was a good feeling; the best for a long time.

Charlotte could see that she had been running forever. First from her parents, and then from her doctor, and then from Mavis Williams and all those men. Gregory Chalmers had shown her love, real love, not just a drunken screw, but he had disappointed her. With Beaty and her cat, she could forgive him. She thought he had died, something to do with her, but her mind seemed unable to focus on negativity.

'How long are you staying?' Beaty asked. Charlotte had found the small cottage online.

'As long as I can.'

'Then I will make sure you have a special rate.'

Beaty showed Charlotte to her room. It was delightful, with a view overlooking the back garden. There was a small stream at the far end, and the sound of it lulled her to sleep at night. Occasionally Felix, the cat, would come in and curl up on the bottom of the bed.

The room, with its floral wallpaper, the morning sun streaming in through the bay window, the homely touches, reminded Charlotte of her childhood. She realised that for the first time in many years she was happy, and the negative thoughts that had plagued her had vanished.

She reflected on her life, and she could only remember the good; the bad, whatever it was, had recessed back into her subconscious.

Three years passed in an instant. A job in the local library, even a boyfriend, but it had not lasted long. For whatever reason, an over-amorous man only complicated her life, and all she wanted was simplicity. She had remembered her parents soon after arriving in the small town, and on Beaty's insistence, she had phoned them.

It had been a short conversation, but Charlotte had been pleased to hear their voices, aware that she could not return to the family home. She did not know why, but it was something serious; she was sure of that. Her parents had been pleasant, but distant; not once offering to come down and visit her, not that she wanted to see them, but it would have shown the love of parents for their child. Their child who had been lost for so many years, but had returned.

It had been Beaty who helped her integrate into the town, and Charlotte grew to love her.

She realised that the medication she carried with her was not needed, and she rarely took it. She threw it in a dustbin.

It had been good with Beaty and the cat but it had ended, badly as always. The cat had strolled out into the lane at the front of the house. Charlotte had warned Beaty how dangerous it was.

'Don't worry, there's no traffic. Felix will be alright.'

The cat did not see the delivery van, or if he did, he was too slow. The driver had not seen the cat, not that he was looking, as he was running late.

'You killed him,' Charlotte shouted.

'Not my fault,' the driver bellowed back from the safety of the vehicle. Charlotte moved her hand to the bag she carried, realised it only contained the day's groceries.

The vehicle hurtled off and was out of sight within twenty seconds.

Charlotte picked up the dead animal and carried it back to the house.

'Felix, Felix, what's happened?' Beaty screamed.

'A van hit him.'

Beaty clutched her chest and fell forward. Charlotte phoned for an ambulance. It arrived too late.

Charlotte buried the cat in the garden, put some flowers on the grave, made a small cross and left for the railway station. Her memories had come flooding back.

She knew what she had to do.

***

The Duke of York in Dering Street looked suitable. Charlotte took a seat close to the bar. A man soon joined her. He was a banker, or at least he said he was. Not that it concerned Charlotte as she had no need of his financial advice, no need of a mortgage, and besides, if she wanted a house, there was one up in Newcastle. At least, once she had removed its two inhabitants.

'Can I buy you a drink?' the banker asked. Charlotte had to admit that he was not a bad-looking man.

'Vodka and Lime.'

Charlotte knew that he was checking the goods on display. She had worn a thick coat and jeans to the pub but changed into a V-necked top and a short skirt on arrival. She knew that she looked cheap.

Let him think I'm an easy lay, she thought.

Dennis Goldman knew a sure bet when he saw one, and this woman was money in the bank. He could see that she wore no bra under the top. It had been a hard week in the city, what with the declining pound and the rise in interest rates. He had made the right call on shorting the pound earlier in the day; he knew that he was making the right call with the woman, especially as she was progressively moving closer to him.

'Are you busy tonight?' he asked the red-haired woman with the winning smile and the beautiful body.

'I'm free. Do you have anything in mind?'

'A meal and then my place,' he said.

If this one doesn't come across, it's still early enough in the evening to find another, he thought.

'How about your place first?'

Excellent, he thought.

'Is it far?' Charlotte asked.

'Five minutes in a taxi, ten if you walk.'

'Then we walk,' she said.

Charlotte drank her vodka and lime; Dennis finished his beer. They left the pub holding hands. Dennis believed himself to be a lucky man, although attracting females came easily to him.

He had the talk down to a fine art. Run through the first few sentences, ensure a result. No result, move on to the next.

London was awash with beautiful women, and he was having the time of his life. He was making plenty of money, sleeping with more than his fair share of women.

This one would be another to add to the tally, he thought.

Dennis's place reflected the man: confident, brash, and modern. It was on the second floor of a converted terrace house, and it commanded a good view over London. Charlotte had to admit that she liked the apartment, even liked the man, but Gregory Chalmers had been a smooth talker, and he had turned out bad.

Besides, he brings me back here, no doubt to screw me and then dump me. I'm not the first one he's brought up here, she thought.

Dennis prepared some snacks, and brought a bottle of wine to the table in the sitting room; Charlotte continued to give the right signals.

The bottle of wine consumed, they moved towards each other. Soon, they were naked and writhing on the carpet. Charlotte was on top, the ideal position for the finale.

'You're beautiful,' Dennis gasped.

'You are suitable,' Charlotte replied.

'I'm ready.'

'Are you sure?'

'Yes.'

Charlotte leant over to her bag. She put her hand in and withdrew the knife.

'What's that for?' he asked.

'You bastard. You think women are just here to satisfy your carnal lusts.'

'What…'

The knife entered his body easily, driven by the force of the palms of both hands pushing down. The man's erection subsided as the blood drained out of his body.

Charlotte, familiar with the act of death, removed the knife; she then drove it back down again, this time harder than before. The man beneath her did not move. She took another knife from her bag, a larger knife, razor-sharp, and slit his throat. The blood spurted out. She rubbed it over her bare breasts and placed her bloodied fingers to her mouth.

'You taste great,' she said.

She then removed herself from the dead man's body and walked slowly to his shower. She washed all the blood off and shampooed her hair, careful to remove all traces of the red dye she had applied earlier in the day. She then dried herself, put on the top and jeans she had worn earlier. Before she left, she helped herself to some food from the refrigerator. She made a sandwich and walked towards the front door.

She looked back at the man lying dead on the carpet as she passed. She admired the skill with which she had carved the number 6 on his chest.

Bastard, she thought as she closed the front door behind her.

***

In one part of London, a woman bathed in the glory of her fame; in another, a police officer was coming to terms with not being in control of the situation.

Detective Chief Inspector Isaac Cook, the star of Homicide, a man slated for senior management, the protégé of Detective Chief Superintendent Richard Goddard, was floundering. He had met senior politicians, charmed them with his good manners. He had met and seduced many women, but now there was one woman who was oblivious to him. The one woman who could undermine his career if she was not stopped, and soon.

She had murdered five, and according to her website, she had killed again. So far, the department had not received any information about another murder, but the website had shown a view from the apartment, and it was clearly London. The photo of a naked man covered in blood was too disturbing for most to see. The London Metropolitan Police had attempted to block the website; it had not been successful. Charlotte Hamilton was fast attaining cult status, with a loyal band of followers: deviants, sadists, and miscreants, not to mention the extreme feminists who saw all men as superfluous.

Monday morning and it was the weekly meeting. Bridget, Wendy, and Larry were in attendance, as well as DI Sara Marshall and DS Sean O'Riordan.

There had only been one subject to discuss, and Sara was still the person with the most intimate knowledge of the woman.

Detective Chief Superintendent Goddard had joined them, at least for the first fifteen minutes. 'It's not looking good, is it?' he said.

'We are working on it, sir,' Isaac replied.

'Without any tangible results. I can find out more information about the murders and this woman on the internet than from you. Doesn't reflect well on this department, and now I have the commissioner of police on the phone asking what I'm doing, and what sort of people I have.'

'He's unreasonable,' Isaac said.

'I know that, but he's the commissioner. I can hardly tell him to go away and to let us get on with the policing, can I?'

'We're a good team, sir.'

'That may be, but this Hamilton woman is better. Mind you, she does not have a commissioner to answer to, only her admiring public. How many followers on her website now?'

'Over twenty-five thousand.'

'She's posted another death,' Goddard said.

'That is the subject of our discussion. So far, we have not received any confirmation of another murder.'

'Apart from her website,' Goddard said. This time she's posted photos.'

'She's mentally sick,' Sara said.

'That's damn obvious to anyone. Still smarter than anyone in this room.'

It was Sara who spoke first after Richard Goddard had left. 'Unfair comment.'

'We go back a long way,' Isaac said. 'His bark's worse than his bite, and besides, he is correct.'

'Have you seen the photos?' Larry asked.

'Yes.'

'Can we deduce where they were taken?' Wendy asked.

'It's not easy. London, and not far from here. You can see the skyline in the background.'

Chapter 16

As Sara and Sean were about to leave the office and return to Twickenham, Isaac's phone rang. He picked it up.

'Hold on,' Isaac shouted at them before returning to the phone.

'Another body?' Wendy asked.

'34 Davies Street, Mayfair. Larry, Sara, you can come with me. We cannot have everyone at the murder scene. Gordon Windsor will go spare if we all come marching in. Sean, Wendy, get ready to conduct a door-to-door. Bridget, open another file.'

Challis Street to Davies Street was no more than two miles. Traffic was heavy mid-morning. Isaac took the portable flashing light out from under his seat and secured it to the roof of his car. With the siren and the light, cars started to pull over to one side to let him through.

'Dramatic,' Gordon Windsor said on their arrival.

'What floor?' Isaac asked.

'Second. Good view, charming apartment, or at least it was.'

'What do you mean?'

'You'll see once you've kitted up.'

Two uniforms were standing outside; the crime scene tape had already been rolled out. Due to the crowd that was building up, barriers were being erected on the other side of the street. As Isaac, Larry and Sara kitted up – gloves, foot protectors, and overalls – a television crew arrived. Barry Wiltshire, their lead crime reporter, saw Isaac and made a beeline for him. Isaac told one of the uniforms to deal with it. He did not have the time to indulge in idle speculation on the street, at least not before he had seen the body and the crime scene, and even then, he did not want to speak to Wiltshire who was an obnoxious toad of a man.

Isaac and his team entered the front door of the building and climbed the two flights of stairs. Once inside the apartment, they followed the obvious route down the hallway. On the floor in the main room was the body of a man: as usual, naked and lying on his back.

'Investment banker, or at least he was. Explains how he could afford this place,' Gordon Windsor said. He had preceded them up the stairs and was standing close to the body.

The white carpet that the body lay on was covered in blood, a lot of blood. Bloodied footprints could be seen on the polished floorboards around the perimeter of the carpet. Larry felt his stomach reacting, as did Sara. Isaac appeared unmoved by the scene.

'That's where she walked after killing him.' Gordon Windsor had seen Sara looking at the footprints, trying to ascertain where they led to.

'Did she shower?' Sara asked.

'Helped herself to the food in the refrigerator too. I would estimate she spent thirty minutes here after she had killed him.'

'Identity of the deceased?' Larry asked.

'Dennis Goldman. Apparently a whiz kid with stocks and shares.'

'How do you know that?' Isaac asked.

'There's a certificate on the wall from his bank.'

Sara's phone rang, and she excused herself from the conversation. Once outside the apartment, she spoke. 'Sara Marshall.'

'Is it?' an enquiring voice asked. Sara recognised it instantly.

'Dr Lake. We are here now. It is almost certainly Charlotte.'

'She phoned me ten minutes ago,' Gladys Lake said.

'What did she say?'

'She sang a song.'

'What song? Do you remember?'

'I will never forget it as long as I live. *Oh, what fun, I slit his throat. Who will be next? Will it be you?*'

Sara felt a shiver down her spine. 'You'll need twenty-four-hour protection.'

'With Charlotte? What's the point?' Gladys Lake said.

'She has only killed men, so far. We have no reason to believe she is targeting you.'

'That may be, but I am scared.'

'Then leave. Go overseas, take an extended vacation until we apprehend her.'

'I will consider that option.'

The phone line went dead. Sara called DI Rory Hewitt in Newcastle. 'I've just had Dr Lake on the phone,' she said.

'She called me five minutes ago. We have assigned immediate protection for her.'

Sara returned to the murder scene and told Isaac about her conversation with Gladys Lake. Gordon Windsor was checking on the condition of the body. 'She did not intend him to live. Very thorough,' he said.

'Was he alive when she cut his throat?' Larry asked.

'Probably not, although his blood would still have been pumping.'

'Friday night?' Isaac asked.

'Judging by the putrefaction, the gases emitting from the body, the defecation, I would agree with that possibility. Why Friday night?'

'That was the date given by his murderer.'

'You realise she enjoys this?' Windsor said.

'She's already threatened someone else,' Isaac said. He checked Charlotte Hamilton's website. It kept being blocked, only to reappear on another server. She now had eighty-four thousand followers.

***

Wendy and Sean were outside when the other members of the team left the murder scene. They were busy organising a door-to-door. Each person assigned to the task had been given a list of questions to ask: did you see anything suspicious, did you know Dennis Goldman, did you see him with a female on Friday night between the hours of 8 p.m. and midnight, and so on.

Wendy and Sean had been given a phone number and address of Dennis Goldman's place of work; they were heading over there.

Sara called Charlotte Hamilton's parents. 'Have you heard from your daughter?'

Charles Hamilton answered the phone. 'My wife is not well enough to talk to you.'

'I'm sorry to hear that,' Sara said. She felt for Charlotte Hamilton's parents. According to Keith Greenstreet, who had met them some years previously, they were decent people who, because of their daughter, the most savage serial killer in England for many years, were now pariahs in society. They were unable to go out of their house, and if they did, then it was to a distant location, hoping they would not be recognised, to purchase the household provisions and then return as quickly as possible to the sanctity of their remote location.

'Is it her?'

'I'm sorry.'

'My wife has suffered a breakdown; attempted suicide.'

'Will she recover?' Sara asked.

'Her body may. We are broken people,' Charles Hamilton said.

'Is there anything I can do?'

'Find our daughter before she kills again.'

***

In an internet café on the northern outskirts of London sat a woman. It was the evening of the previous day, way past 9 p.m. and the café was due to close in fifteen minutes.

Long enough, the woman thought. She had become used to run-down internet facilities with their dodgy screens, keyboards with keys that stuck, especially the most used ones, and cursors that jerked their way across the screen.

A permanent connection was not possible at the bedsit she rented, and a mobile modem would not have had the capacity for the photos she was loading. She was a lonely figure in that café, but she was happy.

She was famous all over the world, her followers a testament to that fact. Each day, in all the newspapers in London, there would be an article on her latest murder, and always a photo of the black police officer.

Her intellect told her that she was taking risks. An internet connection could be checked, even the café where she was now, but she did not care.

She knew that one day all those mad people who saw her as crazy would put her in prison, but it was them, not her, who deserved to be in prison. If they were going to catch her, and she knew they would, then she would lead them on a merry chase first.

She would make the black police officer pay. They said his name was Isaac Cook: she would remember that name. And there, yet again, was that woman, that Sara Stanforth, although now they were reporting her as Sara Marshall. The woman had a husband; what joy to put a knife into him, to watch her suffer.

Maybe she would kill them both. The thought made her smile and then to laugh. The owner of the internet café, a small man with a strong accent, looked at her as she laughed. His interest waned after ten seconds, and he went back to the comic that he had been reading.

He had a motley collection of patrons coming into his café, paying five pounds for a coffee and thirty minutes' free internet, even though the connection was slow. Not that it seemed to concern the woman, a short-haired brunette, her face partially concealed by a large scarf.

If he had looked, he would have noticed that she was attractive, but he was not a man who cared about anything very much. As long as they paid, what did he care? They could be talking to a girlfriend, even indulging in phone sex, learning how to make a bomb, booking accommodation. He only wanted their money, and at five pounds for each patron, he would have enough to make a trip back to India that year.

'Five minutes,' he said.

'Fine,' the reply.

Charlotte Hamilton loaded up some more photos, checked her emails, and pressed enter. The pictures loaded slowly. She wondered what would happen when they went live around the world. Would her parents be shocked? Would Dr Lake? And what about Detective Chief Inspector Isaac Cook? Would he be shocked as well, or would he take them in his stride? She thought he would, but she needed to know. She knew that she needed to meet him.

***

Wendy Gladstone knocked on the door of the house next to Dennis Goldman's apartment. A young woman in her twenties answered the door.

'Are you aware of what has happened next door?' Wendy asked.

'I've just woken up; must have slept for two days.'

'Why?' Wendy asked.

'Just lazy, I suppose.' It did not seem a good enough answer to Wendy.

The woman moved uneasily on her feet. As she lurched forward, Wendy grabbed hold of her and eased her into the house. Dennis Goldman's apartment had been an upmarket conversion of an impressive terrace house. The young woman's house was in its original state.

'Your house?' Wendy asked as the woman revived.

'My parents. They're loaded.'

'And you?'

'I'm just the spoilt kid of the house.'

'Are you proud of that?' Wendy asked.

'I'm not bothered either way. I have a good time, plenty of friends, plenty of money. Why work?'

Wendy could have given the woman a lecture about her responsibilities, but she knew it would be wasted, and besides, she was investigating the death of Dennis Goldman.

'Do you know Dennis Goldman?' Wendy asked.

'He's a friend. We go out drinking together sometimes.'

'I am sorry to inform you that he has been killed.'

The young woman, attractive if she made an effort, put her face in her hands and cried. 'How?' she asked.

'He has been murdered.'

'I saw him on Friday. He asked me out for a drink at the Duke of York on Dering Street.'

The woman said her name was Amanda Brocklehurst. To Wendy, who had grown up in Yorkshire on a farm and who had worked hard all her life, Miss Brocklehurst represented the very worst of people. She was, Wendy thought, one of the Sloane Rangers, if that term was used still, who milled around Sloane Square in Chelsea flaunting their wealth, their titles, their wealthy parents, and their willingness not to work. Still, Wendy assumed they kept the local shopkeepers happy with their gold and platinum credit cards.

'Did he go there often?'

'All the time. So did I, especially if Dennis was there.'

'You fancied him?' Wendy asked. Sara Marshall had told her that he had been a good-looking man.

'Are you sure he's dead?' Amanda Brocklehurst was wilting again. With no one else in the house to look after her, Wendy opened a drinks cabinet in the main room, took a bottle of soda water, poured its contents into a glass and gave it to the young woman. She gulped it down in one go. Wendy had seen a bottle of brandy, the traditional pick-me-up, but did not give it to the woman. It was clear that she was suffering the effects of too much alcohol the previous night.

'I've got a thumping head,' Amanda said.

'Your fault.'

'You're not my mother.'

For that Wendy was thankful. Her sons had come home drunk on a few too many occasions. Her solution with them was a berating at the door on entry, not that it did much good, although the cold shoulder for a few days, and her unwillingness to provide them with three meals a day, did.

'Last night Dennis Goldman brought a woman back with him.'

'That's Dennis.'

'Ladies' man?' Wendy asked.

'He always had someone over for the night.'

'Even you?'

'We had an arrangement.'

'Tell me.'

'If he was lonely, or I was, then we would get together.'

'Sleep together?'

'Just friends, but yes, we would have sex. Not a crime. People do it all the time.'

Wendy could see that the rich and spoilt Amanda Brocklehurst did it all the time and that she had little worth, other than that she was young and attractive. 'Duke of York. Would he have picked the woman up there?'

'Dennis's favourite place for pickups,' Amanda replied.

Chapter 17

'Dering Street,' Wendy said to Larry as they stood in the street outside Goldman's apartment. The team of door-to-doors were slowly working their way up and down the street.

'Good looker,' Larry said. He had seen the young woman from a distance.

'Waste of space,' was Wendy's reply.

The Duke of York had been rebuilt in the nineteenth century, and apparently named after the Grand Old Duke of York who had marched his troops up a hill in France. Wendy remembered the nursery rhyme from childhood; Larry did not.

It was located in St George Hanover Square and was one of the trendy pubs in a trendy part of London.

'Do you know a Dennis Goldman?' Larry asked the woman serving behind the bar. It was still early and the end-of-day crowd had not arrived.

'I'm only new,' the woman replied with an Australian accent.

Another backpacker working for cash and less than the minimum wage, Wendy thought.

'Is the manager here?'

The cash-in-hand wandered off. Two minutes later, a middle-aged man, red in the face, appeared.

'Can I help you?' he asked.

'Detective Inspector Hill, Detective Sergeant Wendy Gladstone. We have a few questions.'

'Fancy a drink? On the house.'

Larry was tempted to ask for a beer but did not. 'Orange juice for me,' he said.

'The same for me,' Wendy replied.

The landlord pulled himself a beer. 'I need to check it anyway. Just changed the barrel.'

'Dennis Goldman.'

'Comes in here several times a week.'

'Friday night,' Larry asked.

'He walked out of here with a woman.'

'Tell us about the woman,' Wendy asked.

'Attractive, red hair, short skirt, tight top. Not much else to tell.'

'Why do you say that?'

'She was giving him the right signals. Coming in close, draping her arm around him. We could see that he was on to a sure thing.'

'We?'

'Those behind the bar.'

'Had you seen the woman before?'

'Never. Anyway, what's this all about?'

'Dennis Goldman was killed between the hours of 10 p.m. on Friday night and 2 a.m. on Saturday morning.'

'Sorry to hear that.'

'Upsets you?'

'It's not something you expect to hear. How did he die?'

'We're from Homicide,' Larry said.

'Do you mean he was murdered?'

'Yes.'

'And the woman?'

'She's our prime suspect.'

'We've got cameras in here,' the landlord said.

***

On the northern outskirts of the city, the woman slept peacefully, or at least as peacefully as could be expected with the heavy traffic outside her window. She dreamt of happy times and happy thoughts interspersed with dark places and dark thoughts. She rolled in her bed, one arm hanging down. The bed, she had known when she agreed to take the room, was old and flea-bitten. She imagined how many sweaty bodies had lain on it, how many fornicating couples had tested its springs, how many murderers had used it.

Charlotte knew the answer to the last question: one.

She moved between rational and despair, anger and melancholy, sweet dreams and nightmares, although the nightmares were becoming more frequent. She wanted to be like everyone else, but they were mad, she was not.

She woke up, the banging at the door disturbing her. 'You owe me for the next month,' the voice said. She had heard the voice before, but she was not sure where.

The door opened, and an old man in his eighties and wearing an old crumpled shirt and a pair of shorts entered. On his feet he wore a pair of slippers.

'The rent,' he said.

She would have paid him, but she had no money. The money she had saved over the years, including some that she had stolen from the men she had killed, was not sufficient. If the man had been younger, she would have given herself to him; it would not be the first time that she had exchanged sexual favours for financial independence.

'No rent, no stay. You know the rules.'

She knew the rules, although he did not. Upset her and her vengeance was absolute, no exceptions.

'I don't have any money.'

'Not my problem.' The man spoke poor English, in spite of having arrived in the country from Eastern Europe thirteen years previously. His country of birth had joined the European Community, and he left it for England and its welfare system. The house he rented, and then sublet, was his only means of income once he had exhausted his adopted country's generosity. When he had arrived in the country, he had had a wife and a family, but they were gone. To him, they were worthless. The accommodation he provided was not legal and did not satisfy any government regulations. There were no insurance policies, no fire prevention systems, no regular pest inspections. Just a bed and a wash basin; the bathroom was at the end of the hall.

'We could exchange,' she said.

'What with?'

'What do you think?'

The old man looked at the woman. He could see that she was young and nubile, not old and haggard as his wife had been. 'Ten years ago, we could have made a deal.'

'You're not too old,' she said. There had been some who had visited her when she was with Mavis Williams who must have been older than the man standing in front of her. Some were able to maintain an erection long enough, most weren't, and the man demanding money appeared to be one of the latter. She could not think of a more disagreeable prospect than seducing this man, but if it was necessary...

She had been there for three months, in that horrible room in that horrible house, and no one had suspected who she was. It was the safest place in London, and she wanted to stay.

'Thirty minutes and you're out of here,' he said. 'Tight arse or no tight arse.'

She knew that she could leave, but he stood in her way. 'We can at least part as friends,' she said.

'It's purely business.'

'I understand.'

The rent collector came and sat on the edge of her bed. She gave him a beer to drink. He opened it and gulped it down. He smelt of rotting fish and sweat. He did not see the knife in her hand, although he felt it enter his chest. He collapsed on the bed. The woman then moved his legs parallel with the length of the bed. Thorough, as always, she slit his throat, careful to stand clear. The shower at the end of the hall was dirty and cold; this time she would forsake the cleanliness. Not wishing to bloody her hands, she took a toothbrush and rubbed it in the blood coming from his throat. One wall in that dingy bedroom was not as dirty as the others. She wrote a number with the toothbrush. It took her five minutes to complete to her satisfaction. Packing her case, she left the room and the house. On the way, she checked the landlord's room. She found nearly ten thousand pounds in cash hidden under his mattress. Now Charlotte had the rent money, but no one to pay it to.

She headed to the railway station: unfinished business.

***

Sara Marshall and Sean O'Riordan headed back to Twickenham to review the events three years before. Isaac headed back to Challis Street from Dennis Goldman's apartment; he knew what was coming.

Not only was he a reluctant celebrity courtesy of Charlotte Hamilton, but he was also a detective chief inspector who had let two murders occur. Graham Dyer was unforeseen, but Dennis Goldman was not. The celebrity of the woman was well known and would have formed the basis of many pub conversations, especially that she would thrust the knife in mid-coitus. The thought of it made Isaac squirm.

Yet an attractive female and Dennis Goldman had been swayed, and almost certainly never gave any thought to the possibility that the woman coming on too easily to him was anything other than a woman with easy virtues. The landlord at the Duke of York had sensed something was amiss, Wendy said, but Isaac did not believe his statement.

Isaac knew that hindsight was all very well, but the landlord, the same as every other man, even he, would have taken Charlotte Hamilton. Isaac knew that he had made mistakes in the past: bedding Linda Harris while pursuing a relationship with Jess O'Neill was the biggest mistake so far, but then Sue Smith had made a dent in his heart, and now she was overseas. He was soon to be forty, and he knew that a man needs someone in his life. He could see himself as a lifelong bachelor; the idea did not appeal.

Wendy disturbed Isaac's thoughts. 'Sir, we still need to find this woman.'

'How can she disappear so easily.'

'She's a Barbie Doll.'

'What do you mean?'

'The woman has no distinctive features, no moles on her face, no rear end that's too large or breasts that protrude. She's the generic young English Rose. Careful makeup, change of clothes, change of hair colour, and she is transformed.'

'You're right, of course. What about the Duke of York? How did you and Larry go?'

'The pub had cameras. Bridget's had a look at the videos.'

'Charlotte Hamilton?'

'Unless you know it's her, you'd not pick her. How about Gordon Windsor? Is he confirming that it was Charlotte Hamilton?' Wendy asked.

'It's her. How many is that now?'

'According to her count, it's six.'

'Isaac, what the hell is going on?' a voice bellowed. Wendy made herself scarce and went to talk to Larry.

'She's killed again.'

'I know that,' DCS Goddard said. 'Not only does she broadcast it in advance, as well as some pictures of you, we now have another body.'

'He should have checked before taking her to his house,' Isaac said by way of a lame excuse.

'Would you?' The DCS knew his DCI well enough to know the answer to that question. 'And now there is a damn press conference. I expect you to put up a good defence. The department's looking very shabby at the present moment, and the commissioner is breathing down my neck. I've spent enough time sweet talking that man; I don't want to blow it with your incompetence.'

'That's not fair,' Isaac said.

'I know it's not fair, but you need reminding. Whatever happens, you're carrying the can for this.'

'I won't let you down, sir.'

'Isaac, you're the best I've got. I cannot afford to lose you, but how many more deaths? The woman's identity is known. Her fingerprints, her DNA are on record. We have photos of her, and then we have her website. I'm trying to get it blocked, but it's not so easy.'

'She will only change the server again. Over one hundred thousand followers now, and they can all find her website easily enough.'

'Misguided fools?' Goddard asked.

'Only a few would be as mental as Charlotte Hamilton.'

'Only!'

'So far, there has been one copycat killer in the UK, two or three in the USA.'

'That's just what we need. Random lunatics aiming to emulate her.'

'That's what being a celebrity does to people.'

'I don't get it,' Goddard said. He left soon after. He had not seen the man so angry before.

Isaac called in Wendy and Larry. 'One week maximum or else.'

'Else what?' Larry asked.

'One week, and I'm off the case.'

'And us?'

'What do you think?'

***

Jason Martin had fancied her from the day she moved in. A casual labourer, he could not afford more than a single room in the converted house. The landlord was a pig of a man, but he minded his business and did not complain about the smell of marijuana in his room.

Martin made little in the way of money, and what he did make he spent on drugs and the occasional woman. He was an unattractive man approaching his forty-fifth year. Each and every day of the year, he wore the same clothes: a tee-shirt, a worn pair of jeans, trainers with holes in the soles, and an anorak. He moved slowly, although he had no impediment. He was a lazy man who would come home after work to smoke and to watch the television, but only the commercial channels. The national broadcaster, devoid of adverts, was not to his taste. 'Intellectual crap,' he would say each time his remote flicked through the channels, briefly pausing to look at a debate or a documentary before flicking on.

He had not had a steady girlfriend in ten years, a fact he put down to their poor taste and his irregular working hours. The new woman, young and just his type, had taken the room next to him. She was polite to him in the corridor and when they queued for the bathroom, he always let her go first as she would clean up, and there was always the smell of her perfume that lingered in the air; also, the meter on the hot water cistern would often have some remaining credit.

He had asked her out once, but she had not accepted. He had decided that she was not good enough for him, although it did not stop him from looking through the crack in the door of the bathroom as she removed her clothes and bathed herself. It also did not stop him widening the crack in the dividing wall between his room and hers, to see her naked. The wall, constructed of cheap panelling, divided a larger room. He thought his half was better than hers.

At night, when it was quiet, he could hear her talking to herself. He imagined that she could hear him. The thought of it excited him.

He had not expected the door to her room to be open when he returned at five in the morning. The urge to look in was irresistible.

He had expected to see an empty room, possibly the woman asleep. He entered, after whispering 'Hello' first.

The bed was initially hidden by the door. He looked through the crack near to the handle; a crack he had used before. He saw a man he recognised. He was not moving.

Slowly Jason, the Peeping Tom, moved forward. He recognised the landlord on the bed, his hands folded over his chest. Not sure of what he saw, Jason Martin touched the red on the man's shirt. He put his finger to his mouth; he knew the taste.

Five minutes later, he phoned for an ambulance.

Chapter 18

At King's Cross Station, the woman carried her worldly belongings. She reflected that it was not much to show for five years. In one hand, she carried a voluminous handbag. On her back, a backpack for her laptop and the photos she cherished. She also dragged a small suitcase.

There had not been time to upload the latest photos; that would be her first task on arriving at her destination. It would only be three hours, and she hoped that the body of the landlord would not be discovered before then, but she knew of the nosey man in the room next door.

As the train pulled out of King's Cross, she broke into song. *Stupid Duncan up at the quarry, along came a sister and gave him a push.*

An elderly couple looked her way, unable to hear the full words due to the noise of the train.

Charlotte smiled back at them.

She remembered little of the trip, other than the train stopping two, maybe three, times to let people off, others on. The elderly couple had left at one of the stops, only to be replaced by a family of four. Charlotte took little notice, although the little boy had tripped over her foot one time. *If he was here on his own,* she thought. She realised her destiny, her purpose with more clarity. The time for subtlety had passed.

From now on, she would intensify her efforts. The elderly couple had seen a bookish woman on the train, not the frivolous tart that had killed the banker. What would she be in Newcastle? Her bag contained all she needed by way of makeup. In her suitcase were clothes suitable for any occasion, any look, any age. So far, she had kept her age close to her own, but she could be young if she wanted, old if needed.

It was five years since she had last been in Newcastle, but it had changed little. She found an internet café close to the railway station. She had covered her face with a scarf, a perfect disguise considering the biting wind.

Four pounds, cheaper than London for forty-five minutes' internet use, a complimentary cup of coffee which was surprisingly good. *Not like the muck they serve down in London*, she thought.

She took out her laptop; the battery still had charge. She removed the connector from the old computer on the table and inserted it into her laptop. She checked the speed; it was adequate.

Ten minutes later, Isaac Cook saw the update on his smartphone. He pulled over to the side of the road and scrolled through the photos.

***

High Barnet, the furthermost station on the Northern Line of the London Underground, was only fifteen miles from the centre of London. Another murder that appeared to be the handiwork of Charlotte Hamilton. The full team had mobilised on hearing of the number on the wall, the knife in the chest, the slit throat.

Jason Martin had been surprisingly articulate once he had calmed himself. He had phoned up emergency services, given a clear description of the man's condition as well as the address.

'54 Normanton Avenue. Send an ambulance, not that it will be much use,' he had said.

The woman on the other end of the phone pressed a computer key to mobilise the police and the ambulance. She maintained the conversation to allow the software on her computer to check the phone number, its approximate location, and the owner's address. They all tallied.

The local DI, Jim Davies, had phoned Isaac on visiting the murder scene. They had met some years previously, and the modus operandi of Charlotte Hamilton was well known.

'It's one of yours,' Davies had said on the phone.

Within five minutes of the phone call, Sara Marshall and Sean O'Riordan were heading north. Wendy Gladstone and Larry Hill were in another car and moving in the same direction. Isaac had decided to take his own.

He phoned Sara after looking at the photos on his phone. 'It's not a pleasant sight,' Isaac said.

'We'll see soon enough.'

Wendy and Larry arrived first. The standard procedure: crime scene tape, barricades to keep the onlookers at a distance, a uniform at the front door of the house, which was a sad example of pre-war architecture.

The crime scene investigators from the local area were taking control. Gordon Windsor was coming up in an advisory capacity, as he had the most recent knowledge of the woman's style of dispatching men.

Wendy took the opportunity to kit up: gloves, foot protectors, overalls. She showed her badge to the uniforms and proceeded to the first floor of the house. She was stopped by Jim Davies before she entered the room.

'I work with DCI Cook,' she explained.

'Fine. Just be careful where you walk.'

Wendy saw the body on the bed; felt as though she wanted to throw up. It had been clear on entering that somebody already had. From what she could see the man was fully clothed, which was in stark contrast to Charlotte Hamilton's usual approach to dispatching her victims.

'Not much to see here, and besides, you're in my way,' the CSE said.

Wendy left the room and went downstairs. Sara and Sean had arrived.

'He's prickly,' Wendy said as Sara kitted up.

'Don't worry. I can deal with him.' Wendy thought she probably could. She would only have to smile at him.

Isaac arrived ten minutes later. He kitted up and went upstairs, which left Wendy and Larry with Jason Martin. The man was calm, and a cigarette hung from his mouth – it was tobacco, although the lingering smell of marijuana remained. Not that Wendy and Larry were concerned with his possible illegal activities. He appeared to be a sensible man and a reliable witness.

'You found the body?' Wendy asked.

'And phoned the police.'

'Can you tell us about the murderer?'

'A good-looking sort. Fancied her myself.'

'Did she respond to your advances? I'm assuming you made some,' Larry asked.

'I tried it on once. Shot down in flames.'

'Did she have a name?'

'Ingrid.'

'Tell us about Ingrid,' Wendy said.

'She arrived some time ago. She lived in the room next to me. Always civil to me when I saw her, but she kept to herself. Apart from that, there's not a lot I can tell you.'

Jason Martin forgot to mention that she had a birthmark just below her left breast, and one breast was larger than the other.

'The landlord. What can you tell us about him?'

'Not a lot. He was an unpleasant man, but he left me alone. She certainly dealt with him.'

'As you say,' Larry agreed.

'Is there any reason why Ingrid would kill him?' Wendy asked.

'He was always looking at her, and then she was struggling to pay the rent. Apart from that, I can't think of a reason.'

Isaac returned with Sara. Sean had been talking to some of the onlookers, to see if anybody knew anything.

'It's Charlotte Hamilton,' Isaac said.

'Where is she, sir?' Wendy asked.

'This time she did not clean up. She panicked, and when a person panics, they make mistakes. Find out where she went after here. This time, it should not be difficult.'

Isaac returned to the office, the others stayed at the murder scene. Isaac knew why he was being summoned back to

142

meet Goddard. His career had been on the line more than once over the years, but this time it looked serious.

Isaac realised he had no defence. The woman moved wherever she wanted, killed whomever she wanted. Unless the team had a break, he was off the case.

It had almost cost the career of Sara Marshall, although she had survived due in part to her being an excellent police officer, in part because she had married her boss.

Isaac, apart from his mentor Richard Goddard, had no one, and this time it looked as though he was about to issue a warning to him, or at least a reprimand.

***

Charlotte walked around the centre of Newcastle looking for accommodation. Nowhere was safe, and for once she was getting desperate.

Even now, the police in Newcastle would be on the lookout for her, although she had walked past two police constables at the station and they had taken no notice. They would have if she had been wearing the same outfit as when she had killed Dennis Goldman, not only because it had been provocative, but also because Newcastle was unusually cold. Before she had gone to London, she had not thought of the climate as so bitter.

She entered a pub, pulling her suitcase.

'Bit heavy for you, luv,' the man behind the bar said.

'I'm looking for accommodation.'

'Room upstairs if you want.'

'How much?'

'We can discuss it afterwards,' the man, who looked to be the worse side of fifty, said. Charlotte noticed the tattoos on his arm and the muscular physique.

She took her luggage upstairs and had a shower. She then dressed inconspicuously and made her way out to St Nicholas Hospital. She stopped on the way to look at her old house. A young couple with a baby were there. A large dog was fetching the ball that the man threw. She had no idea where her parents were, but she would find out. She took some photos.

Charlotte walked around the boundary of St Nicholas Mental Hospital. It had not changed since she had left at the age of nineteen. It was the same foreboding edifice that represented pain and imprisonment and rejection by her parents. She checked out the back fence that she had climbed over in her early teens to meet the local boys. She wondered what had happened to them, although she assumed they were now older and wiser, not foolish and full of bravado as when they had made love to her. To them, she had been a plaything, purely for their own amusement. One of the young men had been friendly to her; Charlotte remembered him with some fondness, but, yet again, he had been deceitful, the same as Gregory Chalmers, professing love, only feeling lust.

Wrapped in a coat with a hood, and wearing warm, sensible clothing, she waited, knowing full well the routine of the one person she wanted to see. She hated the woman for taking her away from her parents, for subjecting her to pain, for giving her medicines that left her depressed or comatose, unable to react.

It was late afternoon when Gladys Lake emerged from the building and walked through a churchyard on the way to her cottage on the far side. Charlotte had been there a few times, part of her therapy and her integration into society. She remembered the lace curtains, the bay window, the old cat. It was evident now that with the Lake woman it had not been therapy, only a way for her to ease her guilty conscience after all that she had subjected her to.

'Another six months and you will be all right,' she had said. Charlotte realised that it had all been lies, and the six months had stretched to one year, then two, and then up to the age of eighteen, when she was free to leave as an adult.

***

Gladys Lake moved slowly across the churchyard, casually glancing at the gravestones as she walked. Under one arm she had some files, across her shoulder the strap of a large bag. She was wrapped up against the weather, and the rain had started again; not that it ever stopped for very long, but now it was turning to sleet.

'You never expected to see me again, did you?' the woman who had emerged from her left said.

'I'm sorry,' Gladys Lake replied.

'Have you forgotten me already?'

The doctor thought the voice was familiar, yet she could not identify the woman, which was not surprising as she had a scarf wrapped around her lower face, and a hood pulled over her forehead. All that she could see were the blue eyes.

'I have never forgiven you,' Charlotte said.

Gladys Lake quickened her pace and attempted to flee. She dropped the files that had been under one arm; she did not stop to pick them up. The woman behind her, younger and fitter, began to close in on her.

'Leave me alone, please.'

'You remember.'

A couple walking their dog entered through the far gate of the graveyard. The dog stopped to sniff the gate post, lifting its leg to make its mark.

'Dr Lake, how are you?' the man said.

'Please, I need your help.'

'Of course.'

'A woman is following me. She is dangerous. I need the police.'

The man looked over the area while the dog continued to sniff. 'I can't see anyone.'

'Please call Detective Inspector Hewitt for me,' Gladys Lake said. She handed the man her phone. He checked the contacts and speed dialled. The doctor had been unable to hold her hands steady enough to press the buttons.

Rory Hewitt found Gladys Lake at her cottage. The couple and the dog who had helped her in the cemetery were there also.

'It was Charlotte Hamilton,' she said.

'Positive?'

Rory phoned Sara who phoned Isaac. The situation had changed. The woman was on the move, and she was making mistakes. She had left a USB memory stick behind after killing the landlord where she had been staying; it only contained photos, and apart from their subject matter, it had revealed nothing more.

The killing of the landlord had been messy; her previous murders had shown a degree of calmness as she had showered, cleaned up, and left. Grace Nelson, the criminal psychologist, said it was to be expected. The shield of invulnerability made Charlotte Hamilton impervious to the possibility of capture.

Isaac set up a meeting at Challis Street. Sara Marshall and Sean O'Riordan came over; Rory Hewitt dialled in.

'Rory, is it confirmed?' Isaac asked.

'Gladys Lake is sure.'

'Is she alright?' Sara asked.

'She's fine,' Rory said, which was not altogether true. Gladys Lake had been scared witless and was under sedation.

'All-points out for her?'

'We have issued a general alert. The woman is dangerous, and she is to be approached with care.'

'Another mistake,' Wendy said.

'If she had killed Gladys Lake, then it would not have been,' Rory said.

'Do you believe she would have?' Isaac asked.

'What else? She kills people, not frightens them. Gladys Lake would have died in that graveyard if a couple walking their dog had not come in. I'm certain of that. So is Dr Lake.'

'Charlotte Hamilton's parents?'

'We're checking on them now, as well as visiting her old house. The Hamiltons' new address is not well known.'

'Do you know it?'

'Yes. We have police cars out there patrolling the area. I intend to visit after I conclude this call.'

'Then you'd better go. She has failed to kill this time. Who are her next targets?'

Chapter 19

DCS Goddard had not lost faith in his DCI, but others had. As far as the Commissioner of the London Metropolitan Police, who sat up high in his ivory tower at Scotland Yard, was concerned it was a fiasco. People were dying, and the murderer was known.

'Look here, Goddard,' the commissioner, a plain-talking man, said. 'I've not seen much to recommend this DCI Isaac Cook. Everyone tells me he is a man on the rise, destined to take my chair one day.'

Not before me, Richard Goddard thought.

'He's a good officer.' Goddard leapt to Isaac's defence.

'Good or bad makes no difference. Sure, he has a few runs on the board: dealt with that Marjorie Frobisher case, found out who had killed a man thirty years ago, and wrapped up the death of the future Lord Penrith, but apart from that… What is it with this Charlotte Hamilton? Does he fancy her?'

The DCS knew that if Isaac survived, he would have to settle down. Aspersions about his performance based on his fraternising with members of the opposite sex were counterproductive.

'That's a scurrilous remark, sir.'

'Don't get smart with me. You're only here because you were friendly with the previous commissioner and because you suck up to the politicians. The prime minister may see something special in you. I don't.'

Goddard knew that his defence of his DCI had placed him in a tenuous position. The previous commissioner had mentored him, but he was now sitting in the House of Lords and unable to protect him.

He had spent years focussing on the chance to become the commissioner of police, but the DCS realised that his efforts werc yet again being thwarted, and this time by a man of little charm and no humour. Goddard knew that Isaac needed to get results, but so far he had achieved none.

Charlotte Hamilton was thumbing her nose at whoever she wanted. Her identity was well known. Her full medical history was available and had been carefully analysed, looking for patterns that would indicate where she would strike next. And now she was in Newcastle, although so far no one had been killed.

Goddard left the commissioner's office in a worse mood than when he had arrived. As much as he disliked the commissioner, and thought him to be a pompous bore, he was right in one aspect: Isaac was not providing results.

***

The Hamiltons were not pleased when Rory Hewitt arrived. He parked his car to one side of the entrance and knocked on the door.

Charles Hamilton opened it. Rory looked in, saw that their previous well-presented house had been replaced by a run-down farm cottage.

It was evident to Rory that the Hamiltons had let themselves go. Charles Hamilton wore an old pair of jeans, dirty from what Rory could see, and a shirt that was fraying at the collar.

'My wife's in bed,' he said.

'Ill?'

'Severe depression. It's as if she has given up.'

'I'm sorry to hear that,' Rory said. He could only imagine the anguish they were going through. He had heard about Fiona Hamilton's attempted suicide, but nothing more since then.

'You'd better come in.'

Rory moved down the hallway to the kitchen. In the sink, there were dirty dishes.

'Sorry about the mess. We don't do much these days.'

'That's fine.'

'You're not here for a social visit, are you?'

'No.'

'We heard about the last murder. It was her, wasn't it?'

'In the north of London?'

'High Barnet.'

'Yes, it was her.'

'Is that why you're here?' Charles Hamilton asked. Rory could see the lines on his face, the downcast eyes. His wife may have been suffering from depression, but it was evident that Charles Hamilton was not well either.

'Charlotte has been seen in Newcastle.'

'My God. Has she killed anyone?'

'Not yet.'

'You suspect she will come here?'

'It's possible.'

'If she comes, we will not stop her.'

'That bad?'

'Our deaths would be no worse than what we are suffering now.'

Rory understood Charles Hamilton's sentiment.

***

Charlotte did not know why she had spoken to Gladys Lake. She had not intended to confront the woman in the graveyard, but she had been there, and it had seemed ideal. No need for a ritual, she had thought, only a knife to the heart and then to the throat. It appeared to be a perfect opportunity: an isolated graveyard, drizzling rain. If she had only killed her, she would not have had to run away. There was a freshly-dug grave; she had wanted to throw the woman in there, but then that couple with that stupid dog peeing everywhere had interrupted her. How she hated them. How she hated that dog.

Dr Lake had deserved to die; it was her duty to rid the world of a woman who took pleasure in the torture of those that she professed to care for.

Charlotte remembered running away from the graveyard, her panic overwhelming her. Now was not the time to get caught. She still had to see her parents one more time; she was sure of that, but she had no address. The Lake woman would have known; maybe that was why she had not killed her. She would have told her as the knife slid into her.

Yes, that was it, she thought.

She knew that her mind was not as sharp as it had been. Why, when she had killed those men, had she felt nothing, yet with failure she felt guilt? She did not know, and it worried her. Her thoughts were muddled, as were her plans.

She had to leave her accommodation over the pub in the centre of town; find somewhere remote, lie low. She needed her parents. They would look after her, and if they did not, then she knew what to do.

And what of the publican? He had agreed to her price, even though she had plenty of money. That miserable penny-pinching man in High Barnet had had over ten thousand pounds hidden under his bed yet he wanted her to pay on time, and then he had rejected her body.

She would have paid him with that, but he was too stupid to appreciate the offer. Many men had used her; most had paid, some had not, some had died, yet he rejected her, even after she had shown him some of the wares. He had been interested, she knew it. The publican in Newcastle had had no such problems. He had appreciated her ten minutes after showing her the room, even neglecting the patrons downstairs waiting for their pints.

***

Isaac avoided the confrontation with Richard Goddard; he and Sara Marshall were on the train to Newcastle. It was only three hours from King's Cross; they would arrive by late afternoon.

With Charlotte Hamilton in Newcastle, and the train and bus stations being monitored, they thought there was a good chance of apprehending her. The woman was making mistakes, too many mistakes, and Isaac knew it was only a matter of time. Whether it would be soon enough to maintain his credibility, even his position on the promotion ladder, was too early to know.

Rory Hewitt met them on arrival. Sara had spoken to him before, but this was the first time meeting him in person.

'Good to see you, Sara.'

'And you,' Sara replied.

'I've booked you into the Marriott,' Rory said. Isaac thought it was outside the department's budget, but accepted graciously.

'I've scheduled an appointment with Gladys Lake.'

'Then let's go. We can check in later,' Isaac said. He was anxious to get on and to try and apprehend Charlotte Hamilton. He knew how it worked. If he came back with the woman in custody, then his career was back on track, as was Sara's. If he did not, then he knew the consequence of that as well. However their visit to Newcastle turned out, it was a crucial turning point in the investigation.

A twenty-minute drive and they arrived at Dr Lake's cottage. A uniform stood outside. Inside, Gladys Lake was relaxed. She was sitting in a chair by the window, a cat on her lap. A policewoman, assigned to stay at the cottage for the next few days, opened the door on their arrival.

'I'm fine now,' Gladys Lake said in answer to Isaac's question. She turned to Sara. 'Good to meet you after so many years,' she said.

'And you, although it's not the best way to meet.'

'Do you believe that she intended to kill me?' Dr Lake asked.

'You're an educated woman. It would be wrong to lie to you,' Isaac said. He had taken a seat on the other side of the small room. An imitation log fire burned in the corner. The cat had left its owner and moved over to him. Isaac was not a great lover of cats, having had asthma as a child that was in part exacerbated by cat fur. This time, he did not push the cat away.

'If those people had not come into the graveyard, she would have killed me.'

'It's probable,' Isaac said. 'You will need to be careful for a few days.'

'I have my patients.'

'We have assigned a policewoman to you. She will accompany you at all times. Also, another officer will be outside this house.'

Isaac asked the standard questions: mental state, what is she likely to do next, where will she be?

Dr Lake concurred with Grace Nelson's conclusions. If Charlotte Hamilton was in Newcastle, she probably had unfinished business. She had failed to kill her, but there were others that she bore a grudge against.

The three police officers left the cottage, the cat clawing Isaac's trousers as he stood up. Sara gave Dr Lake a hug.

Rory started his car and headed out of the city. The night was drawing in, and all three would have preferred to be warm and snug, a view that was echoed by a large number of the Newcastle police who were on high alert. A known serial killer was in the city and roaming free.

Teams of police officers were checking all the hotels, guest houses, and pubs throughout the city, and showing the photo of a woman with blonde hair and then dark hair. For every ten people they asked, one would say that they had seen her. Closer questioning revealed yet again that Charlotte Hamilton's features suited the generic norm, and they were false sightings.

The publican at the Bridge Hotel sat down on learning that the woman who had slept upstairs was a serial killer. He did not admit that he was one of her followers on her website.

'She was here. Not that she looked anything like your photos.'

'Why do you recognise her, then?' the young police sergeant asked.

'There is a small scar just above her left eyebrow.'

The policeman studied the photo. He could see the publican was correct. 'Good eyesight,' he said.

The publican failed to reveal that he had seen it the first night he had slept with the woman.

Chapter 20

Wendy and Larry, still back in London, traced Charlotte Hamilton's former flatmate. Gloria was in Hammersmith, happily married and with a child.

'You are aware of your former flatmate's reappearance,' Wendy said.

'Will she find me?' The child bounced up and down on the woman's lap.

'After three years?'

'She's mad, isn't she?'

'Psychotic, paranoid schizophrenic,' Larry said. Sara Marshall's files had shown that Gloria had been promiscuous. From what he could see, the woman in front of him was subdued, caring and devoted to her husband, Asuko, whom she had met in Lagos.

'She was always strange,' Gloria said.

'Our records indicate that you said she was normal.'

'Three years ago, I may have said that, but now...'

'What do you mean?'

'Her goddamn virginity.'

'You are aware of her history?'

'Who isn't. I sometimes check out her website.'

'Why?'

'Ghoulish, I suppose. She killed Brad Howard, and then put the photos on the internet. What sort of person does that? She's certifiable.'

'She probably is,' Wendy said.

'Is there anything else that may help us in our enquiries?' Larry asked.

'I told DI Stanforth all I knew. Will she find me?'

'At present, she's not in London. That is of two hours ago, but she could return at any time.'

Gloria shifted uncomfortably in her seat. Asuko, her husband, took the baby and left the room.

'Once, when she was not in the flat, I looked in her room.'

'To see what you could steal?' Wendy said. She had read Gloria's file before knocking on her door.

'I was mixed up then.'

'What did you find?'

'A drawing. There were three people. A child and two adults. There was a big cross through the child. What does it mean?'

'You are aware of her brother?'

'No.'

'She killed him when she was ten,' Wendy said.

'And she was my flatmate?'

'Yes. What do you intend to do?'

'I've already spoken to Asuko. We're going back to Nigeria. Until she is in jail or dead, we'll stay there.'

'Have a good trip,' Larry said.

***

By the time Isaac, Sara, and Rory reached the farm cottage it was dark. The only light inside the cottage came from the front room.

Rory knocked on the door; the first time, a gentle tap of the metal door knocker; the second time more vigorously. The sound of footsteps could be heard.

'Who is it?'

'Detective Inspector Hewitt. I'm here with two other police officers.'

The door opened to reveal Charles Hamilton holding a shotgun.

'You'd better give me that, Mr Hamilton,' Rory said.

'It's licensed; it's staying with me.'

'Where is your wife?'

'She's upstairs. We are taking turns to guard the cottage.'

'You would shoot your own daughter?' Sara asked.

'We have heard about Gladys Lake.'

'Dr Lake has suffered no injuries,' Rory said. 'Can we come in?'

'If you must,' Charles Hamilton said, dropping the shotgun to his side. He shouted upstairs. 'It's the police. You can come down.'

A few minutes later, Fiona Hamilton descended the stairs wearing an old dressing gown. She had red slippers on her feet, and her hair was bedraggled. She did not speak on entering the room and took a seat in the corner. The expression on her face was vacant.

'My wife is not well,' Charles Hamilton said. 'It's all been too much for her.'

Sara looked at the woman; she could only feel pity.

'Mr Hamilton, we are concerned that your daughter will come here,' Isaac said. He had found a wooden chair and was sitting on it.

'Our daughter died many years ago,' Hamilton said. His wife sat motionless, only moving to wipe her eyes with a handkerchief. Sara moved over near and put her arm around the woman. It was evident that she had not been eating properly as she was skin and bones underneath the dressing gown.

'Mr Hamilton, are you seriously willing to shoot your daughter?' Rory asked.

'She would have killed Dr Lake. Why would she not kill us, although we have no life now.'

Isaac found it difficult to concentrate: the chair was uncomfortable and the room was cold. 'Has she contacted you?' he asked.

'Not for many years.'

'Does she know where you live?'

'I don't know. It's unlikely.'

'The local police are keeping a watch on the cottage,' Rory said.

'Then tell them to leave. She will follow them,' Hamilton said.

'I'm taking Mrs Hamilton upstairs,' Sara said.

Sara left, leaving the three men together. 'My wife refuses to eat. She just drinks tea and nibbles the occasional biscuit.'

'How about you?' Rory asked.

'I do what I can, nothing more.'

Sara returned five minutes later. 'She's asleep.'

'What is the problem with your wife?' Isaac asked.

'Broken heart, although they call it depression. I suffer the same condition, but I remain resilient for my wife.'

***

Although it was late, the three police officers managed to organise some food at the Marriott. They had checked in: Isaac was on the first floor, Sara on the third.

Sara spent thirty minutes talking to her husband, checking on their son, before joining the two men. A party was in full swing in the bar next door.

Unable to talk about anything else, the three of them went over the case so far. Sara expressed her sorrow for the Hamiltons. Isaac asked about Charlotte, as Rory had seen the woman when she had been ten. He sang the song he had heard her singing, or at least a rendition of it, as he was tone-deaf.

Isaac phoned Wendy and Larry. Wendy was still in the office with Bridget; Larry had left for the day.

'I've upgraded the security for Dr Lake and the Hamiltons,' Rory said.

'Can she find the Hamiltons?' Isaac asked.

'Unlikely.'

The three, exhausted after a strenuous day, then said little more other than pleasantries unrelated to the case. Sara drank a glass of the house white, Rory a beer, and Isaac kept to orange juice.

The party next door was starting to get louder, not that the three minded. The day had been depressing, as had the last few weeks. It was good to see people enjoying themselves. Isaac rose to pay a visit to the toilet. As he moved through the throng at the party, a woman came up to him. 'Take a group photo for us, please.' Isaac obliged the group, young females out celebrating.

'And one with you.'

Isaac stood in the middle, his arm around two of the women. It was not possible to see very clearly as the light in the bar was subdued. The flash of the camera lit up the room briefly.

After the photos had been taken, Isaac received an obligatory kiss on the cheek and continued to the toilet.

'Who were they?' Sara asked on his return.

'No idea. Just some women out having fun. My God, it was her!'

Isaac rushed back to the party. He looked for the two women; he found one easily.

'Your friend?'

'Her?'

'Yes, the other woman in the photo,' Isaac asked. Rory phoned for backup.

'No idea. She just made herself welcome. Started paying for the drinks, as well.'

Two police cars arrived, road blocks were set up, people in the street waylaid. It was to no avail. The woman had disappeared.

***

Two hours later at a run-down internet café on the outskirts of Newcastle a woman took out her laptop. The man that she had paid did not look up as she placed the money on the counter. She had given him five pounds and told him to keep the change. He went back to watching porn on the screen below the counter.

The woman plugged her smartphone into her laptop. She downloaded the images, and then uploaded them to her website.

My favourite police officer, the caption. She then tagged the photo: Detective Chief Inspector Isaac Cook.

She closed the laptop, packed it into her case and left the café. Her accommodation was thirty minutes away. She would sleep well that night.

***

Isaac had tried to sleep, but it had not been possible. He had watched the television for some time, but apart from that he went over how he could have allowed a photo to be taken of him. He had not seen her clearly, and even if the light had been good, her ability at concealing herself was remarkable. He dozed after three hours, only to be woken by his phone ringing.

'You'd better check her website,' Larry said.

Isaac checked. He realised the repercussions.

He phoned Richard Goddard. It was better for him to find out from him than from someone else.

'What the hell is going on here?' Goddard exploded over the phone. 'You can't find her, but she can find you. Maybe I should employ her. The commissioner is going to go ballistic over this. Get yourself down here immediately.'

Isaac packed his case and headed to the railway station. A train left every thirty to forty minutes. He could buy a ticket at the station.

***

By the time Isaac arrived at King's Cross, the newspapers had picked up the photos. Larry met Isaac at the station and drove him to Challis Street Police Station.

Isaac walked up the stairs to Richard Goddard's office.

'I can't protect you on this one,' he said. 'Every time there is an attractive woman, you're there with your tongue hanging out. What is it? Are you lonely, not getting enough?'

'That's unfair, sir. I took a photo at the Marriott. How was I to know that Charlotte Hamilton would be there?'

'That's as may be, but I can't do anything about this. If the commissioner wants your head, he gets it.'

Isaac was aware that this time he was not going to survive. He was an ambitious police officer, yet on more than one occasion his friendly nature had got him into trouble. It had been a late night in Newcastle, and if he had been more alert, he might have studied the features of the woman who coerced him into a photo with her. His willingness to put his arm around her and her newly-acquired friend came naturally. He was a tactile man who was at ease with women as well as with men.

'Sometimes I wonder if you're worth the bother,' the DCS said.

Isaac sat upright on a chair on one side of Goddard's desk; his senior sat on the other. The leather chair he sat on looked precarious as he perched on its front edge. The man was angry, Isaac could see that, and if he had been in his position, he would have been as well.

'What about the commissioner, sir?' Isaac asked.

'I don't know. I've spent enough time with that man to know he does not suffer fools gladly, and that is what you are, a fool.'

'Yes.'

Goddard looked out of the window, unable to look his DCI in the face. He knew what he should do, was reluctant to do it.

'Make yourself scarce, at least for a few days, and just hope you have a breakthrough.'

'I will, sir.'

'Which one do you mean? Making yourself scarce or you'll have a breakthrough.'

'Both.'

'The damage is done. Let's hope we both survive.'

'You, sir?'

'I went out on a limb for you. I told the commissioner you were my best officer and that I had total confidence in you. And yet again you let me down. How many times is this now?'

'A few.'

'Damn right. So far, you've been involved with an operative from MI5 who probably murdered one of the victims in one of your cases.'

'Unproven, sir.'

'And what about Jess O'Neill?'

'Platonic, until Sutherland's murderer was arrested.'

'Charlotte Hamilton's a good-looking woman. Don't go sleeping with her.'

'I'm not a total fool.'

'Find this female, and fast. I can't hold off the commissioner for much longer.'

'The previous commissioner?'

'Shaw? He's now in the House of Lords, clothed in ermine. I doubt if there's much he can do.'

Chapter 21

Isaac's office felt cold when he returned to it after his dressing down by his boss. Some of the other people in the building had been polite as he descended the two flights of stairs. Others had smiled and then sneered when he was not looking, but he had expected that.

There he was, one of the stars of the Met, the man most likely to make it up to commissioner, the first black man to lead the most respected police force in the world. Those who sneered – he knew their names – were those who resented the idea that someone other than a pure-bred Anglo-Saxon could be allowed to hold the top job.

It had upset Farhan Ahmed, his Pakistan-born former DI. Isaac had told him to develop a thick skin and to brush it off, and now his skin was not as thick as it had been.

Charlotte Hamilton obviously had a fixation on him, as had others, and now he was on her website and the front page of at least two of the major newspapers in the country.

There was to be a press conference that afternoon. For once, Isaac's parents would not be tuning in to watch him. His attendance was not required, although his name would be on everyone's lips.

'*My date with a serial killer,*' was the headline in one of the newspapers. The other said, '*The long arm of the law,*' referring to his arm around Charlotte Hamilton.

Isaac entered his office and closed the door. He sat down, his hands behind his head, his eyes closed.

It was Larry, his DI, who knocked on the door. 'No point in dwelling on it. We still have a murderer to catch.'

'What do we know?' Isaac asked.

'They could not find the woman after…'

'After I had been photographed.'

Larry did not answer.

'We know she moved out of the pub in town,' Isaac said. 'Any idea where she went after that?'

'Not yet. I could go up to Newcastle,' Larry said.

'Best if you stay here. Rory Hewitt is a good man, and it's his part of the world.'

'Is she returning to London?'

'It's impossible to know. There's unfinished business for her up north. She failed in her bid to kill Gladys Lake, and her parents are targets.'

'Do they have protection?'

'Protection, yes. I'm not confident that it is sufficient,' Isaac said.

'With Charlotte Hamilton, it's probably not,' Larry agreed.

***

Psychotic, crazy thoughts swirled in Charlotte's mind; thoughts she knew were right, yet were wrong. An intelligent woman, she saw it all so clearly now.

The black police officer had been attractive, and she realised that she liked him, but he wanted her in jail. Her parents wanted her there as well, as did the Lake woman. She had failed there; she had to rectify her mistake, but how?

The authorities were crushing her, as they had when she was a child. Her parents had questioned her over the death of her brother. She had seen the police officer who had taken so much interest in her song that morning in the garden. She had seen the notebook and his writing down of every word. He was older now, and his hair was thinning, but it was the same man. She remembered the song: *Stupid Duncan up at the quarry, along came a sister and gave him a push.*

She had wanted to sing it for her parents, knowing they would not have liked it, but she did not. They knew of her hatred for her brother, or they should have. It was always him; he was always the favourite.

At Christmas, she had wanted another doll, but they had given her a book. They said she was too old, but what did they know. They had given Duncan what he wanted, not her. She was only a female, and they had wanted sons, not daughters. She knew that she hated them. They deserved to die, the same as the others.

***

Gladys Lake was not an easy person to protect. She was impetuous, rushing here and there. The instructions from DI Hewitt had been precise. 'Don't move without one police constable, don't allow him or her out of your sight, and lock all your doors.'

Initially, mindful to follow instructions, she had been diligent, but those who had been assigned to keep a watch on her were complaining.

Rory had been warned by the head administrator at St Nicholas that Dr Lake could be a nightmare. 'Brilliant doctor, but a scatterbrain.'

The man had been right, Rory concluded. He had seen her office with Keith Greenstreet, and it was a mess. Her cottage was better, but not much. In the kitchen, cups and saucers were not in the right place. In the main room, files were on the floor, on the table, even where the cat sat.

Gladys Lake had been asked to speak at a conference in London, and she was going. Rory had advised against it, but she had been adamant.

He knew that down there he could not protect her, and there was no reason to believe that Charlotte Hamilton intended to let her live.

Charlotte Hamilton's attention to detail and to cleanliness was well documented. It took a logical mind to kill someone and then shower, even hanging the towel up and drying the floor.

If Gladys Lake was still on Charlotte's hit list, London would represent the best opportunity.

***

Sara Marshall had been forewarned. If Isaac Cook was removed from the case, she was to take over. Her fortunes had been resurrected, and once again she was in her detective superintendent's good books.

Not that she wanted to take the lead position. She had a young child, and he was at an awkward age. He needed her to be around, but she had a career and a murder case.

Charlotte Hamilton frightened her. It was clear that she was devoid of emotion, and she would have no problems with harming anyone close to those who hurt her.

The team believed the woman to still be in Newcastle, but that was unproven, purely a supposition.

Sara and Sean O'Riordan were back in Twickenham, communicating with the team at Challis Street on a constant basis.

After the attack on Gladys Lake, it had gone quiet. It had only been six days, but it felt like an eternity.

Sara knew that Charlotte was still around somewhere. Instinct told her that, and that she would strike again very soon. Anyone as brazen as she had been in having her photo taken with Isaac Cook does not disappear for long.

The question remained as to where. Was it to be London or Newcastle? Nobody could be sure. Sara believed she would strike again in Newcastle.

***

An isolated farm cottage was not the most secure of locations, and it was fine as long as its occupants stayed there, but occasionally they needed to go out.

Charles and Fiona Hamilton made the trip to the supermarket. They had, at least for the last seven weeks, driven forty miles away to avoid confronting the locals.

This one time, they followed the police advice and drove to the town only two miles away. Charles went to get money out of the cash machine; his wife took a trolley and was filling it up with provisions for four weeks. The two police officers waited in their car, the heater on full blast. The season was changing from cold to even colder. They wondered how Charles Hamilton could walk around in just a shirt. Too many events had clouded his ability to think, to even register the climate.

His wife, Fiona, was slowly withering away; another three months and she would be dead. Charles Hamilton considered his position as he waited for his wife. He was sixty-five and still fit, but without his wife he could not continue, would not want to, and he knew their lives were forfeit.

He returned to the present and entered the supermarket. He found his wife in the second aisle loading up with cereal. She was moving slowly, not looking at what she was buying. He returned some items to where she had found them, and then took another trolley.

'Cash or credit?' the lady at the checkout counter asked.

'Cash,' Charles Hamilton's reply.

Together, Charles and Fiona Hamilton wheeled the trolleys out to their car. Charles pressed the key on his remote. The lid of the boot opened. After putting the provisions in the car, they drove out of the car park.

Neither they nor the police had noticed the woman on the other side of the road.

***

Detective Chief Superintendent Richard Goddard did not like press conferences. There were always some attending who felt the need to monopolise proceedings. The investigation was not going well, and it was hard to defend their lack of progress. Against his better judgement, he had been instructed to bring his DCI with him.

The commissioner had been adamant. 'You're a wet fish once they stick a camera in your face. Cook may be a bloody idiot, but he handles himself well. He can deal with the flak when they start asking their stupid questions.'

As usual, Goddard made the official presentation: long on content, short on fact.

At the end of his statement, the hands went up.

'DCI Cook, what is the situation with you and Charlotte Hamilton. Are you protecting her?' It was not unexpected. Liz Devon, who typically did not attend police press conferences, was a columnist for one of the gutter press publications. She did not care about the murders, only salacious gossip.

'Miss Devon, you are aware of the circumstances surrounding that photo,' Isaac said.

'You had your arm around her.'

'I was asked by a group of women partying in the hotel; it was late at night. I believe that I acted correctly when approached to take a photo of them.'

'Brent MacDonald, BBC. It is apparent that this woman is making a mockery of the police.'

'That is not the case,' Richard Goddard replied.

'The question was directed at DCI Cook,' MacDonald said.

The conference was not going well.

'I believe that she made a mockery of me, not the police force,' Isaac replied, aware that the best defence was to divert the blame, confuse the audience.

'Are you saying you are incompetent?'

'Not at all. Let me ask you, Mr MacDonald. What would you have done if you had been asked to take some photos?'

'I would have refused.' Isaac knew the man was a miserable sod and he had given a truthful answer.

'Detective Chief Superintendent, do you have confidence in DCI Cook's ability to bring this woman to justice?'

'I have total confidence,' Goddard replied.

'After six murders?' Brent McDonald persisted, aiming to evoke a response from Richard Goddard. The murder of Duncan Hamilton was generally not known about, and the official count stood at six, not seven.

'Detective Chief Inspector Cook has an impeccable record. He will apprehend this woman soon.'

'And where is she now?'

'She was last seen in Newcastle.'

'With your inspector's arm around her. It's a shame it wasn't handcuffs. Although with the incompetence of the police, DCI Cook would have been cuffed to a radiator.'

The room burst into laughter. Only two faces remained impassive.

'That is an ill-founded assertion,' Goddard said.

'You're wasting your time with this lot,' Isaac whispered to him. 'It would be better to wrap it up.'

Richard Goddard took his DCI's advice. 'Ladies and gentlemen, let me assure you that we are working hard to find this woman and detain her. You will need to excuse us.'

Both of the police officers beat a hasty retreat.

'Disaster, sir,' Isaac said.

'Unmitigated.' Goddard's monosyllabic response.

Chapter 22

Charlotte Hamilton had remembered the area that her parents had liked. It was pure chance that she had seen them that day. She could see that her mother was looking older, although her father, always the fitter of the two, had not changed.

She felt some compassion on seeing them; almost had wanted to rush up and throw her hands around them. Her love for them had been unconditional, but it was never returned, only given to her brother, her dead brother, squashed like a melon at the bottom of a quarry. She smiled at the thought of it.

It had not been difficult to find out where they lived from the overly talkative woman at the supermarket. 'We never see them here,' the lady had said. 'It's a sad story.'

'Where do they live?'

'Up the road, about five miles. There's a road off to the left, go up there until you see a small cottage. You can't miss it.'

Charlotte left the supermarket and found a car that had been left with its engine running. She got in and drove off.

The road was easy to find. As she drove along it, she saw a police car off to one side. The officer was talking on his mobile.

It was clear that reaching the cottage unseen was not possible by road, as her car would be visible from where the police car was parked. Two miles further on, she pulled the car off to one side. It was higher up the side of the hill, and the road had snaked back on itself. Down below, not more than five hundred yards away, she could see the cottage, with smoke billowing out of the chimney. It looked picture perfect to her.

There was a gate to a field. She opened it and drove the car through, parking so that it was hidden from the road. The wind was bitterly cold, but she had brought warm clothes. Satisfied that no one would see her, she walked down through the fields to the house. As she got nearer, she saw the car that she had seen at the supermarket. It was the right place.

Through the small window at the rear of the cottage she could see her father. Her mother was not visible.

Crouching down, she edged along the wall outside. The weather was getting colder, and she could feel herself shaking. She ignored her discomfort and continued to edge forward.

The door, she could see, was secured by a latch. She lifted it gently. It opened, and she entered the cottage. Her father was in the other room. It was warmer inside than out, and she removed her coat.

'Father,' she murmured.

'Charlotte!' her father exclaimed. He put down the cup that he was holding. 'What are you doing here?' He wanted to call the police but knew he could not. His mobile phone was on the table behind his daughter, a person who he had not seen for five years. A person that he loved, hated, loved. A person who had come to kill him and her mother.

'How's mother?' Charlotte asked.

'She's not well.'

'I want to see her.'

'Why are you here?'

'I needed to see you one more time before...'

'Before what?' Her father cut her conversation short. He had to admit she had changed. She had been blonde with a beautiful face the last time he had seen her. From what he could see, she had dark, shoulder-length hair, and the complexion that had been perfect was now blotchy. He could see the anger in her eyes, and hear the venom in her speech. She knew why she was there; he knew what he had to do. But could he? Could he kill his own daughter in cold blood to protect the mother? Was that possible?

He was a man who had cherished life, and now faced the ultimate dilemma: the death of his child or that of his wife. It was not a decision he could make, a decision that anyone should be forced to make, and the situation was irresolvable. His daughter was psychotic, mad, and she had killed seven times already. In her twisted mind, the killing of her parents would just be another notch in the belt, he realised.

'Are you here to kill us?'

At that moment, Charlotte realised the anger in her had subsided. It was if she was back in the village where she had spent three years with Beaty and her cat. She relaxed her guard and embraced her father.

'Why, Charlotte?' he asked as he hugged her in return. Tears were streaming down his face. At that moment, he held the loving daughter that they had known before that day: that day when Duncan had died. He pulled back from her, the daughter he loved, the murderer of his son.

'You don't love me, you never did,' she said.

'We always loved you, but you killed Duncan.'

'He deserved to die.'

'But why?'

'He broke my doll,' she said. The anger in her eyes had returned. Charles Hamilton was afraid again; afraid for his wife.

'You cannot stay here,' he said.

'This is my home.'

'The police will return. They will see you.'

'I can hide.'

'We still have your doll,' Charlotte's father said. If she stayed, he would have to call the authorities; he knew that.

'I want it.'

'Wait here, and I'll get it for you.'

Charles Hamilton went to the other room and picked up his wife's phone. He pressed speed dial to a prearranged number. The alarm flashed in the police car down the road.

'You've called the police,' Charlotte screamed. Her mother appeared at the top of the stairs.

'Go back, Fiona. Lock yourself in your room.'

Charlotte came forward, a knife in her hand. She was ready to kill her father.

'You bastard. I killed Duncan, the irritating little fool. Now I will kill you.'

The father, desperate to protect his wife, unable to kill his daughter, grabbed a vase holding some flowers and hit her across the head. Charlotte, momentarily stunned, fell back against the door separating the main room from the kitchen. Her father rushed forward to restrain her, receiving a slash across the face from a stiletto knife. He pulled back; the police car drew closer.

Regaining her senses, Charlotte retreated out through the back door and into the cold weather. She had not picked up her coat. Charles Hamilton could see her running up the hill, her warm breath visible in the almost freezing air.

The police car arrived. 'Backups are coming,' the police officer behind the wheel said.

'Anyone injured?' he asked.

'We are fine.'

'Your daughter?'

'Yes.'

'Where is she?'

'Unconscious in the kitchen.' Charles Hamilton lied. He could not kill his daughter, nor could he allow her to be caught. He knew he was wrong, and that it was a decision he would have to live with for the rest of his life.

***

Charlotte Hamilton reached the car; she was out of breath. She started the car and drove off at speed. The car had a full tank of fuel, sufficient for where she was going.

Rory Hewitt arrived at the cottage within forty minutes. 'Where is she?' he asked Charles Hamilton.

'She must have regained consciousness and left.'

Rory Hewitt knew that he had lied, but then what would he have done in a similar situation?

'Your wife?'

'I gave her a sedative. In her condition, she may not survive.'

'What do you mean? Has she been harmed?'

'No. She's let herself go, and now with Charlotte having been here, the stress may be too much.'

'She should be in the hospital.'

'An ambulance is coming.'

The team in London were notified of developments. Isaac had been trying to deal with paperwork but failing miserably as the situation with the photo in Newcastle continued to bother him.

Wendy had tried to buck him up, but with little success.

Sara Marshall was in the car and heading over to Challis Street as soon as Rory Hewitt had phoned her. She arrived in the office puffing, as she had run up the stairs. 'She's making mistakes. We'll have her soon.'

'Where is she now?' Larry asked.

'They're looking for her. She cannot have got far. It's remote up there.'

'Never assume anything with this woman,' Isaac said. 'The moment you believe she's cornered, she disappears, and the next time we find her, there's a dead body.'

'She just missed out on 8 and 9,' Sara said.

'Dr Lake. Is she safe?' Isaac asked.

'DI Hewitt has removed her to a safe location, regardless of the woman's protestations.'

'Charlotte Hamilton's coming back here,' Larry said.

'That may be, but where and when and who will she target this time?' Isaac asked.

'You may need protection, sir,' Wendy said.

'I will, as well,' Sara said.

***

Charlotte drove ten miles before realising the stolen car had probably been reported to the police. She had to dump it. All she had now was her backpack; it still contained her laptop and a change of clothes. It was clear she could not return to Newcastle. Instead, she drove to a small town in County Durham; she remembered she had an aunt there, although she would not be visiting.

From there she was sure she could take local buses and trains until she reached her destination. Her episodes of paranoia were increasing in their frequency and their intensity, but in her lucid moments she could feel tenderness for her parents, sorrow that her father had rejected her.

She knew that her time was drawing to a close, yet there was unfinished business. The Lake woman had deserved to die, but somehow she had survived. Her father, she had wanted to love, but he had rejected her. And, as for her mother, she could go to Hell.

There were others that had made her life miserable. She remembered them well. She ticked them off in her mind: 8, 9, 10.

It was a good number, but first she had to get back down south. She felt in the front pocket of her backpack; the ten thousand pounds in cash was still there. She could always buy new clothes, new disguises, and this time they would be quality.

Chapter 23

Fiona Hamilton died twenty-four hours after her daughter had visited the cottage. Her husband said it was a blessing.

Once they had been well liked and respected, but they had become outcasts. Rory Hewitt could only feel sadness for the man.

'Broken heart,' Hamilton said.

The doctor's official statement was heart failure exacerbated by a weakened physical condition due to poor nutrition.

Rory phoned the team in London. Wendy, although she had not met the woman, cried on hearing the news, as did Sara Marshall. It brought a lump to Isaac's throat as well.

Rory left the hospital at the same time as Charles Hamilton. He intended to return to the cottage on his own.

Back in London, Isaac called the team together. 'The car she stole has been found.'

'Where?' Larry asked.

'Consett, County Durham.'

'Was she seen?'

'We're checking, but the local police believe she would have taken a bus and left the town.'

'Direction?'

'She can't go to Newcastle unless it's to deal with unfinished business.'

'Gladys Lake,' Larry said.

'She will not find her.'

'Safe location?'

'Very safe. There's no way Charlotte Hamilton can find her.'

'That's what you said about her parents, sir,' Wendy reminded him. Isaac chose not to answer.

Sara Marshall and Sean O'Riordan joined the team at Challis Street.

'Why can't we find this woman?' Sara asked. She looked nervous.

'What's the problem?' Isaac asked.

'We're targets. You realise that?'

'It had crossed my mind.'

'I have a child. This woman is willing to kill her own parents. She would not have any issues with an infant.'

'You'd better find somewhere for your son,' Isaac said.

'She can't do that,' Wendy said. 'No mother would part with their child indefinitely.'

'Not even when their child may be at risk?'

'Isaac's right,' Sara said. 'If I stay with my son, she will find us eventually, and besides, I can't disappear. I know her from three years ago, and so far, Isaac and myself are the only ones who have been close to her.'

Larry felt inclined to make a comment. Isaac was still smarting over the rollicking that he had received from Richard Goddard, and was not in the mood to be reminded of the scurrilous reports in the newspapers and on the internet, not to mention the remarks in the police station.

Sara left the office. If Charlotte Hamilton were on her way, it would only be hours before she arrived. Sara had a place to take her son; she only hoped he would be safe there.

Isaac, aware that he was also in danger, organised a gun for himself. He offered to arrange one for Sara, but she declined.

Wendy and Larry went out to the Chalmers' home. Eventually, after the kitchen had been cleaned and repainted, Stephanie Chalmers had moved back in. The area where her husband had died had been bricked off. It reduced the size of the kitchen, and Stephanie did not like to spend time in there. She had organised a cook to prepare all the meals.

Charlotte Hamilton was coming back, and it was important to visit all the places, all the people that she had been involved with, to reanalyse any item of interest that could possibly help them to find her. The police had been given a directive to approach the woman with care, as she was extremely dangerous. If she did not accede to an order, they were licensed to use a Taser. If there was further resistance, they had the authority to shoot.

Charlotte's website had been updated. Her ramblings were more incoherent, although that did not seem to concern her followers, whose numbers continued to increase.

***

Stephanie Chalmers had not been able to help much. Her life appeared to have returned to pre-Ingrid Bentham. Wendy and Larry saw little to be gained by interviewing her more. Gloria was out of the country and safe, and there could only be three obvious targets: Isaac Cook, Sara Marshall, and Gladys Lake.

The movements of all three were being monitored, although Gladys Lake was the most difficult to protect. She had an agenda, and a presentation at a conference on mental health in London was more important to her than her personal safety. She had been warned not to go out on her own enough times, but she continued to ignore the advice.

There had been a couple of times at St Nicholas Hospital when she had absent-mindedly wandered off on her own. The assumption that she was safe within the confines of the building were incorrect. It was not a prison, purely a secure location.

After the death of Fiona Hamilton, Rory had kept in contact with Charles Hamilton. His wife was buried in a moving ceremony attended by Hamilton's immediate family, a few morbid onlookers, Rory, and three members of the press. Apart from that, there was no one else.

The priest had followed the traditional service, omitting any mention of the Hamilton's children. Charles Hamilton read a eulogy. He mentioned the son, but not the daughter. Rory thought the man looked old, even though he was only two years older than him. He had been a university lecturer, but at the lectern in the small church he had mumbled, sometimes incoherently, as though his mind was going. Rory put it down to grief. He wondered what would happen to the man now that he had no one to look after.

After the events at the Hamiltons' cottage, the local police had searched for Charlotte Hamilton. The car found further south indicated that she had returned to London, although that had not been confirmed.

A local bus driver in Consett thought he remembered a woman matching the description, but he had not been sure. After that, no further sightings.

***

An unpleasant, dishevelled man with bad breath and body odour was not what Charlotte Hamilton wanted to see on her return to London, but he offered anonymity, no questions asked. 'It's not much, but you can have it for twenty pounds a night,' he said.

She had not wanted to enter the building located to the east of the city of London, but her options were few. She knew that she could afford the best hotel in the city, but the police would be everywhere.

'It's fine. It's been a long trip.' The room was worth no more than ten, but Charlotte realised that the chances of being discovered were slim. It was clear that the local prostitutes brought men there, took their money, and then kicked them out of the door. The room still had the smell of cheap perfume and sweating men, even without the man who had shown her in. He had looked her up and down, imagined her naked. She knew what he deserved but lucidity had kicked in again, and she realised the cards were stacked against her. She knew she had to complete her task, yet she had not decided how.

The events in the north of the country had shaken her. No longer the success she'd had before, and the way forward was unclear. Random killings seemed to offer no satisfaction, although targeted ones still did, but when, and how?

And now she was back in London and time was running out.

Not sure where to go, Charlotte wandered the streets without purpose. Her hair was now red, her skin complexion two shades darker due to tanning cream. No longer wearing the mini skirt and the tight top that had so enticed Dennis Goldman, she was now dressed dowdily, courtesy of a shop selling old clothes for some charity or other. Conditioned as she was to disguise herself, she slouched and ambled, indicative of an older woman; she was pleased with the result.

With no purpose and no direction, subconsciously she revisited old haunts. She saw where she had killed Gregory Chalmers, even the window of the bedroom where he had first seduced her. She thought back to that night when he had taken delight in making love to her on the marital bed. In the small garden at the front, she could see the two children playing; children that she had loved as if they were her own. Stephanie Chalmers had come to the downstairs window to call them in for a meal. Charlotte could only reflect that they had been happy times, and if it had been her at the window instead of Stephanie, she could have been happy. She knew she would have been a better mother than Stephanie: always worrying about her business and whether it was a good week or bad, instead of focussing on little Billy and his sister.

She could see that the children were grown, almost at her height, especially Billy. She had been sorry that she had attacked their mother that night, but now she was sorry that she had not completed the job. Charlotte's mind was whirring, aiming to make sense of all that had transpired, seeing it all clearly, confused at the same time.

She thought about knocking on the door and pretending to be an old woman down on her luck, but she decided against it.

She had ambled past the police station in Twickenham, and seen the policewoman, Detective Inspector Sara Stanforth, now Sara Marshall. A woman who had hunted her, now married, maybe with a child, and yet she, Charlotte Hamilton, was alone and unloved and childless.

She had seen the man in Challis Street who had put his strong arm around her in Newcastle. She knew she wanted him. She wondered if it was still possible; were her disguises good enough to fool him. A dowdy old woman wearing clothes that smelt of moth balls would not succeed, although if she dressed young and seductively, then maybe she would.

Chapter 24

Newcastle Station was a foreboding sight as Gladys Lake walked through the concourse. Time had moved on since her encounter with Charlotte in the graveyard, although she took the advice of Detective Inspector Rory Hewitt and shortened her stay in London from three nights to two, which explained why she was taking the early train.

Rory Hewitt's argument had been cogent, in that Charlotte had been identified at King's Cross Station. Not that it helped as it had taken a check of two days' worth of security videos before she had been found and by then the woman had vanished. But she was in London, no one was in any doubt of that one fact, and now Gladys Lake was entering the lair of a desperate woman. A woman who had failed in her first attempt to kill her. Gladys Lake did not need Rory Hewitt or a criminal psychologist to tell her that. She knew full well what Charlotte Hamilton was capable of. After all, she had seen her in the graveyard.

The train pulled out of Newcastle Station at six in the morning for the three-hour trip to London.

With Gladys Lake leaving Newcastle, Police Sergeant Liz Castle had been relieved of guard duty. A policeman would take over in London.

'Look out for Police Constable Rob Grantham on your arrival. You have his phone number, and please, whatever you do, don't leave King's Cross Station without him,' Liz Castle said, glad of the chance to get back to some real policing. She knew she was new at the station, only three months, but so far she had been assigned the menial tasks reserved for juniors. Still, she reasoned, it would only be a matter of time before she was given a real job to do.

Three hours later the train drew into King's Cross. Gladys Lake failed to follow instructions and did not contact PC Grantham, and he was late anyway due to an accident near King's Cross. The speech she was due to give was not until two in the afternoon, and it was still only nine o'clock. She had the chance of a few hours' rest. She hailed a taxi. 'St Pancras Renaissance Hotel, please.'

Unbeknown to her, she had been seen. Charlotte Hamilton was a smart woman, everyone agreed on that, even if she was mad. She had phoned the hospital in Newcastle and had found out Dr Lake's plans. It was pure luck for her that Dr Lake was attending the conference in London.

It had not been difficult to wait at the railway station, knowing full well that Gladys Lake had a fear of flying and did not drive, so it had to be the train. It was quicker anyway. For two days, Charlotte had waited in the station, watching Platform 2 from the comfort of a café for some of the time, or else wandering around the concourse. No one would have noticed her. She had to admit that her ability to disguise herself was good. One day old and dowdy, another young and tarty, as her facial features were still young and her body had not turned to flab, unlike her mother, although the last time at the farmhouse she had looked almost anorexic.

***

The taxi driver at King's Cross Station had complained when presented with a fifty-pound note for a fare that was only fifteen, but Charlotte had no time to wait. 'Keep the change,' she said. Another time, she would have argued with the man, but Gladys Lake had left her taxi that they had been following and was heading into the hotel.

'An old friend, I've just missed her at the station. She'll be surprised when she sees me,' Charlotte said when the driver queried why they were following another taxi.

Dressed in disguise, Charlotte was able to approach the reception and hear the woman check in.

'Room 232, ma'am,' a small, bespectacled man behind the reception said. Charlotte thought he looked like a gnome, but she managed to repress a smirk. She realised her mood was whimsical, whereas her intent was malevolent. She stood back when Gladys Lake turned around briefly. To Charlotte, it appeared to be a sign of nervousness on the woman's part; she hoped it was. She wanted the woman to suffer, as she had suffered for all those years.

Gladys Lake picked up her bag and moved towards the lift. A smartly-dressed porter took the bag from her and pressed the button inside the lift. Charlotte stood back, pretending not to look in their direction but watching intently out of the corner of one eye. The conference was scheduled for two days; no need to hurry this time.

And besides, there was still the unresolved matter of Detective Chief Inspector Cook. She was not sure what to do about him. Somehow, vengeance for those who had troubled her seemed the most suitable way forward.

Charlotte returned to her accommodation, grabbing a bite to eat at a local fish and chip shop. Always aware of her figure before, she no longer felt the need to worry. She knew her time was not long, and she had no need to be attractive and fashionable. Her wardrobe, no more than what she could carry in a suitcase, was looking the worse for wear. The ten thousand pounds she had taken from the dead landlord was still intact, apart from several hundred pounds that she had laid out on the trip to Newcastle and the incidentals necessary to maintain a low profile: wigs, dowdy clothes, shoddy accommodation.

She knew that in the past she would have cared, but now she did not.

The man who had first shown her the room at her hotel was behind the reception counter when she got back. He offered an inappropriate comment; she chose to ignore him. He was a poor quality of man, not even worthy of contempt. Charlotte took the key for her room from him with a disparaging shrug of her shoulders, and climbed the two flights of stairs. Her room smelt of damp and decay, as did the rest of the hotel. A quick shower and she lay down on the bed. Her mind was full of the days ahead, knowing full well that she was to become more visible than ever before. She realised that the police would be looking for her, and they would not be far from Gladys Lake, her primary target.

There were two days for her to deal with Gladys Lake, and, if possible, Detective Chief Inspector Isaac Cook. She counted those that she had dispatched, starting with her brother. It pleased her enough to bring a smile to her face.

***

Even with the full force of the Met behind him, Isaac did not know where Charlotte Hamilton was hiding out. Apart from being certain that she had arrived in London, no more had been seen of the woman. Gladys Lake was being subjected to continued surveillance by the police, hopeful that she was safe. Rory Hewitt had received a few choice words from Isaac because he had allowed Gladys Lake to travel unaccompanied from Newcastle to London, an ideal opportunity for a devious woman to commit murder. Police Constable Grantham, who should have been at King's Cross Station on Gladys Lake's arrival, was also given an official reprimand.

'What's the latest?' Isaac asked in his office. He had called the full team together. Police Constable Grantham was permanently assigned to Gladys Lake, as were two other junior police officers. The doctor's protection was paramount, although it was believed that close proximity to her would also present the best opportunity to catch Charlotte. Isaac was still smarting from the photo that she had taken with him in Newcastle.

Isaac knew that his career could not suffer another embarrassing incident. Even now, he was confining his movements to the office, his policing duties and his empty flat. Socialising, even if there was time, was strictly off the agenda.

Charlotte Hamilton could appear at any time; an inappropriate approach engineered by her with a photo posted on the internet, and he would be suspended. His career could not take the ignominy, he knew that. He had to catch her and ensure she was put behind bars; no doubt hospital bars as it was clear that she was criminally insane.

Regardless of the lax security, Dr Lake was in London. Protection had been assigned to her day and night, although Isaac and his team felt that, going on previous form, Charlotte Hamilton would not be easily deterred.

Wendy was the first to speak that morning in the office. As usual, she was upbeat and optimistic, in sharp contrast to Isaac.

Wendy, perceptive and having known him longer than anyone else in the office, sympathised. She was used to seeing a fit, upright black police inspector, not the man in front of her now with a worried look on his face. 'Don't worry, sir. We'll find her soon enough.'

She realised it was probably a futile statement of encouragement. Apart from knowing Charlotte Hamilton was in London, they knew little more. Gladys Lake was still safe, although she was a woman not used to restrictions, and despite the best efforts of the police, all in the office knew that she still represented an easy target.

'Don't relax your guard for a minute,' Isaac had warned her when they met at her hotel for a coffee. 'Charlotte Hamilton is not far away, and she's not used to failure.'

Gladys Lake, appreciative of Isaac's visit to warn her, could only agree. 'I understand, but I can hardly hide away until you find her. Besides, I don't believe she wanted to harm her parents. All she wanted from them was unconditional love and a respite from her killing spree.'

'Can you empathise with Charlotte?' Isaac asked, not sure that the doctor was correct.

'Empathise, certainly. I need to do that with all my patients, try to understand the world from their point of view, aim to bring them back to reality.'

186

'And did Charlotte understand the reality? Do you believe she is aware that what she is doing is wrong?'

'I believe I've had this discussion with your people before.'

'Maybe, but I would appreciate your informing me.'

'Depends on her medication, her current state of mind, but she probably does not believe she is at fault. However, like everyone she needs love, unconditional love. Her parents would be the obvious choice to give her that, and they attempted to in the past.'

'That's before they realised that Charlotte had killed her brother, their son,' Isaac reminded Gladys Lake.

'As you say, before they realised. And it's clear they could not give her the love she wants now, and when she confronted them in their house the other week, it was always going to end badly.'

'So she could have gone to their house hopeful of a warm welcome.'

'Probably, but that's not what happened, is it?'

'No, her parents reacted badly. And your reaction if you're cornered by her? Will you be able to empathise, to show her the love and trust she craves?' Isaac asked.

'Outwardly, I probably will, but I will be shaking like a leaf. Charlotte scares me, and I know she blames me for what has gone wrong in her life.'

'Yet you do not take the appropriate precautions. You should have stayed in Newcastle,' Isaac reminded her.

'The conference I am attending is important. I needed to come.'

'Important enough to risk your life?'

'Not that important, I suppose, but I'll be careful.'

Isaac realised that his discussion with Dr Lake, pleasurable as it had been, had achieved little. Even if there were someone with her at all times, it would not be difficult in a crowded conference room to get in close and to stab her. Still, Isaac realised that he had done his best, and her fate, as well as his future, were in the hands of a delusional woman who continued to evade justice.

***

Sara Marshall, fearful for her safety but mainly for her child, had asked her mother to look after the infant for a few days. Sara instinctively knew that the current case was coming to a conclusion; she didn't know why, other than she could feel all the intricacies, all the components, of the case coming together. She had been involved with Charlotte Hamilton for too many years to believe that she would not go after Gladys Lake, and she intended to stay close to her, even if there was other protection close by. An assigned police constable, even with a photo and a description of Charlotte, would not recognise her easily, especially if she was disguised, and she was clearly proficient in that.

Sara knew more about the woman than anyone else, and she would be looking for mannerisms, the way she walked, the look in her eyes, similarities to her parents. No one else was more capable of recognising the woman, she was sure of that; no one else could save Gladys Lake.

Sean O'Riordan, Sara's constable during Charlotte Hamilton's first murdering rampage three years earlier, and now an integral member of Isaac's team at Homicide, continued to look for the woman. His girlfriend, although used to his extended working hours and his time labouring over the books at home to obtain the qualifications to raise himself from constable to inspector and hopefully as high as commander, continued to complain, although her complaints were muted in comparison to the past. Sean and Sara had agreed to work together on Gladys Lake's protection. They had run it past Isaac; he had been in agreement. If Sara was not with Dr Lake, then Sean would substitute.

Wendy Gladstone, always the best person to track someone down, and Larry Hill were involved with trying to find Charlotte Hamilton, although it was proving difficult. Her presence had not been confirmed in London, although the police officer's sixth sense told them she was there, but it was a huge city: needle in a haystack, according to Wendy, but she didn't give in easily.

And besides, if she wasn't in London, where else could she be? The people who concerned her the most – Sara Marshall, Isaac Cook and now Gladys Lake – were all in the city.

Chapter 25

A lone woman sitting in an internet café in north London raised no interest. The others sitting at their terminals were all focussed on the screens in front of them, tapping away at the keyboards. Some were surfing the web, some talking to loved ones overseas, others looking for employment; only one was planning violence.

Charlotte's mood was calm. Even though the weather was mild, she wore a thick coat, its collar turned up. Dark sunglasses, incongruous when looking at a computer screen, were not ideal, but they helped to conceal her identity. On her head, she wore a baseball cap.

It was necessary to be careful now, as her face was well known throughout the country. Even the newspaper that the man behind the desk was reading when she had paid for thirty minutes on the internet had her face on the front of it, with her history, and a warning to be on the lookout for her. She had to admit she liked the notoriety, even if it impinged on her movements, but regardless, she was hardly recognisable as she sat there in front of the well-used computer.

Her accommodation did not have Wi-Fi, in fact, it didn't have much of anything, and she was not inclined to purchase a USB modem for her laptop in case the authorities could monitor it. Once they knew her laptop's IP (internet protocol), then each time she logged on, they would be able to record all that she wrote, as well as find out where she was. No, she realised, it was better to use internet cafés, a different one each time.

As she tapped away at the computer, her mind focussed on the plan ahead. She knew where all those who were the bane of her life were. Sara Marshall was in Twickenham, Isaac Cook at Challis Street, and Gladys Lake at her hotel or the conference centre. She toyed with the idea of a romantic encounter with the black policeman before she stuck a knife into his heart, but rejected the idea, even if it brought a smile to her face. She knew that in an intimate encounter she would not be able to conceal her identity. If she wanted DCI Cook dead, then that was what would happen. Sara Marshall was another target, but not the prime one. She was a police officer, and apart from wanting to arrest her, she had done no wrong, although she still hated the woman. Gladys Lake, however, was a different matter.

Still, the need to be close to Detective Chief Inspector Isaac Cook ran strong in her veins. She knew she could not be closer, but another photo for the website, and the embarrassment it would cause him, seemed possible.

***

Wendy Gladstone and Larry Hill were out on the street; they had organised a team of one hundred constables to question people on the street at locations that seemed possible as the hiding place of Charlotte Hamilton. Without more accurate information, they had focussed close to the scenes of the past murders: Twickenham, Holland Park and Mayfair, as well as where she had killed the landlord at the cheap accommodation with the Peeping Tom, Jason Martin. That was discounted as the least likely area although it was still a good place to hide. They even ventured out to Joey's in Kingston where Liam Fogarty had been stabbed in the heart, but no one had seen the woman there, although the club was still annoying the neighbours with the noise from the rowdy drunks into the early hours of the morning. Yet Charlotte Hamilton remained elusive, so much so that Isaac felt increasingly frustrated. It wasn't helped by the ambivalence of DCS Goddard, his friend and mentor, towards him, and Isaac was no longer sure about the former of the two descriptors, as his DCS had been less than friendly since the unfortunate incident of the photogenic Isaac and the equally photogenic Charlotte appearing across the social media and on every newspaper front page, not to mention the hilarity on the early morning breakfast shows on television.

It was Wendy, his ever-loyal sergeant, who snapped him out of his inertia after she had returned from pounding the streets. She had seen him in his chair looking despondent.

'It's not that bad, sir. It'll blow over,' she said.

Isaac, forced to focus, could only agree. 'I suppose you're right,' he said. Regardless, he was the SIO on the case, and it was for him to get his backside out of his chair and to do his job. A meeting that afternoon seemed the best approach to breathe life into the search for Charlotte Hamilton.

At the nominated time, Isaac's team assembled. He had to acknowledge that they were a finely-honed team and he had been primarily responsible for bringing them together.

Larry Hill reappeared in the office five minutes before the meeting started. 'Bugger of a day. No sign of the woman,' he said. It was clear that he was not in a good mood; Isaac put it down to his wife's latest macrobiotic diet, which he was obliged to share or else feel her wrath and get the cold shoulder from her.

Larry confirmed Isaac's suspicions. 'I could do with a good plate of steak and chips.'

'Why don't you?' Isaac asked.

'My wife's right, of course,' Larry admitted, 'although it doesn't help with the hours we work.' Isaac said no more; he understood. Jess O'Neill, before she moved out of his place, had been keen on eating properly, so much so that he had tried to modify his eating habits of grabbing a bite here and there, and to wait until he was home with her. On some occasions that was very late at night, as both were busy people with demanding jobs.

Sara Marshall and Sean O'Riordan were both present, as was Bridget, who continued to do a sterling job dealing with the paperwork, assisting Isaac with his when she could.

'Any luck?' Isaac asked, looking over in the direction of Sara and Sean. Sara was looking worried.

'Not really,' Sara said. 'We know she's in London somewhere.'

'Apart from picking her up on camera at King's Cross, she's not been seen since,' Isaac said.

'She could hardly go back to Newcastle,' Sean said. 'Rory Hewitt and his team would have apprehended her if she had.'

'Are you joking?' Larry said. 'Why should they have any more luck than us? Besides, she updated on social media that she was coming to London.'

'And we trust her to be truthful?' Isaac interjected.

'She has unfinished business,' Sara reminded the team.

'Gladys Lake?'

'Yes.'

'And you, sir,' Wendy reminded Isaac.

Isaac, usually a mild-mannered man, was becoming frustrated. Apart from Larry consuming the biscuits, he couldn't see what they were achieving. Charlotte Hamilton continued to intrigue the media, although she had not killed for some time, and each time police ineptitude was implied, and on more than one occasion referred to overtly. His name had been mentioned more times than he appreciated, and whereas he had achieved some degree of celebrity, and someone had once said that any publicity was good, it didn't ring true in his case. He had become accustomed to reading accolades about himself, receiving phone calls from Richard Goddard congratulating him on excellent policing, even from the commissioner, the head of the Met, on one occasion. But now every phone call from a superior asked the same questions: when will there be an arrest, what are you doing to find this woman? Isaac realised there was one question being asked amongst his superiors: Is DCI Cook up to the task or should he be relieved of command?

He felt sure that Goddard would protect him; after all, he had ensured that Isaac was on the promotion ladder, and he had protected him well enough in the past. However, his DCS was a political animal, and he was not going to allow his career to be hindered by defending the indefensible.

***

Charlotte Hamilton, safely ensconced in her room at the flea-bitten accommodation she had found, sat on her bed. Her mood was ebullient, even if her life was in tatters.

She quietly sang a song: *stupid Duncan up at the quarry, along came a sister and gave him a push.* Although now she had another verse: *the black policeman thought he was smart until I stuck a knife in his heart.*

The melodious singing was interrupted by the sound of a jackhammer on the road outside. She looked around the room. It wasn't much for someone who had close to ten thousand pounds in her backpack.

A night in a good hotel will do me good, she thought. *Maybe the hotel where the Lake bitch is staying. So much easier to deal with her if I am close.*

She opened her bag and took out the clothes she needed: an old woollen skirt she had purchased in a charity shop, a blue jumper, some sensible black shoes, a brunette wig. She changed, applied makeup to age her face, and walked out of the door.

'The bastard can wait for his money,' she said under her breath. She still owed for two nights' accommodation, but she had no intention of coming back to pay. It was a five-minute walk to the train, although she made it in four. As the train rattled towards its final destination, she looked round the carriage. *If only they knew who was on the train,* she thought.

Virtually everyone was looking at their smartphones; some had iPads, but only one person had a newspaper. Even from where she was sitting, she could see a reference to her on the front page, as well as a picture of two men at a press conference. She recognised one, his black complexion unmistakable. A woman to one side of her looked at her for a while and looked away. Maybe the woman recognised her, she thought, but discounted it. Charlotte knew her ability to disguise herself was excellent, and that she would have no problems checking into Gladys Lake's hotel.

Thirty minutes later, Charlotte left the train at King's Cross and walked down Euston Road, heading for the hotel, and the woman who remained her main focus. An attentive receptionist at the St Pancras Renaissance Hotel signed her in, although she had used a false name and address. She paid in advance with cash and asked for the minibar to be emptied. Even so, she had taken a step back when she saw Inspector Sara Marshall sitting in the foyer drinking coffee. Charlotte felt for the knife in her pocket, resisting the urge to move closer and to insert it into the police officer's chest, as she realised that her carefully constructed plan would then be in shreds. She had already decided: first Gladys Lake, followed by Isaac Cook, followed by Sara Marshall. To Charlotte, in need of a friend, a shoulder to cry on, someone to love, Sara Marshall would have been ideal, but she was the enemy. She was someone who should understand her desire for vengeance on men, but probably would not.

Charlotte's mind swirled with impossible thoughts: a happy family, Isaac Cook, even Gloria, her former flatmate, and even Gregory Chalmers whom she had killed so long ago. If only he had loved her, she would have looked after him and his children, but knew it could not have been. She recognised that her earlier ebullience had been tinged with sadness and regret.

'Room 334,' a voice snapped her back to reality. She realised that she had been daydreaming. She hoped it wasn't noticeable, as the receptionist said nothing, and she could see that Sara Marshall was still sipping her coffee, talking to someone on her phone. Otherwise, the foyer of the hotel was quiet. Dispensing with anyone to show her to the room, Charlotte pressed the button of the lift. The room she had booked was as elegant as her previous accommodation had been flea-bitten. Appreciating the luxury, she took a lingering bath. Her mood tempered in the warm water, and for a moment, sanity reigned; the anger that she had felt had abated. Realising that her life had come full course and that there was no going back, she drew herself out of the bath, dried herself on the towel hanging behind the door and lay down on the bed.

When she awoke it was dark outside; she had been asleep for at least eight hours. Charlotte looked at the clock; it was 9 p.m. She dressed, careful to maintain her disguise, and left the room, unsure as to where she was going, although a good meal was first on her list of things to do.

As she left the hotel, she noticed her nemesis talking to someone she recognised: the police officer who worked with Sara Marshall, although she could not remember his name. Careful to give them only a sideways glance, she walked out of the front door and down the street. Feeling better after a pizza, she strolled around the area for some time, looking in shop windows, idly speculating on what could be. She saw couples walking arm in arm, elderly people hobbling down the street, even a baby in a pram being pushed by its mother. Charlotte daydreamed yet again about what her life could have been without her stupid brother, her uncaring parents, men who had wronged her, men who had used her body.

A car beeping its horn soon brought her back to reality as she walked out in the middle of the traffic, not looking where she was going. She knew that her mind was playing tricks when it was a time to be rational. There was a plan to execute, and she needed maximum focus, she knew that.

Charlotte returned to the hotel, noticing that Gladys Lake was not to be seen. She thought that it would be easy to knock on her door and to kill her there and then, but she needed to deal with others first. If she could not kill Isaac Cook, she could at least humiliate him again; that sounded fun to her. In her bag, she carried tablets that would calm her down, allow her to think clearly, but she knew that they would take away the anger, bring the regret for what she had done. She flushed them down the toilet.

***

Detective Chief Superintendent Richard Goddard was feeling the heat. A summons to the office of the Commissioner of the London Metropolitan Police was not what he wanted, especially as his relationship with the current commissioner was less than ideal.

A plain-talking man who Goddard kept his distance from if he could, the commissioner was in no mood to mince words. 'What the hell are you doing, DCS?'

Goddard had no defence, although he needed to put on a good show. The previous commissioner, a friend as well as his boss, would have been sympathetic, offering to give assistance and advice, but the new commissioner was a blunt man who spoke his mind, sometimes too freely. He was in no mood to accord the DCS standing in front of him any words of encouragement.

'We believe she's in London.'

'For Christ's sake, there's how many people in London? Eight, ten million? What chance do you have?'

'We're following up on all leads, conducting door-to-door, checking surveillance cameras.'

'That's just verbiage, and you know it. Admit it, you haven't a clue where the mad woman is.'

'Her ability to vanish is remarkable.'

'And you and your team's ability to display extreme incompetence is outstanding. Maybe I should bring in some people from my previous command to show you how to run an investigation.'

'That's not necessary, sir. My people are all competent and working hard to bring this case to a conclusion.'

'How many people dead now, eight or nine?'

'Six officially, sir.'

'What do you mean by officially?'

'Her brother's death is still recorded as accidental, and besides, she would have been a minor then.'

'Cook. What are you doing with him?'

'He's still the senior investigating officer.'

'Any more photos of him wrapped around the main suspect?'

'None.'

'You're a bloody fool to keep him in that position. I've been looking through his records: excellent policeman, but he has a habit of making a fool of himself,' the commissioner said.

'As you say, an excellent policeman who occasionally makes an error of judgement.'

'Occasionally! You should have put him on restricted duties after that photo, brought someone else in.'

'I realise that, sir.'

The DCS sensed a lessening in the commissioner's venom, although he was premature in his assessment.

'If there'is no breakthrough, then you and your team will be out. I need not add that your career and that of your star DCI will be down the drain.'

'Yes, sir.'

'Don't underestimate my resolve. The previous commissioner and your political friends will not be able to save you if I decide to act. Is that clear?'

'Clear, sir.'

'Good. Now leave and get on with it.'

Richard Goddard, with the exalted title of detective chief superintendent, left the room like an errant schoolboy summoned to the teacher's office for a dressing down. He was not in the best temper when he left. He needed someone on whom to take out his frustration; Isaac seemed the best person for that.

Chapter 26

'Isaac, I've received a right bollocking from the commissioner.' It was unusual for the DCS to use bad language, a clear indication that his visit was not social. Isaac braced himself for what was to come.

'It's to be expected, sir,' Isaac replied to Goddard's opening comment, after the DCS had firmly closed Isaac's office door behind him.

'Just because you're stuffing around, I'm forced to allow the commissioner to take it out on me. I may resent the man, but he's still our boss.'

'Under the circumstances, the team is working well,' Isaac said.

'What is it with this woman? It's not as if you don't know who the guilty person is.'

'Agreed, sir, but she blends in easily.'

'We know that already, but what are you doing to find her?'

'Sergeant Gladstone and Larry Hill are out in the field looking for her, conducting door-to-doors. Inspector Marshall and Sergeant O'Riordan are checking out old haunts, previous murder locations.'

'The woman is hardly likely to do that; but then again, she and the commissioner may be right, this department under your tutelage is incompetent.'

'I resent that, sir.'

'Maybe you do, but I'm tired of taking flak from his holiness in his ivory tower at Scotland Yard. He instructed me once before to put you on restricted duties, even to suspend you, but I didn't. And now it's on my record that I acted against advice. If she kills again, the commissioner will have me on restricted duties along with you, and I do not intend to allow that to happen. He wants to bring in someone else to run this investigation; someone from his previous command, although what good that will do, coming in cold to the case, is unclear.'

'Understood.'

Goddard, after venting his spleen on Isaac, felt his frustration at the meeting with the commissioner subside. He took a seat. Bridget, outside, noticing the mellowing atmosphere in Isaac's office and regarding it as safe to enter, came in with a cup of tea for each of the two men.

'Isaac, what can be done?' Goddard said calmly after Bridget had left.

'You're right, DCS. It should be easy. All we have to do now is to protect the living and to find one woman.'

'So why can't you find her?'

'She just has an uncanny ability. She always disguises herself, and she's not using bank or credit cards.'

'She must have money then.'

'The last man she killed had money hidden under his bed.'

'She stole it?'

'It's the only explanation. The man's ex-wife turned up at the crime scene soon after the body had been discovered. We used her for a positive ID later. Anyway, she was convinced that he had stashed his money somewhere. Called him a miserable old skinflint.'

'You checked?'

'Of course, sir. Found some money, but not much.'

'The commissioner's receiving flak over this woman.'

'You don't care much for him, sir?'

'Not the issue, is it?'

***

Since the incident with the photo in Newcastle the investigation had been progressing satisfactorily, and thankfully there had been no further deaths. Standard policing was being followed, and the paperwork, always too much, was up to date and in line with regulations. The new commissioner regarded the process as important, and while Isaac did not enjoy that side of his job, he had to reluctantly admit that it was necessary. Get a smart lawyer for the defence and any shoddy paperwork would soon be relegated to the rubbish bin as inadmissible evidence.

It had happened a few times in the past, even to Isaac, and nothing irked more than to see a guilty person walk free, thumbing their nose at the police. Isaac did not intend for that to happen this time. He was still smarting from the embarrassing photo, and the woman was already thumbing her nose, and she was not even in custody.

Admittedly, she was not doing it as much as in the past, as the woman's attempts to use social media had mostly been curtailed. Each time she posted, it was from another location. It had been possible to trace the locations, and they were always internet cafés, spread throughout the country. Her last post had been close in to London.

Wendy and Larry, hot on the trail, had missed Charlotte by no more than two hours at the last internet café. The man behind the counter had been surly when questioned, claiming that he had seen no one suspicious. Questioned further, he admitted he had seen a woman matching the woman in the photo that Larry showed him. The café, no more than twenty miles from London, had provided further proof that Charlotte was close by, although the only witness was vague and could hardly be regarded as reliable.

***

Charlotte reclined on her bed at the hotel. She was not sure what to do next. The key players were all in position, but how to execute her plan concerned her. She knew that when she made her first move, she would become more visible.

There she was in plain view, and no one had seen her, not Gladys Lake nor Sara Marshall. She had not seen DCI Cook yet, but she was determined to obtain one more photo.

The first time in Newcastle, with a frivolous group of women, the DCI had been easy to corner. She could see even then that he was attracted to women, even to her, judging by the way he gripped her around the waist when the photo had been taken. She fantasised over him, yet knew it was not possible. Tired of staring at the television and daydreaming, she left the hotel; it was the end-of-day rush hour, and the city was milling with people.

She thought about leaving the city, to get maybe twenty to thirty miles out from the centre and find somewhere to use the internet. She walked up Euston Road as far as the entrance to the London Underground. Flashing her Oyster Card at the ticket barrier she looked for the next train.

As she descended on the escalator, safely ensconced in the melee of people, she looked to the right. Ascending on the other side was Sara Marshall. Unable to resist, Charlotte looked across at her. Even as well disguised as she was, there was no way the police inspector would not recognise her. Immediately Sara started pushing her way up past the people, attempting to flash her badge and to shout 'Police'.

Equally alarmed, Charlotte pushed her way down and jumped into a train that was about to pull out, its destination unknown and unimportant.

Sara was now at the top of the escalator and on speed dial to Isaac and the team. Not waiting for a reply, she hurtled down the escalator in an attempt to catch up with Charlotte, her pulse racing at the realisation of who she had just seen. Isaac, on the other line, was unable to speak to Sara, but was able to register the noise and the activity on her end of the phone.

He quickly fired up the team, using another phone on a group call. 'Sara's in trouble.'

Sean O'Riordan answered first. 'She was heading over to meet me at Gladys Lake's hotel.'

'Wendy, Larry, get over there now,' Isaac said.

'We're on our way,' Larry's reply.

Thirty seconds later, Sara's voice was heard. 'Charlotte Hamilton, I've just seen her. St Pancras Underground.'

'Where is she now?' Isaac asked.

'No idea. By the time I could get down the escalator, she had jumped on a train and left. Probably the Victoria line, heading south.'

Isaac phoned for support. An APW was instigated: focus on all stations downline from St Pancras. Soon, every station on the line was being converged on by police cars and police officers on foot; the woman's importance ensured a maximum response from all police authorities.

Forty minutes later came the inevitable negative response from all stations. Isaac, annoyed that yet again she had eluded them, phoned his boss.

'DCS, Charlotte Hamilton confirmed in London.'

'You've caught her?'

'Not yet, but she's running scared now.'

'I'll phone the commissioner. May help to give you some time, but don't count on it.'

Sara, deducing that St Pancras Underground and Gladys Lake's hotel were too close to be a coincidence, rushed to the hotel after ensuring the police who were pouring into the station were updated. She found Gladys Lake in her room with Sean O'Riordan, two uniforms on the door outside.

'Was she coming for me?' Gladys Lake asked.

'I don't think so. She was heading in the wrong direction,' Sara replied.

'Staking out the area?' Sean asked.

'It's possible. You'd better get Wendy and Larry to check.'

***

A desperate woman took stock of the situation. Charlotte had not expected to see Sara Marshall in the underground station; she chastised herself for looking her way.

If it had not been for the eye contact, there was no way that anyone, even a police officer, would have recognised her. If the train had not been there when she ran off the escalator, she knew she could have been caught. And now there was the problem of money. Checking her bag, she still had two thousand pounds; the rest was in her room back at the hotel, along with her disguises.

If I hadn't got off one station down, she thought, having realised that the police would soon be mobilised to look for her. Her estimation was correct, and as soon as she left the station at Euston, she moved quickly away on foot. Hailing a taxi, she took it to Windsor, a small town to the west of London. Unable to think straight, too many issues to consider, she checked into a budget hotel using the name of Ingrid Bentham.

Once in the room, Charlotte took stock of the situation. 'Two thousand pounds, the clothes I'm wearing,' she said out loud to herself. She took a shower and then slept for two hours. Later, she went to a local supermarket and bought herself a few essentials: toothbrush, toothpaste, change of underwear. Apart from that, she decided to leave the rest of what she required for the next day.

She realised that the net was closing in on her. She saw clearly that the next few days would be crucial and she could not evade the police for much longer.

Wendy and Larry focussed on St Pancras; Bridget was looking at the CCTV. If Charlotte had been there, then it was clear that she knew where Gladys Lake was; it was too much of a coincidence to be discounted. Sara had been able to give a good description: red hair (obviously a wig), dark blue skirt, knee-length, blue top, possibly wool, as well as a calf-length coat, dark brown. From where she had been on the other side of the escalator, Sara had not been able to see what shoes Charlotte Hamilton was wearing.

'If she hadn't looked at me,' Sara had said, 'I wouldn't have known it was her.'

'Just hope she didn't get a photo of you,' Isaac's reply. He had been close to Charlotte Hamilton, admittedly in the dark, but he had failed to recognise her too, so he was in no position to offer any further comment.

Gladys Lake was adamant that she would continue with her presentation, regardless of the protestations from Isaac, who had come to the hotel to meet her personally. 'We can give you protective custody for the next few days,' he said. 'Charlotte's rattled now. It won't be long before we catch her.'

'That may be, but I've been preparing for this conference for the last three months. I don't intend to miss it, Charlotte Hamilton or no Charlotte Hamilton.'

'Sara, Sean, stay with Dr Lake. Day and night if you have to,' Isaac said realising the futility of further debate.

'Will do, sir,' Sean replied. Sara, concerned that her child had a nasty cough and she should be with him, nodded her head weakly.

Chapter 27

Charlotte was disturbed after the incident at St Pancras Underground Station; her manner in the train as it pulled out of the station had caused others to look at her. She had sworn out loud in anguish. She had nearly been caught and all because of a stupid error; if she hadn't looked, the woman police officer would never have recognised her. She realised she had become too nonchalant about her ability to move freely, thumbing her nose at the incompetent police officers, which was how she saw them.

She had seen Sara Marshall on more than one occasion, even walked past her in the street close to the hotel one day, almost felt like sitting close to her in the foyer of the hotel. It was arrogance on her part; she knew it now. She determined to lift her game, although events were moving quickly.

A visit to a shop selling wigs in Windsor, not far from the castle, and she was a brunette; a charity shop provided the clothes she required. The subject matter of the conference where the evil doctor would speak was academic. Charlotte had read it carefully: Human Rights and Mental Health. She knew what it meant: how to make people's lives miserable. Charlotte, knowing full well how Gladys Lake dressed, decided to dress in the same style, which made for sensible clothes and sensible shoes; not the style of clothes which she had affected when she had seduced and killed four of her previous victims.

Back at her hotel, she changed into the clothes she had bought, putting her money securely in the small bag she carried. She left her remaining meagre belongings in her hotel room and walked out of the door. She was not sure if she would be returning, but it did not matter. Her life had come full circle now, and if she could strike a blow on behalf of all those who had suffered at the hands of malevolent doctors, in buildings called hospitals but were no more than prisons, then all was fine. Whatever the day brought, she would accept it with grace.

***

Isaac, early in the office after a sleepless night, sat at his desk pondering Richard Goddard's visit the previous day.

He had left the office the previous night close to midnight, and he had returned at five in the morning. The situation weighed heavily on his mind.

Bridget and Wendy had been working together to ascertain Charlotte Hamilton's movements after the incident with Sara Marshall; not so easy considering that it had been rush hour, and the clothing described by Sara could have matched at least five per cent of all the women travelling at that time. Facial recognition, especially a retinal scan, was the best way to confirm one hundred per cent that it was the right person, but that was deemed not possible in this case. For one thing, the camera lenses at most underground stations were dirty, and secondly, their resolution was not ideal. The most that could be hoped for was a close match on the clothing.

The previous night Bridget had stayed in the office with Wendy, who kept up the supply of coffee until two in the morning. They had phoned Isaac on leaving to let him know they had a possible lead, and they would update him in the morning.

Wendy walked into the office at six in the morning, an hour after Isaac. 'The alarm didn't go off,' she said.

'That's fine,' Isaac said. 'Grab yourself a tea, and we can talk.'

'Bridget's on the way, so is Larry.'

'Fine, we'll wait for them.'

'It's going to be alright, sir.'

Isaac realised that Bridget had been talking to Wendy about the DCS's visit to his office.

Ten minutes later, all four sat down in Isaac's office.

'What do you have?' Isaac asked.

'We believe we've identified Charlotte Hamilton at Euston Underground,' Bridget said.

'Confirmed?'

'The clothing matches, as does the time.'

'Assuming it's her, what then?'

'We sent a photo to DI Marshall. She's certain it's her, as well.'

We're closing in on her.' Isaac visibly relaxed at the news, so much so that Wendy felt obliged to comment.

'We still need her under lock and key, sir.'

'Understood. Any further sightings?' Isaac asked.

'We think we picked her up outside on the street hailing a cab,' Wendy said.

'Details?'

'Not possible to identify the cab. We'll be dealing with that today; it shouldn't be too much of a problem.'

'Maybe an address?'

'Always possible. The woman's making mistakes; we should catch her soon.'

'Hopefully before she kills again.'

'And Gladys Lake?' Larry asked.

'Inspector Marshall and Sergeant O'Riordan are sticking close to her. Once she's out of London, the better it is for us.'

'And when will that be?' Wendy asked.

'Tomorrow, hopefully. So that's the agenda for today: protect Dr Lake, find and arrest Charlotte Hamilton.'

'You make it sound easy, sir.'

'It has to be, or else they'll bring in another team.' Isaac realised that he should have berated them in the same way that he had been by Richard Goddard, but he saw that as unnecessary; they wouldn't let him down.'

'We'll succeed,' Wendy said. The others acknowledged with nods of their heads.

***

Gladys Lake woke early. Today was a big day for her, and she was excited. Her approach to the welfare of the mentally ill was to be commended for its record of success. She had been allocated forty minutes for the presentation; she could have done with sixty, but there were other speakers, and the organising committee had been adamant about her allocated time.

A shower, then breakfast in her room, a concession she had been forced to make after Charlotte Hamilton had been seen close by. She would have preferred the restaurant downstairs with its greater choice of food, but even she could see that it was possibly dangerous to be so exposed, especially after it had been discovered that Charlotte had spent two nights in the same hotel as her. After she had been spotted nearby, Sean and Sara had conducted a check of the hotel's records and discovered the room that Charlotte had been using, along with eight thousand pounds and some clothes.

After breakfast, Dr Lake checked her presentation and went through it one more time. Satisfied that it was in order, she lay down on her bed again. She fell asleep until the phone rang. *Oh, what fun, I slit his throat. Who will be next? Will it be you?'*

Gladys Lake slammed down the phone and screamed for help. The two police officers stationed outside her door came rushing in.

'What is it?' the more senior of the two asked.

'She's been on the phone.'

Sean O'Riordan arrived first. He had been at the hotel since early morning and was just eating breakfast when the phone call came through from Sara Marshall. She was on her way, due in twenty minutes.

She phoned Isaac. 'Charlotte's called Dr Lake.'

'Trace on the phone?'

'Not sure yet. It looks like she used a public phone.'

'Anyway, we need it located.'

Sara arrived at the hotel to find Gladys Lake calm but still upset.

'You need to cancel your presentation,' Sara said.

'I'll be okay. I intend to honour my obligation.'

Aware, after so many times of trying, that she would not be able to dissuade the woman, Sara acquiesced. The plan she outlined to those charged with protecting the doctor was that they would take her to the event at 11 a.m. for the pre-conference get-together.

At all times, one police officer was to be at her side, which would be, unless advised otherwise, either Sara Marshall or Sean O'Riordan. Two police officers would be stationed at the main entrances to the venue, and police would be interspersed throughout the building. All persons entering would be checked and their credentials established.

As it was a two-day event, it was clear that Charlotte Hamilton's window of opportunity was limited, at least in London. At the conclusion of the day's activities, Dr Lake was to be taken back to the hotel and protected at all times. On the third morning after arriving, she would travel to the railway station to catch an early train back to Newcastle. A discreet police escort consisting of six officers, including Sara and Sean, would accompany her to Newcastle where she would be placed under the protection of Rory Hewitt and his team. At no time, and Sara was adamant about this, was Gladys Lake allowed to be out of sight of the police.

As Sara explained, it was not only about protecting Dr Lake. It was also about capturing Charlotte Hamilton who was preparing to take some action, although where and when was not known.

***

Wendy and Larry were at Euston Underground. The security videos had identified Charlotte Hamilton but not where she had gone after leaving the station.

The taxi rank offered the best opportunity, and six officers, as well as Wendy, were working the taxis one by one, although the drivers were not pleased to be delayed. However, they could not avoid the police, and it was always best to keep on the right side of the law; they knew that.

Larry was the first to make a breakthrough. 'That's her. She was a nervous woman, kept asking me to drive faster,' an Indian Sikh driver said.

'What can you tell me about her?' Larry asked.

'Can't it wait? It's the best time of the day to make money.'

'Official police enquiry.'

'Then be quick.'

'Where did you take the woman?'

'Windsor, an excellent fare at that time of night. There's a train out there, but for some reason she preferred to come with me.'

'Address?'

'Just in front of the castle, that's all. Can I go now?'

'Subject to giving your details. We'll need a statement later from you.'

'That's fine. I'm a good citizen. Always willing to help.'

The Sikh driver gave his details. Larry could see no reason to detain him further. However, he had not been able to provide a precise address.

'Important, is she?'

'Very.'

'Okay. You have my phone number, but as I said, I dropped her in front of the castle. No more than that.'

Isaac, now aware of where Charlotte had gone, was soon on the phone to the police station in Windsor. Larry and Wendy left Euston soon after Larry's success, and with their team headed towards the small town, twenty miles to the west, that was invariably swamped by tourists hoping for a glimpse of royalty. It was still early; there was a chance they could stop Charlotte before she left there.

Sergeant Bevin Downton met them on arrival at the police station in Alma Road, no more than a mile from Windsor Castle, and the last known location of Charlotte Hamilton.

'What can I do for you?' Downton, a tall man with dark wavy hair, asked.

'Your team is ready?' Larry asked.

'One step ahead. Once you phoned and explained the situation, we had people out on the street asking passers-by. Also, we're checking the hotels now. If, as you say, she's running scared, she may have stayed close to the city centre, or moved on somewhere else.'

'Not likely that she's moved,' Wendy said. 'Time's against her now, and she knows it. We believe that she will strike today in London. She's already phoned the target; scared the living daylights out of her.'

'Give us three hours, and we should have checked the main possibilities,' Downton said.

***

Charlotte wandered down by the river, throwing some bread for the ducks to eat. It was still early, too early to complete what remained unfinished from Newcastle. Usually, she would skip breakfast, but today, for no apparent reason, she decided that a full stomach was needed.

'Full English breakfast, dear?' the waitress at the small café asked.

'Yes, please,' Charlotte replied. She checked inside her bag; all that she needed was there.

Ten minutes later, her breakfast arrived: tomatoes, eggs, bacon and sausages. Charlotte gulped down the meal, paid the bill and left the café. She walked to the railway station in Windsor and took the 7.55 a.m. to Waterloo. From there it was a one-mile walk across Waterloo Bridge to Chancery Lane, and the London International Medical Centre where the conference was to be held, although she intended to leave the train at Vauxhall, two miles further away from the venue.

She realised that there would be police at Waterloo looking for her; her phone call to Gladys Lake would have alerted them to her primary target. A rational person would not have made such an error, but she was no longer rational, only focussed. If she was to die in the attempt, so be it, but Gladys Lake had to die first.

The train moved rapidly to its destination, Charlotte barely registering the movement. It was only when she heard the driver announce 'Vauxhall next stop' that she raised herself from her seat.

As she had predicted, there was no police presence at the station, only railway security, and they weren't looking for her. She left the station on the side closest to the river and walked up the Albert Embankment; it was only 9.30 a.m., and time was on her side. A police car came hurtling by, its siren blaring. For a moment, Charlotte moved over to one side, closer to the river, but the car did not stop. She resumed her steady pace up the road, passing Lambeth Bridge, Westminster Bridge and the Houses of Parliament; at any other time scenically impressive, but not for Charlotte. She came to Waterloo Bridge and looked around for a heightened police presence; she could see none. The crowds had started to form on the bridge: locals going about their usual business, tourists with iPhones taking photos, mainly selfies to post on social media. None of them interested her as she maintained her pace over the bridge, looking left and right, straight ahead, not noticing the River Thames flowing beneath her. Leaving the river, she reached the Strand and turned right, eventually reaching Chancery Lane and her destination. The police car outside was the first sign of trouble; the second, the two police officers checking everyone entering the building.

Anxious to ensure that her plan was not thwarted, she walked around the edifice looking for another way in. She found Clifford's Inn Passage, a lane to one side of the building. History would have told her that the name referred to an Inn of Chancery, one of the country's legal institutions that had been founded in 1344, but she was not interested in that, only in whether the passage would afford her entrance into where she wanted to go. Moving up the lane, she found a small door; it was unlocked. She turned the handle and entered the basement of the conference centre. She ascended a flight of stairs: yet again, police. A cupboard solved the problem; it contained cleaning utensils and a cleaner's uniform. She put it on and moved around the building, pretending to clean. Soon she reached the room where Gladys Lake was to present her paper; it was empty. Easing herself into a space beneath the elevated stage, she waited.

It had been luck that the room was empty when she had entered. Within a few minutes, people started to file in, ready for the opening speech at midday. Gladys Lake entered the room just before it started, in the company of Sara Marshall. Charlotte watched them come down the stairs through a crack in the raised-floor's plinth. Up on the stage, the microphones were being given a final test: 'One, two, three. Can you hear me at the back?' They could.

Charlotte listened to the boring speeches about subjects that she had knowledge of after years in a hospital. Gladys Lake was due to speak at 2 p.m.

Charlotte, unsure how to proceed, waited patiently, although it was dusty where she was, and there was evidence of vermin. Regardless, she kept still, hoping that an opportunity would present itself. She saw the doctor fiddling with her notes, talking to Sara Marshall, looking around the room nervously. At ten minutes before her nominated time, Gladys Lake rose and left the room in the company of the police officer. Charlotte cursed, unable to follow them. She moved back, finding an exit. Quickly, unseen, she moved around behind some partitions to the rear of the room and through a side door into the corridor outside. At the other end, she could see the Ladies toilet; her assumption was that was where the two women had gone. She gingerly approached the door, listening for voices, hearing muffled sounds from the other side. Charlotte checked her bag and withdrew the knife she carried.

Carefully she pushed opened the door; it squeaked. Once through it, she concealed herself behind a pillar. Certain of her target, she moved forward.

'What the –' Sara Marshall shouted in surprise, instinctively shielding her body from the knife that Charlotte held.

'Where is she?' Charlotte demanded. Her face was red with anger.

Sara realised that Dr Lake was safe as long as she stayed in the cubicle. She shouted to her, 'Don't move.'

'In there, is she?'

'There's no way out,' Sara, her pulse racing, said. She knew that if she could reach her phone, there would be police officers nearby to take down the woman confronting her.

'There was no way in, but here I am. I intend to finish what I started. To show those doctors in the other room what happens when you torture innocent people.'

Sara used all her training in negotiation to attempt to calm the woman. She was a strong woman, and in her state, unpredictable. Sara moved away from protecting Dr Lake's cubicle, aiming to distance herself from the knife. She hoped the doctor would have the good sense to remain where she was.

Charlotte moved forward, matching the distance between her knife and Sara Marshall. Sara could feel her panic increasing and attempted to calm her nerves. She was a seasoned police officer, similar scenarios had been practised in training, but here was the real thing, and it was nothing like she had been taught. Then, there had been an element of make-believe, and there was no way that any harm would befall those who failed the test, but now: one mistake, one wrong word, one action, and there would be death.

'Two for one,' Charlotte said, grimacing. Sara could see that the situation was precarious. She thought of her child without a mother, all because of her chosen career and a mad woman.

'It's over, Charlotte. You cannot escape,' Sara said.

'With Dr Lake dead, what do I care?'

'You need help, Charlotte,' Sara said, hoping to delay the woman's next action. Sara pressed her hand against her left pocket; her phone was there, but there was no way to use it, not while the woman was watching her intently. One wrong move and the knife would be propelled forward.

'I'm coming for you,' Charlotte taunted the woman in the cubicle.

'Please, Charlotte, dear Charlotte. I always cared for you, did what I thought was right.' The sound of Gladys Lake's voice indicated the fear she was feeling.

'Electric shocks and cold baths, is that how you care? Nobody cared for me, not my father, not my mother, and not that brother of mine.'

'You killed your brother?' Sara asked.

'He deserved to die.'

'Nobody deserves to die,' Gladys Lake said.

'Those men who treated me badly did.'

Sara could see that the conversation was weakening the resolve of the woman in front of her; the knife was not held as erect as before. She kept talking.

'What did you plan to do after here?' Sara asked.

'I have no plans. I've already told you.'

'There is help available for you, you know that.'

'Help! Drugged out of my mind until I'm no more than a vegetable. No thanks.' The knife grip firmed.

Sara moved further back, unable to avoid the direct impact of the blade. At the crucial moment, she managed to step sideways to avoid the full length of the blade entering her body. Charlotte came in again, Sara feebly trying to push her away. Gladys Lake, aware of what was happening, opened the cubicle door. It was the wrong move.

At that moment the door from the corridor opened and two women entered.

'Help,' one of them screamed. Charlotte, taking advantage of the situation, bolted for the door, pushing the two women to one side. She ran along the corridor, somehow avoiding the other police officers in the building and found the stairs to the basement. She hurtled down them and out of the door and back into Clifford's Inn Passage. She could hear police sirens in the distance, coming closer. She removed the uniform she had been wearing, as well as the brunette wig, and walked, almost ran, down the street, aiming to distance herself from the police.

Chapter 28

Five minutes after the events at the conference centre, Isaac was in his car and on the way, the blue flashing light and the siren easing him through the traffic. A police officer down, the most serious offence in an officer's book.

What concerned him was that one of his team had been stabbed. Details were sketchy. Her husband, Bob Marshall, had been notified.

Arriving at the conference centre, Isaac parked his car, taking no notice of whether he was interfering with the usual flow of traffic, and headed into the building. He rushed up the stairs, a policeman on the door showing him the way. Thankfully, the constable had recognised him and waved him through. An ambulance had arrived just before him; a medic bent over Sara's still body. Gladys Lake was also administering assistance, holding Sara's head in her lap, although it was evident to Isaac that the doctor was in need of aid too.

The doctor looked up at Isaac as he entered. 'She's going to be alright,' she said. 'The knife did not go too deep.'

Bob Marshall arrived ten minutes later. Sara, by that time conscious, although sedated and bandaged, meekly acknowledged his presence.

After the initial concern about Sara, Isaac took stock of the situation. He noticed the delegates at the conference filing out, their names and a brief statement obtained, although there was no need to detain them for long. Once again, Isaac realised, Charlotte Hamilton had made fools of them; he knew what was coming next.

Wendy phoned Isaac from Windsor. Bridget had phoned her. 'DI Marshall?'

'She'll survive. Luckily, she managed to avoid the full force of the knife. She'll be sore for a while and out of action for a few weeks, but she'll live.'

'We found where she was staying. She registered as Ingrid Bentham.'

'She's not thinking straight,' Isaac said.

'Not much else to tell you. We found a bag and some clothing. Apart from that, nothing.'

'It's probably not relevant now. She's here in London, and not far away.'

'What about the police at the conference centre? How did they let her get in?' Wendy asked.

'Good question,' Isaac said. 'Someone will need to do some serious explaining later, but for now we need to find this woman. If there's no more where you are, then you and Larry had better get back to Challis Street as soon as possible.'

'We'll leave in five minutes.'

***

DCS Goddard phoned, as expected. 'Sara Marshall?'

'Her condition is stable,' Isaac replied.

'And Dr Lake?'

'Shaken, but otherwise unharmed.'

'Good. Now tell me what happened.'

'Charlotte Hamilton attacked DI Marshall in the Ladies toilet. Gladys Lake was in one of the cubicles and protected.'

'How did Charlotte Hamilton get in there? I thought the place was secured.'

'I had asked the local police station to provide security.'

'And they failed?'

'Correct.'

'I'll need a full report on my desk by tomorrow morning.'

'Yes, sir.'

'I've already had the commissioner on the phone. He wants a full internal enquiry as to how a known murderer can walk into a secured location and then attempt to kill a police officer.'

'She wasn't after Sara Marshall.'

'That's as may be, but she's been attacked, and the commissioner intends that heads will roll; yours and mine, if he can arrange it.'

'Understood, but our primary concern is finding Charlotte Hamilton.'

'You'd better find her within twenty-four hours, or you're off the case.'

'Harsh, sir.'

'Not harsh. It's a directive from the commissioner. Your replacement is due in London within a day. I can't stop this, and with a police officer almost fatally wounded, I'm not in a position to put forward a case for your retention.'

Isaac sat down on a nearby chair. He had had some tight scrapes in his career, but this was the most severe. He wasn't usually a drinker, but if he had been at home, he would have opened the bottle of brandy that he kept for such occasions.

***

Charlotte walked and ran down Fleet Street, the former home of the major newspapers in the country. She could not think, only run, and remove herself from the area of the conference centre. As she hurtled down the street, she glanced in the occasional shop window. Without the wig, she could see Charlotte Hamilton staring back at her, not an old lady or a tarty female, but the Charlotte Hamilton that she knew, as did the police.

What a mess, she thought.

She turned right down Salisbury Court and Dorset Rise, joining Tudor Street. Once out of the immediate area, she slowed her pace to a brisk walk. Her breathing was still heavy, and she was perspiring. With no feelings of guilt about what had occurred, she found a café.

'Cappuccino and a slice of cheesecake, please,' she said, when asked by the waitress.

A police car drove past; it took no notice of where she was sitting close to the front window. Charlotte discounted it.

The waitress brought her the coffee and the cake. Charlotte took her time to drink and eat. She thought through what had just occurred, and what to do next. Outwardly, she resembled an average person just going about their daily business: worrying about their job, their children, how to pay next month's mortgage.

She left the café and walked down the street, turning right on Farringdon Street. She crossed Blackfriars Bridge, keeping her head low. Where to head for was uncertain, but she knew it had to be out of London.

***

'Your career's finished. You know that,' Detective Chief Superintendent Goddard said.

'Yes, sir,' DCI Cook said. For once, the friendly handshake with his superior and mentor was dispensed with. Isaac was standing upright in the DCS's office; Goddard was sitting down, although he looked ready to burst.

'I've had the commissioner on the phone three times today already. If Marshall had died, can you imagine the problems that would have caused?'

'Full inquiry.'

'And the rest. They would have my head on a plate for letting you continue with this case. All that nonsense about you being the future commissioner of the Met down the drain.'

'I never held much store to it,' Isaac said, which was not altogether true. He had been working his way up to the top by exceptional policing, obtaining the right qualifications, and, if needed, charming those who could help.

Richard Goddard had guided his career from the start, from when he had been a junior constable and Goddard an inspector. The previous commissioner had seen something in him, but the new commissioner did not like Isaac, any more than he liked the DCS, and Isaac was clearly Goddard's man.

Isaac's good relationship with the former government whip Angus McTavish would not help as he was now sitting in the House of Lords. He was unlikely to want to sully himself with a DCI whose latest case had resulted in six murders, almost a seventh.

'You'd better sit down, Isaac,' Goddard said. 'Let's see if we can salvage anything out of this sorry mess.'

'Sara Marshall is going to be fine,' Isaac said, attempting to alleviate the tension in Goddard's office.

'I know that, and from all accounts, she handled herself well. No doubt she'll receive an award for exceptional courage, probably the Queen's Police Medal. At least, she'll have my recommendation and the commissioner's, that's if I'm still around.'

'That bad, sir?'

'What do you think?' Goddard's mood changed again. 'You were given this case when the death count stood at four. Or was it five?'

'Four. Graham Dyer was the first, in Holland Park.'

'And the count now?'

'Six.'

'How can I defend you? It's not as if you didn't know who the murderer was. This Charlotte Hamilton has made us laughing stocks.'

'Three were murdered some years previously when DI Marshall was running the investigation of the crimes down in Twickenham.'

'Hardly a defence for your ineptitude, and besides, she was relatively inexperienced, her first murder case. You're a DCI with an exceptional track record; plenty of convictions under your belt. What can I say? What can I do?'

'Have you explained this to the commissioner?'

'The man's an arrogant fool,' Goddard said.

'First time you've said that.'

'First time I've not cared if he hears or not. Isaac, I can't defend you on this one.'

'I know that. Protect yourself if you can.'

'It doesn't work like that, and you know it. If one goes, we both go. Anyway, enough complaining and criticising. What do we have? And make us both a cup of tea.'

For a few minutes, the conversation turned away from Charlotte Hamilton, and the two men spoke as friends and colleagues. The commissioner phoned Goddard, who answered in an obsequious manner.

'Your replacement will be here within the hour,' Goddard said.

'What do you want me to do?' Isaac asked.

'Play it by the book. Give him all the assistance he needs, although he may bring his own people, start from scratch.'

'That would be sheer madness. Charlotte Hamilton's out there, probably not far from here, and she failed with Gladys Lake. There's no way of knowing when she'll strike next.'

'Agreed. Your team is still with you, although the new SIO may purloin them.'

'They'll be reluctant to afford him the support they gave me.'

'That's understood, but they're professionals. They'll do their duty. You'd better tell them that. Now, what can you tell me about Charlotte Hamilton?'

'Since the attack on Sara Marshall, nothing.'

'What do you mean?'

'She vanished.'

'But how did she get out? You had the venue surrounded.'

'We did, but she slipped through a door at the rear of the building.'

'She's not Harry Houdini. Didn't your people cover all possible points of entry?'

'They missed that one. We've put out an APW on her; she can't have gone far. All the bus and train stations are being monitored.'

'In the rush hour!'

'She blends in well.'

'Okay. What's the situation with Gladys Lake?'

'She's returning to Newcastle earlier than planned.'

'Is she safe there?'

'She intends to secure herself at her hospital. It's safer than here, and we believe Charlotte Hamilton to be close to London.'

'But she could return to Newcastle.'

'We realise that possibility, but regardless, the mental hospital she works at does have good security. Also, DI Rory Hewitt, up in Newcastle, knows Charlotte Hamilton by sight.'

'Very well. Outline the plan.'

'Gladys Lake will be taken to King's Cross by a police car at two in the afternoon. That's the earliest we could arrange adequate protection. She will board the train. There will be six police officers in plain clothes on the train, as well.'

'Are you expecting the Hamilton woman to reappear?'

'It's a possibility.'

'And where will you be?'

'I'll be travelling with Dr Lake, as will some of my team. Assuming that my team is not occupied with the new SIO.'

'If they are, make sure they are out of the office in time. Make up a ruse if you must.'

'That's what I planned.'

'Is Gladys Lake the bait?'

'Not really, but if Charlotte Hamilton makes an appearance, we'll be there to nab her.'

'Good plan, as long as no one else is killed. And if the new SIO starts causing trouble, act professionally. If you catch this woman, the accolades go to you.'

'And you, sir.'

'Correct. But if she's caught on the new SIO's watch...'

'He's the hero of the hour, and you and I are dead meat,' Isaac said as he left his DCS's office.

Goddard shrugged his shoulders in agreement.

***

Charlotte continued to move away from where she would be recognised. She had considered her life expendable, if only it would ensure the death of her torturer, but now…

If only that woman had not got in my way, she thought.

She reflected on the events at the conference centre: the Ladies toilet, the knife in her hand, Sara Marshall separating her from her target, the knife entering her body, Dr Lake in the cubicle, inches from her. If only those two women had not come in, she would have completed her task. Now the plan was in shreds again, and she had nowhere to hide. She knew that she needed sanctuary. She needed her friend, where she had spent three years; she needed Beaty. But Beaty was dead; dead as a result of the shock of seeing her dead cat.

Charlotte realised that she had been the only person who had really cared for her, and if she wasn't there, at least the area would be.

She walked towards Southwark, careful to avoid being too visible. A discount clothing store on the way gave her the opportunity to buy a thick coat; she had dispensed with the previous one in Windsor. Although it was not the coldest day of the year, it did not look out of place to the people scurrying along the street.

Taking stock of her appearance, she realised that she was still too recognisable. She bought a hat, which under normal circumstances she would not be seen dead in.

She chuckled at her appearance, but she knew she would not be recognised, at least by a patrolling police car; not even by a police officer on the street.

Slowing her pace, Charlotte reviewed the situation. She knew she still had a task to complete, but when and how? Gladys Lake, she knew, would be protected. As for Sara Marshall, she did not care whether she lived or died. The knife which she had used was at the conference centre, discarded as she left the building. She needed another.

Once at Southwark, realising that there was no transport available to her destination, she continued to head south, joining up with Old Kent Road. Another two miles, and she boarded a bus. She smiled to herself as she sat in its warmth and the comfort, thinking how easy it was for her to fool the police.

Chapter 29

Nothing had changed from what Charlotte could see, apart from Beaty, her friend, the only person who had cared for her, being dead and buried in the local churchyard. Although not religious, Charlotte visited the grave, placing on it some flowers which she had purchased from a florist.

'Cathy,' a voice startled Charlotte. It was a name she had not used since she had lived with Beaty.

'Mrs Jenkins, how are you?'

'Fine. We haven't seen you for a long time.' The woman had been a friend of Beaty and Charlotte, or Cathy as she was known then. Charlotte remembered that she had bad eyesight, surprised that she had recognised her, and that she never watched television or read a newspaper, which was as well.

'I couldn't stay after what happened.'

'I know. We were all fond of Beaty, although she preferred you to all of us,' Mrs Jenkins said.

'I was so upset I had to leave that day. Not only Beaty but Felix.'

'His grave's still in the garden. Do you want to visit?'

'Yes, please,' Charlotte replied. 'I hope Beaty won't mind, but I'll take one of her flowers for Felix.'

'I'm sure she won't.'

Mrs Jenkins, a similar age to Beaty, chatted away as they walked the short distance to Beaty's cottage. She gave Charlotte all the gossip: who had married whom, who had left whom, even who was having an affair. She even updated Charlotte on the boyfriend she'd had in the town, and that he had married and was now the father of twins. Charlotte felt as though she had come home.

Beaty's cottage was now occupied by a couple from London who had relocated to avoid the hustle and bustle of the big city. They invited the two women in for tea. Charlotte put on some sunglasses and darkened her face with tanning cream, remembered it from when she had left some years ago, although the furniture had changed, and Felix the cat had been replaced by Ben, the Jack Russell Terrier, who instinctively liked her and came and sat beside her. Charlotte patted the dog and remembered Felix the cat and Beaty; a tear came to her eye. 'Pleasant memories,' she said, which was true.

She gave a thought to her past and could feel no anger, only regret about what she had done. She wanted to stay in that chair with that dog and that open fire forever.

'Stay the night,' the couple said.

'Thank you. Too many memories here for me, but thanks all the same.'

Charlotte went out to Felix's grave. Even though there were new owners, the small cross she had put there was still in place. She tidied the area surrounding it and laid the single flower on the grave.

She said a little prayer and silently mouthed a few words. 'Forgive me Beaty and Felix for what I have done. You were the only two that loved me, I know that now.'

***

Isaac returned from Richard Goddard's office to find the new man in place – Detective Chief Inspector Seth Caddick. He had arrived early.

'Pleased to meet you, DCI Caddick,' Isaac said as he shook the man's hand firmly.

'Fine mess you've got yourself into here,' was the reply from the man, a Welsh accent unmistakable. 'You'd better bring me up to speed if I'm to catch this woman. How many have died now?'

'Six, possibly seven.'

'It's not going to look good on your record, is it?' Caddick's reply.

Isaac, a man not willing to judge people too harshly on first meeting, could only come up with one conclusion: he didn't like him. To Isaac, who was willing to encourage and only criticise when necessary, his replacement was the complete opposite. Isaac studied the man more carefully than when he had first walked in the door. Caddick was as tall as he was; although he carried at least another twenty pounds, it was muscle, not flab. He had a full head of hair, although it was greying at the sides. Isaac judged his age to be about forty-five.

'Where's your team, apart from the one who was stabbed?'

'Out looking for Charlotte Hamilton.'

'Do they have a plan or are they just aimlessly wandering around?'

'They're professionals. They don't just wander around,' Isaac's curt reply.

'Maybe, but I'll be bringing in some of my people in the next couple of days, to deal with this Charlotte Hamilton woman.'

'Your prerogative, DCI,' Isaac said.

'I'll need your office.'

'I'll move out for you.'

Isaac found a desk close to Larry's and settled himself there. He could see Caddick making himself at home. He was on the phone, not attempting to lower his voice. 'No worries, commissioner. I'll soon lick this team into shape.'

Isaac had judged the man correctly; he was a sycophant who ingratiated himself with his superiors at every opportunity.

Larry entered the office, a look of surprise on his face at seeing his DCI sitting at the desk next to his. He looked over at Isaac's old office, saw the new man in place. He rolled his eyes at Isaac; Isaac nodded.

'Detective Inspector Larry Hill, sir.' Larry introduced himself to the new man.

'Caddick, DCI Caddick,' the man replied. He shook Larry's hand with a bear-like grip.

'Pleased to meet you.'

'Where have you been?' It seemed to Larry a criticism, not a question.

'I've been with our people trying to find out where Charlotte Hamilton has disappeared to.'

'From what I know of her and Challis Street, she's probably outside here having a coffee.'

'Unlikely,' Larry said, not sure how to handle the man's surly attitude.

'That may be, but I need to be updated by the team if we are to prevent any more murders.'

'She seems to be focussed on Dr Lake at the present moment. CI Cook has ensured that she is well protected.'

'She was meant to be well protected at the damn conference, but the woman got through, almost killed DI Marshall,' Caddick said.

'That's true.'

Larry, summarily dismissed, sat down at his desk.

'You've met our new SIO,' Isaac said.

'Gruff sort of man.'

'DCI,' a voice shouted from the other side of the room.

'Our master beckons,' Larry murmured.

Isaac re-entered his former office.

'Yes, DCI,' Isaac said.

'I need to meet the team as soon as possible.'

'They're busy at the present moment.'

'Where?'

'Apart from DI Marshall, who you know about, Sergeant O'Riordan is staying close to Dr Lake in case Charlotte Hamilton reappears.'

'Unfinished business?'

'That's what we believe.'

'Who else?'

'You've just met DI Hill, and Sergeant Wendy Gladstone is looking for the woman.'

'I was told that she was excellent at finding missing people.'

230

'She is.'

'But not this woman.'

'Not entirely true, but with this woman we've always been one step behind. DI Hill and Sergeant Gladstone found where she stayed in Windsor, but she had left by then.'

'Not much use then, is it?'

'I can't agree with you on that. Any evidence or information assists.'

'Agreed, but policing by the book isn't working. What's the latest on this woman?'

'After the conference centre, we traced her movements down as far as Blackfriars Bridge.'

'How?'

'CCTV monitoring the traffic picked her up. That's why Bridget Halloran, our CCTV viewing officer, is not here.'

'She's out checking the videos?'

'We're looking south of the Thames.'

'And then?'

'Hopefully, we'll find out where she's gone.'

'What's the psychologist's analysis of the woman.'

'Dr Lake believes she's fixated on her. There have been two attempts on her life, so far. Charlotte Hamilton has succceded with every previous victim.

'Is Dr Lake, the best person to give an analysis?'

'You've brought yourself up to speed on this case?'

'Not totally.' It was a frank admission from the new SIO. Isaac knew that this was not about a new broom to resolve the case; this was the commissioner looking after his people. Ousting him, and no doubt Richard Goddard, his DCS.

It was evident to Isaac that Detective Chief Inspector Seth Caddick would not be up to speed for some time, and if there was to be a resolution to the case, it was up to him.

***

Charlotte woke up the next morning when a cup of tea was brought to her. She had slept well. As it had been with Beaty, so it was with Mrs Jenkins. A cat which had climbed up on her bed during the night slept peacefully.

'That's Brutus. He's been out ratting all night. If you don't mind, I'll leave him there.'

'I don't mind,' Charlotte said.

'Bacon and eggs?'

'It sounds lovely.'

'Twenty minutes. You can have a shower; I've put a towel there for you. Also, I washed and ironed the clothes that you wore yesterday. I hope you don't mind.'

'You're too kind.'

'Not at all. I know how much Beaty and Felix loved you. It's the least I can do.'

Charlotte remembered back to her time in the town before; how much she had loved it there and how much she had loved Beaty, more than her own parents. She determined to stay in Sevenoaks and to forget about her past, even though she could not resist the need to phone the St Pancras Renaissance Hotel and to ask about Gladys Lake.

As she sat down to breakfast, Mrs Jenkins spoke. 'You can stay here as long as you like. At least until you are settled.'

'I would like that very much,' Charlotte said as she ate her breakfast.

She had spent three years with Beaty, the best years of her life, when there had been no medication, no doctors, no anguish on her part, and no recriminations for the murders she had committed. She wondered if they had only been imaginings on her part, a result of her schizophrenia.

'More toast?'

'Yes, please, and some of your jam.'

'Made it myself.'

'I remember your jam from before.'

'Where did you go?' Mrs Jenkins asked.

'After Beaty and Felix?'

'Yes.'

'I was so upset. They meant everything to me.'

'But you had friends here; friends who would have cared for you.'

'It's complicated.'

'Let's talk no more about it. You're here now. That's all that matters.'

'I'm here now, and this time I'll stay.'

It was eight in the morning as Charlotte wandered around the town, that she saw him. It was the driver of the truck that had killed Felix. Her anger flared, and she reached into her bag for a knife. It was not there, and he was gone.

She left the town by the next train. Her peace was gone, only to be replaced by an uncontrollable rage and a desire to inflict a fatal wound on the woman who had destroyed her life – Dr Gladys Lake.

***

'She took a bus to Sevenoaks, thirty miles south from here,' Wendy said on the phone to Isaac.

'Our new SIO is here.'

'What's he like? As charming as you, sir?'

'Charming is not a word I would use.'

'Don't worry. We'll soon have this woman. We'll make sure you get the credit for her capture.'

'Thanks. What can you tell us about Charlotte?'

Larry sat alongside Isaac, the phone on speaker. Caddick sat in his office, looking through the reports.

'How did you find her?' Larry asked.

'Bridget found her on Old Kent Road, CCTV cameras. After that, good old-fashioned legwork. A couple of local constables with me, and we started showing Charlotte's most recent photo. That's how we found her.'

'Are you going to Sevenoaks.'

'I'm on the road now. I've got the two locals from Southwark with me. I'll be there in forty minutes. Also, I've phoned the local station there.'

'Do you need Larry?'

'It would help.'

'I'm on my way,' Larry said. 'Give me one hour.'

'How about you, sir?' Wendy asked.

'I'm travelling to Newcastle with Dr Lake. Sean O'Riordan is coming with me.'

'She should be safe.'

'With Charlotte Hamilton?'

'You're right. If she's in Sevenoaks, we'll find her.'

'And if you don't, she's still coming after Dr Lake.'

'She's tenacious.'

'And deadly.'

'Don't get too close. She'll either take your photo or stick a knife in you.'

'She'll probably do both if she gets the chance,' Isaac said.

***

Careful not to be seen, Charlotte left the train two stations before its final destination at Charing Cross. She realised that London Bridge Station was not the ideal location, but she could not delay. It was already mid-morning, and Gladys Lake was due to check out around two in the afternoon. That could only mean that she intended to catch the 4.15 p.m. train from King's Cross.

Charlotte checked her bag; she still had fifteen hundred pounds. A local shop provided a change of clothes and a cheap wig. She also purchased a kitchen knife in a discount store.

She walked across London Bridge and up Princes Street, before turning into Cheapside Street, eventually connecting with Farrington Road which took her close to King's Cross Station. She found a small restaurant and ate a good meal.

She knew she was early, but she needed to check out the area: entry and exit points, roads and side streets to vanish down if the police were there.

Charlotte sang her song quietly, repeating all the verses as she waited for the woman.

Stupid Duncan up at the quarry, along came a sister and gave him a push.

Liam thought he was a stud until I stuck a knife in his heart.
Oh, what fun, I slit his throat. Who will be next? Will it be you?
The black policeman thought he was smart, but I killed him anyway.

Charlotte knew that Dr Lake would be accompanied by the police, and it would not be possible to board the train at King's Cross, as they were bound to be on the lookout for her. She had attempted to kill the woman twice now, once in Newcastle, the other time in London, and they knew that she was determined and unlikely to desist.

Once the knife had entered the doctor's body, she knew she would have no further use for life. Until she had that blood-soaked knife, there was no freedom from the torment that cursed her: fluctuating between sanity and malevolence, the loving environment of Beaty and Felix, the torture in Newcastle at the mental hospital, the love of her parents for her brother Duncan and their disinterest in her.

The weather had turned colder, and a biting wind blew. Charlotte knew that if Dr Lake was coming, it would be soon.

As expected, ten minutes later, a police car drew up at the station. Gladys Lake emerged, clearly visible. Charlotte felt a nervous tingle knowing that her prey was so close, yet so far. Also visible was the black policeman, DCI Cook, and another police officer that she recognised. The man she had seen with Inspector Marshall at Joey's, the night she had killed Liam Fogarty, the least satisfying of her murders.

She wanted to rush across the road and to deal with the doctor there and then, but it had an element of risk. Besides, she wanted to savour the moment, not just a quick thrust in and out. She wanted to enjoy the doctor's death, to hear her plead for mercy.

Realising that killing the doctor was not possible at King's Cross, Charlotte put her backup plan into action. She walked around the immediate area. A woman struggling with the key to the door of her house, her arms laden with shopping, her car on the street with its engine running. Charlotte jumped into the driver's seat and took off. In the rear-view mirror, she could see the woman running down the street. The time was 2.20 p.m.

***

Larry Hill, in Sevenoaks, phoned Isaac as he was boarding the train at King's Cross Station. 'The local police in Sevenoaks identified her. Apparently, she was seen at the railway station earlier in the day. Also, she went by the name of Cathy Agnew here, and she was well known in the town.'

'Which train did she catch?' Isaac asked.

'Early, 8.45 a.m.'

'London?' Isaac asked a rhetorical question.

'Charing Cross. Unfortunately, she's back up there with you.'

'Don't worry. This time we're armed, and we're sticking close to Dr Lake.'

'She's going to try again, you know that.'

'We know it. I've stationed plain clothes in every carriage, and I'll be with Sean O'Riordan and Dr Lake from here to Newcastle. After that, she's Rory Hewitt's responsibility.

'There's not much Wendy and I can do to help,' Larry said.

'Agreed. It's probably best if you both get back to Challis Street and update DCI Caddick.'

'I can't say I like him much.'

'That's as may be, but he's got the ear of the commissioner. If he's to take over on a permanent basis, then you'd better stay on his side.'

'What about DCS Goddard? Can he do something?'

'If we catch Charlotte Hamilton, then anything is possible. Without a result, both the DCS and I are out and back on traffic duty.'

'A bit dramatic.'

'At the least demoted or transferred out to the suburbs.'

An announcement sounded in the station. *The 4.15 p.m. to Newcastle is leaving in ten minutes from Platform 4. First stop Peterborough.*

***

Charlotte, using the GPS installed in the BMW, made good time; twenty minutes after stealing the car she was on the A1 and heading to Peterborough. She had travelled on the train from Newcastle many times, and she knew it would arrive in Peterborough at 5 p.m. She had a greater distance to travel, and the train was quicker. The drive should take two hours; she had one hour and fifty minutes.

Exceeding the speed limit on more than one occasion, she made the trip in one hour and forty-two minutes. She left the car and rushed into the railway station. Quickly purchasing a ticket, she waited for the train from London to pull in. It arrived on time. Charlotte looked for familiar faces; she saw none.

As the train stopped, she climbed into the second carriage. She knew she would need to search the train. Her disguise was good, she knew that, but there was no way to fool the DCI again, as she had that night in Newcastle.

Charlotte sat patiently in her seat waiting for the train to leave. It was still some distance to Newcastle; she had time. Carefully she looked around the carriage; no one she knew. She felt safe.

In the fourth carriage, Isaac stood. He looked around, phoned his men up and down the train: nothing.

'Looks like we're okay,' he said.

'What happened to her?' Sean asked. Both he and Isaac were sitting close to Gladys Lake on the trip from London: one on either side of her.

'I won't feel safe until I'm back in Newcastle,' Dr Lake said.

'We'll be there soon enough,' Isaac replied.

The train pulled out five minutes after it had arrived in Peterborough; its next destination, Doncaster.

Charlotte felt the knife in her bag. It would be dark outside before the train arrived in Newcastle; she decided to wait for another ninety minutes.

Sean went and purchased some food and drinks for his party of three; Charlotte ate nothing, not moving from her seat. She didn't even complain when the child in the seat behind kept prodding the back of hers with his feet. She felt as if it was the end of a long journey.

The light outside the train started to dull, a sign of the impending night. Unwilling to wait any longer, she pulled up the collar of her coat, ensured the hat she wore concealed her face, and moved forward in the train. She walked through the first carriage, scanning left and right; attempting to move her eyes, not her face. There was no sign of her prey and her bodyguard.

She retraced her steps, back through the second carriage where she had been sitting; the third carriage was the same as the first. She took a seat.

A suspicious woman, at least to Charlotte stood at one end of the third carriage. Charlotte arose from her seat and moved into the fourth carriage. Immediately a message on Isaac's phone: 'She's heading your way from the front of the train.'

Charlotte saw the woman on the phone, realised that she had been spotted. She lunged at the woman, caught her a glancing blow with her fist, causing the woman police officer to fall back and onto the floor. Charlotte moved forward, oblivious to the danger and the outcome. Sean was first to spot her. 'Stop,' he yelled.

Charlotte took no notice and kept moving forward. Sean went to draw his gun from its holster, but the train was full. A child was running up and down the corridor between him and the woman. Charlotte pushed the child to one side with her foot and continued forward, reaching Sean. He attempted to grab her. She pulled her knife out from her bag and slashed him badly across the face; he fell to one side, holding his face and attempting to control the bleeding.

Isaac was right behind Sean. He pulled his gun. 'Stop, or I'll shoot.'

'Shoot then. I only want that bastard woman.'

The passengers on the train, confused about what was happening, craned their necks; one man stood up.

'Sit down!' Isaac shouted. 'Police. This woman is extremely dangerous.'

In the confusion, Charlotte moved forward again. Gladys Lake stood up. 'Charlotte, please stop, you need help.'

'Not your help,' Charlotte replied.

Isaac stood between Charlotte and her target. Some of the passengers were screaming in fear; some had hidden in their seats. A child cried.

'Charlotte, stop,' Isaac warned her again.

She ignored him. The distance between the two of them was no more than six feet. Isaac realised that he had no option but to pull the trigger. The bullet hit her in the left leg, causing her to falter. His police training had taught him to aim for the torso, but the risk of hitting people in the carriage was too high.

Undeterred and apparently impervious to the injury, she continued. Isaac pulled the trigger again, this time hitting the other leg. Charlotte, unable to continue, fell forward. 'You bastard,' she mumbled weakly, blood trickling down her legs.

As she fell, she raised the knife in front of her. She collapsed into Isaac's arms, the knife piercing his shoulder. By this time, Sean, temporarily recovered, had taken control of the situation. One of the plain clothes had phoned for an ambulance to be at the next station, five miles away.

Charlotte, wounded but not fatally, was treated by Gladys Lake on the train as it headed to the station. Isaac, not so badly injured, although in a lot of pain, held a towel that he had been given by one of the passengers to his wound, the blood soaking it.

'Don't worry, Charlotte. I'll look after you,' Dr Lake said.

Charlotte, unable to speak, looked horrified.

Sean O'Riordan phoned DCS Goddard to update him, then DCI Caddick. After the situation had stabilised, he phoned Wendy and Larry. Sara Marshall, on hearing the news, phoned Charlotte's father.

'I'll make sure she is treated well,' the sad man replied.

Charlotte had killed seven people, including her own brother, yet her father still loved her.

The End

ALSO BY THE AUTHOR

Murder House – A DCI Cook Thriller

A corpse in the fireplace of an old house. It's been there for thirty years, but who is it?

It's clearly murder, but who is the victim and what connection does the body have to the previous owners of the house. What is the motive? And why is the body in a fireplace? It was bound to be discovered eventually but was that what the murderer wanted? The main suspects are all old and dying, or already dead.

Isaac Cook and his team have their work cut out trying to put the pieces together. Those who know are not talking because of an old-fashioned belief that a family's dirty laundry should not to be aired in public, and certainly not to a policeman – even if that means the murderer is never brought to justice!

Murder is a Tricky Business – A DCI Cook Thriller

A television actress is missing, and DCI Isaac Cook, the Senior Investigation Officer of the Murder Investigation Team at Challis Street Police Station in London, is searching for her.

Why has he been taken away from more important crimes to search for the woman? It's not the first time she's gone missing, and why does everyone assume she's been murdered?

There's a secret, that much is certain, but who knows? The missing woman? The executive producer, his eavesdropping assistant? Or the actor who portrayed her fictional brother on the Soap Opera?

Murder Without Reason – A DCI Cook Thriller

DCI Cook, now a Senior Member of London's Anti-Terrorism Command, faces his Greatest Challenge. The Islamic State is waging war in England, and they are winning.

Not only does Isaac Cook have to contend with finding the perpetrators, but he is being forced to commit to actions contrary to his mandate as a police officer.

And then, there is Anne Argento, the Prime Minister's Deputy. The man has proven himself to be a pacifist and is not up to the task. She needs to take his job if the country is to fight back against the Islamists.

Vane and Martin have provided the solution. Will DCI Cook and Anne Argento be willing to follow through? Are they able to act for the good of England, knowing that a criminal and murderous activity is about to take place? Do they have any option?

Hostage of Islam

Kate McDonald's fate hangs in the balance. The Slave Trader has the money for her, so does her father and he wants her back. Can Steve Case's team rescue her and her friend, Helen in time?

Three Americans are to die at the Baptist Mission in Nigeria - the Pastor and his wife in a blazing chapel. Another, gunned down while trying to defend them from the Islamists.

Kate is offered to a slave trader who intends to sell her virginity to an Arab Prince. Helen, to ensure their survival, gives herself to the leader of the raid at the mission and the murderer of her friends.

The Haberman Virus

A remote and isolated village in the Hindu Kush mountain range in North Eastern Afghanistan is wiped out by a virus unlike any seen before.

A mysterious visitor checks his handiwork clad in a space suit, and American female doctor succumbs to the disease, and the woman sent to trap the person responsible, falls in love with the man who would be responsible for the death of millions.

Malika's Revenge

Malika, a drug-addicted prostitute waits in a smugglers' village for the next Afghan tribesman or Tajik gangster to pay her price, a few scraps of heroin.

Yusup Baroyev, a drug lord enjoys a lifestyle many would envy. An Afghan warlord sees the resurgence of the Taliban. A Russian white-collar criminal portrays himself as a good and honest citizen in Moscow.

They are entwined in an audacious plan to raise the quantity of heroin shipped out of Afghanistan and into Russia and ultimately the West.

Some will succeed, some will die, some will be resurrected from their plight and others will rue the day they became involved.

ABOUT THE AUTHOR

Phillip Strang was born in England in the late nineteen forties, during the post-war baby boom in England. He had a comfortable middle-class upbringing in small town seventy miles west of London.

His childhood and formative years were a time of innocence. There were relatively few rules, and as a teenager he had complete freedom, thanks to a bicycle – a three-speed Raleigh – and a trusting community. It was in the days before mobile phones, the internet, terrorism and wanton violence. He was an avid reader of science fiction in his teenage years: Isaac Asimov and Frank Herbert, the masters of the genre. How much of what they and others mentioned has now become reality? Science fiction has now become science fact. Still an avid reader, the author now mainly reads thrillers.

In his early twenties, the author, with a degree in electronics engineering and desire to see the world, left the cold, damp climes of England for Sydney, Australia – his first semi-circulation of the globe. Now, forty years later, he still resides in Australia, although many intervening years were spent in a myriad of countries, some calm and safe, others no more than war zones.

Printed in Great Britain
by Amazon